# The Cure
# for the Healer

ALORA CRAIGHTON

THE CURE FOR THE HEALER

Printed in the United States of America

Self-published
by Alora Craighton
lovebyalora.com

Copyright © 2025 by Alora Craighton

Copyediting and book production by Bestsellers with Brooke-Sidney™
Design and typeset by Bestsellers with Brooke-Sidney™
brookesidneybooks.com

Manufactured in the United States
10 9 8 7 6 5 4 3 2 1

Library of Congress Cataloging-in-Publication Data
has been applied for.
ISBN: 979-8-9923602-0-2

*For* **Z**

# Acknowledgments

Thank you to my family: Z, Shelly, Shad, Eli, Lia, and Deb. You inspire me every day. Thank you to my mother for her prayers for success. Thank you to my A-team: Frida, Ronnie, Michelle, Shelby, Dr. KK, Heather, and Jim.

Thank you, Brooke-Sidney and team, for your expertise and guidance.

And finally, to you, the reader… Thank you for taking this journey with me. I hope you enjoy reading *The Cure for the Healer* as much as I enjoyed writing it.

# Contents

# Prologue

## (Liam)

I always knew this day would come. In so many ways, today is a day that I planned for, anticipated, but most of all, dreaded. Burying my mother today was the hardest thing I've ever had to do. My mom was a beauty, inside and out. She had long, beautiful, red hair and blue eyes. Liam, my father, had dark brown hair, brown eyes and easily cleared six feet. I inherited his name, size, and hair, but my eyes and my smile were all from my mom. She was everything to me.

My earliest memory of my mother was of her on her hands and knees, crying and screaming at my father to stay home with us. It was the first time I remember seeing him hit my mother. She threatened to leave him. He just smirked and continued getting ready for his date. She told him she would take me with her. That's when he turned and rushed to grab her by the throat. He lifted her and slammed her into the floor-length mirror, breaking the glass in their walk-in closet. "Bitch, I will hunt you down and kill you if you so much as think about taking my fucking son anywhere." Then, he calmly dropped her on the floor and stepped over her. He chose one of his many women over his family that night and would continue to choose them over me for my entire childhood. My mother, on the other hand, chose herself. One might assume that the choice caused a rift between my mother and me, but it didn't. It was my first lesson in strength and self-preservation. I was five.

The next thirteen years of my life, my father hired nannies to care for me while he continued to do whatever it was that he did. They were all women of color. He treated them horribly, but paid them well. Liam verbally abused them and would go out of his way to let them know he thought they were beneath him. He mocked their cultures and encouraged me to do the same, but even as a young child, it felt wrong. One of the first things my mother taught me was to be respectful and show kindness. "An ounce of kindness goes a long way, Lee," she would always say. When I refused to belittle my nannies, he called me weak, stupid, and any other name he could think of. I think my nannies took pity on me and stayed longer than they should have.

There was Delilah. She was Jamaican, kind, and smart. Delilah would take me to the park and pretend that she didn't see my mother when my mom would sneak to spend time with me. She would sing to me to calm me when we had to leave my mom; she had the voice of an angel. Delilah left me after she finished her degree in child psychology. Then, there was Anna. She was Mexican and fun to be around, but she was afraid of my father. The first time she spotted my mother in the park, she threatened to tell my father. Liam had told Anna he would have his friends come and take her sick abuela back to Mexico. But my mom knew my father well, so she would give Anna extra money and help her get medical care for her grandmother. Anna left me not long after her abuela passed away; I was ten. Then, there was Ms. Cassie, the second most important woman in my life.

Ms. Cassie was, for all practical purposes, my grandmother. My mother's mother disowned her when she married Liam because my paternal grandfather had financially ruined my maternal grandfather. Liam's mother disappeared when he was a teenager, so I never met my biological grandmothers. Ms. Cassie was a Black woman, older than my other nannies. She was born and raised in Mississippi but moved to California with her husband to raise their children in a more liberal environment. I guess Liam's attitude towards Black people was a bitter taste of home for her. Ms. Cassie was different from the others. She didn't respond the same way to my father's threats and demeaning attitude. I once asked her how she could stand the names he called her. She said, "Chile, I've been called everything by white folks but a child of God. I stay because when I look in your eyes, I see your heart. If I can help keep your heart kind, then tolerating Mr. Sinclair's nonsense is worth it." That's when I asked her to walk with me to the park.

At eleven, I was more than capable of walking to the park on my own in our affluent, costal neighborhood of Palos

Verdes Estates in southern California. Ms. Cassie asked me, "Why do you always go to the park? You have this huge mansion with sprawling lawns, a pool, a tennis court, and a basketball court. Your father even let you put in that ridiculous half pipe ramp thing for you to ride your skateboard. What does that park have that you don't have here?"

My answer was simple, "Come with me and find out."

That was the day Ms. Cassie met my mother. Unlike my nannies before her, she fully embraced my mother and wanted to get to know her. She affectionately called my mom Jessie, short for Jessica. It was the start of a beautiful relationship. Ms. Cassie didn't just look after me, she also became a stand-in mother for my mother. My mother cried just as much as Ms. Cassie's own children at her funeral. We buried her twenty years ago right after I turned twenty-one. Ms. Cassie died from flu complications. Something that could have been prevented, but no one listened to her. I was studying abroad at Oxford that semester. I would have fought harder for her if I had been there. It was my mother who encouraged me to turn my frustrations into action by studying infectious diseases. Now, they are both gone. Hopefully, this journey home will help clear my head. My trek back from civilization will take about three days if I don't run into any trouble. *Wow, I really am a coward. All that talk about social justice, but all I've done is hide out on my mountain for the past three years.*

After I finished my B.S. in business, I worked part-time at my family's finance company. Liam was upset I chose not to pursue my MBA. Instead, I earned an MS in molecular pharmacology and toxicology from the University of Southern California. I stayed local so I could check in on the firm. Then I earned a PhD in biological sciences in public health from Harvard. After graduation, I was already published and had several job offers, but I did something no one really expected, least of all Liam. I went to work full-time at the firm. What people didn't understand was that I knew what was coming. I could see the trends in the medical field and the shift in power in the social constructs of our country. And so, the first pandemic wave and the uprising against white power were not surprising to me.

Ms. Cassie would say, "Don't fear your dreams. It is the universe's way of preparing you for what's coming." I started having dreams about the shift in power eight years before it happened. Once Liam passed away of a heart attack, I became owner and CFO of the company. Not only did I branch out and start diversifying, I began investing in my friends' businesses. I also made a few medical breakthroughs and sold the patents. Money was more abundant than ever before. That's when I started anonymously hiring contractors to build small parts of my large compound in the mountains. I figured the area I selected was remote enough that no one would ever come looking. Shit really got real when I went to pitch the cure that I found for a blood disorder that disproportionately affects Black children. Not even two hours after that pitch meeting, they tried to have me executed. I took two bullets to the chest.

I called Christopher Ito, one of my best friends, really a brother, from undergrad. He joined the military and eventually became a SEAL. When he was discharged, he opened a security company. Chris provided me with a security detail, but more importantly, he trained me in weaponry and hand-to-hand combat.

I've done a lot of construction and hunting over the last five years, so I realize how threatening I must look at 6'2" and 225 pounds of pure muscle. I guess I'm not the nerdy weakling my father always told me I was. Well, I'll always be a nerd. *Okay, okay, I need to get my head ready.* I'm about a mile outside of the last checkpoint before I'm able to head into the forest and up the mountain.

The checkpoint is just outside of the small port town of Port Jaron, right on the border of California and Oregon. It's used as a trading post and a port where they separate people of color from whites, but this time it's the whites getting the short end of the stick. People of color board buses and boats to take them somewhere nice while whites are shipped off to some shitty destination if they don't have a trade that is useful around the port. I guess some people become the same monsters they hate when they get tired of having a boot on their necks, literally and figuratively. At least we finally have people from all walks of life in D.C. working together to make America truly a place where all are accepted. Hopefully, their efforts will reach everywhere soon, and these pockets of guerrilla warfare will end.

I purchased a huge piece of land here that leads into the forest. Some of my favorite memories are of the annual camping trips I would take up here with my environmental studies club in high school. It always meant peace, and time away from Liam. I built a luxury resort on the land. When the tables turned, I signed the land and the resort over to one of my other closest friends, Thaddeus Masters. Thaddeus is Black and shorter than me, 5'10", average build with just a little extra around the middle these days. His dark skin and perfect teeth always kept the ladies around. It also helped that he is super cool with a relaxed vibe. Thaddeus is versatile and can blend in with royalty or hang with the fellas on the Shaw. He once took me to meet his family in Windsor Hills and then to hang out on Crenshaw. I stuck out like a sore thumb, but once people got to know me, they saw I was cool. Thad has always had my back. Let's hope my drop-in doesn't cause any problems for either of us.

# CHAPTER 1
# A MOTHER'S LOVE

(Liam)

---

*Okay, here we go.* Ducking into an abandoned burnt building, I get to the second floor quickly for a better vantage point. I pull out my binoculars and take out my high-tech breathing gear that I personally designed. Assholes got bold after the first wave of the first pandemic. That may have been an accident, but some of this other shit they've released into the air is not. Whites say it's the Blacks trying to wipe us out, but in my heart, I know it's the whites retaliating.

The resort is visible from here. I can also see the port and most of the hotspot trading stations. Zooming in on the docks with my binoculars, there appears to be a situation brewing. There is a group of Black people, about five to seven people, surrounded by Black guards. They all bear a resemblance; they must be a family. "I don't get it. What's the issue there?" That's when I see her. There's a woman

18

arguing with a guard. *Why is she crying? Did he just snatch her mask off her face?* My concern and fear for them spill out audibly. "Oh, no, she hit him! Please don't hurt her! Shit, I don't want to see him kill her." Her family members are surrounding her and holding their hands up in surrender. Now she's hugging them. It looks like she's saying goodbye. *I'm so confused.* The circle disperses and I finally see what the commotion was about. She has a son, looks like he's mixed-race. They're both crying and hugging. "Okay, where's her husband? He must be hiding somewhere. Coward. How could you let them face that alone?" I watch for a few more minutes, but no one shows. I grab my backpack and drape my rifle over my body with it pointing down and head out of the structure.

"Hey Clorox, where are you going?" I turn and see a guard preparing to approach me. That's when I reach into my pocket and pull out a pre-wadded roll of ten hundred-dollar bills.

"Hey man, I'm not looking for any trouble. I'm simply passing through."

"Yeah well, I don't know when the fuck in time you think you are, but whitey ain't allowed to stroll through this town bearing arms."

"Yeah, I get that, and I mean no disrespect. I'm just looking for safe passage from here to the other side of the port. Can I offer you a grand to just look the other way?"

Snatching the wadded money from my hand, he says, "Whatever, Clorox. Take yo' ass on. I hope you have something for the next guard."

I continue and can see the front of the resort. There's a long line of diverse people hoping to find somewhere to lay their heads for the night. One of my requests to Thaddeus before signing over the property was that everyone would be welcome here.

As I approach the entrance to the resort, I see a man standing in the line in front of the mother and her son. "Hey bitch, you think you and your little pale bastard are going to get shelter here? If they have any sense at all, they'll throw you out on the street where you belong." He's too close to them.

I walk up right behind the woman and her son and calmly, but sternly, say, "They're with me." He looks up, preparing to challenge me, but I have about six inches on him and outweigh him by at least forty pounds. Then, he notices my rifle. His eyes double in size and I ask, "Are we cool here?" He turns back around.

Now that I'm standing inches away from her, I see that she's a short, little woman. I'm at least a full foot taller than her. When she turns to look up at me, our eyes meet over our masks, and I swear she looks straight into my soul. Her eyes are filled with fear and anguish, but not defeat. *Hmm, she's a fighter. I like that.* She grabs her son even tighter and holds him close. I reach for her arm to guide her to the front counter. Probably afraid that my white skin will bring her extra unwanted attention, she jerks away. I look deep into her eyes. "Please, let me help you. I promise you I can help." She gives me a wary look, but nods. I continue to push my way through the crowd.

"Hey Casper, it's a new day. Did you miss the memo? You're not running shit around here anymore," someone shouts. Many hurl other obscenities my way, but I keep us moving. We pass other white people who stand in line sheepishly with their heads down. I nod in acknowledgement, but they all quickly turn away.

Finally, we reach the front desk. "Excuse me, ma'am. Would you be so kind as to ask Mr. Thaddeus Masters if he would come to the front desk?"

Rolling her eyes, she looks in my direction, but appears to be looking through me. "As the gentleman you pushed by told you, you are not running anything. You need to wait in line like everyone else."

"Actually, this one we'll make an exception for." The voice of another woman sounds behind her. A beautiful Black woman appears wearing an expensive designer, coral colored dress, and heels. She has dark, flawless skin and shoulder length natural hair. I recognize her as Thaddeus' wife. "Well, look what the cat dragged in. I was beginning to think you were dead. It's been what, like three years?"

I nod. "Yes, sorry about that. How are you, Alicia? Thad around?"

"Yeah, he's around, somewhere. How about I get you settled into your room?" She grabs the sister key to mine for the dual lock system on my room. One of my conditions for giving Thad the resort was that I get to keep a room that no one else enters without me, but of course I kept a copy of their sister key. She begins to lead the way and then notices that I have guests. "So, I see you have company." Holding

21

out her hand, she says, "Hi, I'm Alicia." My guest shakes Alicia's hand but says nothing.

"I'm sorry. Please forgive her. She's had a rough day," I respond.

"No worries. We all have those. Here we are. You ready? On three. One, two…" We turn our keys simultaneously. "So, how long are you planning to be with us?"

"Not long. Thanks for everything, Alicia. Will you please ask Thad to call me before he stops by the room?"

Whispering, "She's skittish, I get it. Yeah, sure thing." She walks away.

The room I kept for myself was once the presidential suite, so there's plenty of room for three people to spread out. There are two bedrooms, but I had to turn one into a makeshift infirmary, lab, and armory in case I ever run into trouble while passing through. I remove my mask and turn to my guests. I hold out my hand, but don't advance toward them. "You're safe now. Hi, I'm Liam, Liam Sinclair." They remove their masks and I try not to react. I know it's been a long time since I've been in the company of a woman, but goddamn she's beautiful. Caramel skin, big brown, doe eyes, high cheekbones, her hair is pulled back in a ponytail, but it's clear that once released, it flows down her back. I can't see her body yet because she's layered her clothes like many do to lighten the load they carry. Even though it's early-spring, it's cool out. *Shit, they're both wearing sneakers. That's not going to cut it on our trek up the mountain.*

She slowly reaches for my hand and shakes it. "Hi, I'm Nicole Simmons and this is my son, Zion. I apologize for

22

being so skeptical, but they tried to take my son from me." She breaks out into tears and pulls her son close to her side. "I'll be damned if anyone is going to take my son away from me! I carried him, birthed him, nursed him, and…"

"Shhh. It's ok now." I tell her, but I dare not touch her. Zion is just as traumatized; I can see it all over his little face. I can feel their pain and, without thinking, I blurt out, "No one is going to take your son! I promise."

Her eyes dart up to me as she regains her composure. "Thank you, Mr. Sinclair, but I don't think you're in a position to make that call. I appreciate you helping us out, but I can't pay you anything. And why are you helping us anyway?"

I'm not really a fan of how she called me Mr. Sinclair. "Please call me Liam, or Lee. I saw what happened with your family on the dock. It was bullshit, and I didn't like it. So, let's just say that I have a soft spot for mothers and their sons."

"You didn't exactly answer my question, Mist… Liam. Why help? You don't know us, and I can't pay you back right now."

"I don't want anything from you. I'm helping you because I can. My mother taught me that if you can help, you should help. Why don't the two of you get comfortable, maybe take a bath. In this day and age, you never know the next time you may have access to hot water. Come on, let me show you around the suite. That is, if I have answered your question to your satisfaction." I take off my jacket and throw it on the sofa.

They follow and take off their jackets. Underneath, she's wearing a hoodie and jeans. She removes her hoodie to reveal a fitted, v-neck, long sleeve t-shirt. *Damn!* Her ass and hips are pure perfection. Her waist curves in, creating that classic hourglass silhouette. It accentuates her round ass. Those hips are baby-making hips. Thad taught me that one. She has lots of curves. I've always liked a voluptuous woman. She turns around after hanging their jackets on the back of the chair on the other side of the room. *Well, damn! Those must be double Ds. Hmm, I bet they would bounce wildly while I bounce her up and down on my cock. Shit, her expression just changed. She must have noticed me looking at her breasts. Damn, man, pull yourself together!* Her voice pulls me out of my head.

Turning Zion away from me, she says, "So, should we take the tour on our own?"

I blink and wipe the stupid smirk off my face. "No, right this way," I say to Nicole, gesturing with my hand. Walking next to Zion I tell him, "What a handsome young man you are." Zion has pale skin, maybe just a shade darker than mine, a head full of dark brown loose curls, and freckles. He has his mother's eyes.

With a healthy sense of stranger danger, he shyly says, "Thank you."

## Chapter 2

# WE'LL GET OUT OF YOUR HAIR

## (Nicole)

A deep, stern voice sounded behind me. I turn around to see... *Oh sweet Jesus! Who is this crazy ass white man? He's either going to get us killed or kill us.* He grabs my arm and pulls me out of line, and I think to myself, *I know the fuck he did not just grab my arm! He's a big guy, but I'm not going out without a fight. It is my God-given right to protect my child and I will, by any means necessary.*

Then, he whispers that he can help me as he leads me past the other people waiting, straight to the front desk. All the while, I'm thinking he must be on drugs. *He thinks he can help me? God, please don't let us die today.* This lady is looking at him like the nutcase he is. *Seriously, look lady, I really don't know him. Please don't call the guards over here. I can't take another run in with them today.*

Just then, a well-dressed, beautiful Black woman appears who looks like she knows him. *Oh, thank you, Lord! I can't believe we made it past the mob and the front desk. Who is this white man?* He finally takes off his mask and introduces himself.

I burst out in tears at the thought of how close I came to losing my child earlier. This day just keeps getting better and better. There was a time in my life I would have never let anyone see me cry. I lost it twice today in front of complete strangers. Then, he promises me that no one will take Zion away from me. *Now might be a good time to tell him I won't be staying with him long enough for him to fulfill his promise.* After taking off our jackets, I turn back to face him.

*Well, hello, Mr. Liam Sinclair! God forgive me, I know this isn't the right time, but you know I've always had a thing for light-bright Black boys and white boys. And this white boy is very easy on the eyes! I can't remember the last time I saw a white man this clean. Oh, hold up, did he just check me out?*

"Right this way," he says.

"Lead the way."

"This is one of the bedrooms. I had to fix it up a bit, make it more practical. I'll use this bathroom and sleep out front on the sofa. That way, I can guard the door. This is the kitchen area, but we won't be here long enough to use it." We walk across the dining room and through the large living room and enter the master bedroom where he says Zion and I will stay tonight. "Please, make yourselves at home. I'm going to go look for my buddy and I'll have dinner brought up."

"Ok, thank you again, Liam. I promise we won't be any trouble and we'll be out of your hair in the morning."

"Out of my hair? What exactly is that supposed to mean?"

"Uh, it's a fairly known expression," I say sarcastically. Zion tugs my arm for me to follow him into the room.

"I know what the expression means. What I'm confused about is where exactly do you think you're going? How far do you think the two of you are going to get?"

Pulling Zion farther behind me and slightly closing the bedroom door between Liam and me, I respond with, "Just because you're helping us get out of the cold for tonight, doesn't mean I'm following you anywhere."

His gaze intensifies, not with anger, but with concern. He lowers his voice, seemingly being sensitive about Zion overhearing his words. "Look, I know we don't know each other, and I have to earn your trust, but you need to believe me when I tell you that I will never touch you or your son in a manner that is not respectful. I have witnessed women being raped in these streets and I wouldn't be able to live with myself, not knowing if the two of you are safe or not, dead or alive. I have somewhere safe where you both can relax and not look over your shoulders."

"I'm sorry, Liam. I know you mean well, but you expect what from me? I just lost my family today, and I have every intention of finding them as soon as I can." His expression turns very dark, sad really. *What's that look?* I wonder if I'm being too aggressive in my protest, so I ask him, "Liam, are you ok?"

27

"Yeah, I'm sorry. Look, I know you want to find your family, but I can help you do that in a safe way. Just think about it. I'm going out. Don't open the door for anyone."

I close and lock the bedroom door and hear the suite door close. I turn to Zion, looking at him. I scoop him up and toss him on to the king-sized bed. He giggles uncontrollably. Yes, I want to hug him and be serious, but I haven't seen my seven-year-old smile in days. This is hard on me, and I'm an adult. After several minutes of joking, jumping on the bed, and giggling, I grab him into the tightest embrace he's ever had. My voice breaks a little as I try to speak. "Zion, you know I love you, right?"

"Yes, Mommy. And Mommy, you know you're still my favorite person, right?"

"Yes, baby, I know, and you're mine. Listen, I know things are really scary right now, but I want you to know that you're not scared by yourself; I'm scared too. The thing that scares me the most is losing you. I know it hurt today when we lost Tee-tee and your cousins. Auntie Renee's not just my sister, she's my best friend, after you. I miss all of them so much."

"I know Mommy." He pauses and then continues, "Mommy, who is the man that's helping us? Can he really help us find Tee-tee? He's white like me. I like him."

"His name is Mr. Sinclair. I don't know if he can help us find Tee-tee. And for the millionth time, you're not white!" I tickle him and we giggle. "Why do you like him?"

"He doesn't let people push him around. And Mom, if I'm not white, they would have let us go with Tee-tee."

Wow, this kid always knows how to shut me up. "First of all, you know I hate it when you call me mom, makes me feel like my baby is growing up too fast. Come on, I think it's time for a bath and maybe when Mr. Sinclair comes back, we can ask him if we can have ice cream for dessert. What do you think about that?"

He squeals, "YES!"

# CHAPTER 3
# TEAM LIAM

## (Liam)

---

It only takes me a few minutes to find Thaddeus. He greets me with a hug. "Hey Lee, buddy! Sorry to hear about your mom, man." Contrary to popular belief, Thad and I keep in touch. There's a whole underground communications system that most people don't know about. That's because I invented it with my friends during our undergraduate years when I created special projects for my friends and their rich daddies. You know, the kind of projects that always skimmed off a couple of hundred grand for me and my buddies. None of our fathers needed any more money.

"Thanks, man. Listen, I sort of met someone today. She's upstairs in my suite."

"There you go, man! Leave it to your white ass to be able to still pull pussy even with a target on your back." We both laugh.

"Look, it's not even like that. I mean, don't get me wrong, she is beautiful, but right now I just want her to trust me enough to let me help her and her son."

"Oh, shit! She has a kid?"

"Yeah. The guards separated them from their family because he's biracial."

"Wait, I heard about that. How did you get involved?"

"I saw the whole thing from the burnt out building up the street. When I got here, she was waiting downstairs trying to get in."

"Look Lee, no offense, man, but ain't no Black woman getting ready to follow you into the forest. She's probably thinking you're going to kill her."

"I know, but what other choice does she have? She can't protect herself and her kid out there." The thought of her being violated angers me to my core. "Thad, if she refuses to go with me, can you give her a job?"

"You know I'd do anything to help you out. You're my brother and I wouldn't have this amazing spot without you."

I cut him off, "But?"

"But I can't take the heat the kid would bring. Your best bet is to turn up the charm tonight and convince her to go with you. Hey... it's the mother-son connection, huh?"

I look away and nod in acknowledgment. "Yeah, it is. Listen, I'm going to need food for three for the next three days, four if you can spare it."

"Spare it? Man, I got you! Plus, you're talking to the owner of the best joint in the land! And you know this!"

"Yeah, yeah, yeah. Will you please send up dinner for us? I need to get back up there before she starts freaking out."

Thad grabs me around the shoulders and smiles ever so cool. "I got you."

I leave Thad and head back to the room. When I enter, I hear them talking. I shouldn't listen in on their private conversation, but I need to know where her head is at.

*"Mommy, who is the man that's helping us? Can he really help us find Tee-tee? He's white like me. I like him."*

*"His name is Mr. Sinclair. I don't know if he can help find Tee-tee. And for the millionth time, you're not white!"* I hear laughter. *"Why do you like him?"*

*"He doesn't let people push him around. And Mom, if I wasn't white, they would have let us go with Tee-tee."* His struggle with his identity breaks my heart a little. He's a little kid. He shouldn't need to worry about these things.

*"First of all, you know I hate it when you call me mom, makes me feel like my baby is growing up too fast. Come on, I think it's time for a bath and maybe when Mr. Sinclair comes back, we can ask him if we can have ice cream for dessert. What do you think about that?"*

I pull out my phone and text Thaddeus.

**Me:** Will you please send up ice cream for dessert?

**Thad:** Sure, what flavor?

**Me:** Don't know and I can't ask. I was eavesdropping. Vanilla? Strawberry? Chocolate? Cookies and Cream?

**Thad:** I'll mix it up. You need all the help you can get!

The food arrives just before they come out of the bedroom. She almost looks startled to see me back. Zion stays behind his mother. Knowing that he's Team Liam, I decide to take a chance. "Hey buddy. I'm Liam."

He peeks around Nicole. "My mom says I have to call you Mr. Sinclair."

"Well, I'm okay with you calling me Lee; it's what my friends call me. That is, if it's okay with your mom." She looks at me, then at him, and nods. *Score one for Liam!* "Let's see what's for dinner. I have it on good authority that we're having ice cream for dessert." He smiles big and heads over to the table.

*Thad, my man!* He sent up steak for me, jambalaya for her, and pizza for Zion. Though steak is my favorite, I look at Nicole and apologize. "I'm sorry. I just asked him to send up food. I didn't ask you about allergies or preferences. Which plate do you prefer?"

"I love jambalaya! It's one of my favorite meals." And for the first time, she smiles. That smile sucked all the air out of my lungs, and I swear she glowed. Then again, it was probably just the lack of oxygen to my brain.

We sit down to eat at the long table. I sit at the head and she and Zion each skip a seat away from me to sit across from each other. Time to see what I can find out about her. "So, Nicole, tell me about yourself."

"Why?" She snaps at me without looking up from her plate.

"Just trying to get to know you."

"Why?" This time she looks up at me with one raised eyebrow.

This woman is going to be tough to crack. "Because that's how you start a friendship."

"I want to be your friend." Zion chimes in. "Can I ask you a question?"

"Zi," Nicole says firmly as if reminding him of his manners.

He looks at her and says, "May." Then he turns back to me. "May I ask you a question?"

I smile, "Absolutely buddy, ask me anything."

Nicole chuckles and says, "Good luck with that."

Zion continues, "Where did you live before you came here?"

"Rancho Palos Verdes near Los Angeles." I smile, remembering the good times and the parties I threw when my father went out of town.

"We're from Los Angeles too!" He beams, acknowledging that we have something in common.

"How old are you, Zion?

"Seven. How old are you?"

"Forty-one."

"You're older than Mommy. She's thirty-eight."

"ZION!" Her tone scolds him for the over-share.

"Sorry Mommy."

Laughing hysterically, I smile at her and say to Zion, "That can't be true. Your mom doesn't look a day over twenty-five."

Blushing, she says, "Well, you know, Black don't crack, but thanks."

"So, Zion, what else can you tell me about your mom?"

"I can tell you a lot about my mom, but if I do, I'll probably get in trouble." He curiously looks over at his mother.

"Hey Mommy, what are you going to take away now if I get in trouble? I don't have any of my games or devices."

"You like video games?" I ask. "What's your favorite thing to play?"

"Roblox, Minecraft, Fortnite. I love gaming."

"Sweet! Maybe we can play for a little while after dinner, but we should all go to bed early since we need to leave early in the morning." I look over at Nicole and see the disagreement in her face. *I'm sorry, Ms. Nicole Simmons, you're coming with me whether you like it or not.*

"Where are we going? Is it far? How are we getting there? And can you really help us find my Tee-tee?"

"And there it is. Zion, looks like your pizza is finished. Are you ready for dessert? Let's see what kind of ice cream we have." His mother tries to redirect the conversation.

I jump up to grab the ice cream out of the freezer before she can stand. "I'm told there's cookies and cream, vanilla, and chocolate. Who wants what?"

Zion screeches, "Cookies and cream is my favorite."

Nicole follows with, "I love my vanilla!"

I audibly grunt, "And chocolate has always been my favorite." My eyes lock with Nicole's and we both laugh at our flavor selections, not missing the innuendo. "It's been a while since I've had ice cream. It was always my favorite treat growing up. My mother took me out for ice cream when I lost my first tooth." Sadness fills my chest. I can't let her see my pain, not yet.

We finish up the ice cream and I invite Zion into the living room to check out Roblox. Nicole follows closely behind us. With the flip of a switch the massive screen descends from the ceiling. Zion squeals with excitement.

"Impressive," Nicole says from behind me.

With Zion already comfortably on the sofa and Nicole lounging in the comfy chair several feet behind him, I circle around the sofa instead of cutting across. I slow down just enough to whisper to Nicole, "We need to talk." I don't stop long enough to give her a chance to respond. Zion and I both sign-in to our accounts on the split screen and play for barely an hour before I notice his avatar stop moving on the screen.

"He's out," I say softly over my shoulder to Nicole. She stands and wipes her face. She's been crying. My eyes well up with tears at the memory of my own mother silently crying in the corner while I played without a care in the world. She walks over to pick up her son. "No, Nicole, let me." I pick him up and we both walk him to the bedroom and I place him on the bed. Walking back toward the bedroom door, I stop in front of her where she's leaning up against the wall with her arms crossed. "Do you want to talk now, or do you need a few minutes?"

"Do you mind if I take a shower first?"

"Not at all. I'll go take a shower too and we'll meet in the living room afterwards. Okay?"

"Yes. And Liam, thank you."

I nod and leave the room. She closes and locks the door behind me. Hopefully, I can earn her trust, make her feel safe. I walk across the huge suite to the bedroom on the other side. It's been a long day even though it's barely 7 p.m. I take off my clothes and step into the shower where for the first time,

I allow myself to feel the weight of the day. The warm water falls all over my whole body from the rain showerhead and tears fall down my face. Even though the funeral had been closed casket, her husband allowed me a few minutes with my mom where I was allowed to see her. She lay there in a navy-blue dress with the sapphire earrings I gave her on her sixtieth birthday. She told me then that she hoped I never wanted them back because she was taking them to the grave with her. With all my knowledge of the human body and pharmaceuticals, there still wasn't anything I could do to prevent her death. My mother was a great mother. She loved and cared for me even when her own life was threatened. I think that's the kind of mother Nicole is.

My thoughts shift to Nicole. Nicole, she's so beautiful. Just the thought of her makes my cock stiffen a little. I've grown use to ignoring myself, so I didn't give the urge to stroke my myself a second thought. Besides, it would be disrespectful, and I need to go talk to her. The last thing I need, she needs, is for me to have a flashback of me fucking her in my mind just moments before.

I never gave my mother a grandchild or a daughter-in-law. Yeah, I had my share of women, but I never took the time to get to know any of them. I was always too busy trying to overthrow my father. I came close once when I was twenty-eight, but after six months, she decided I was too wrapped up in trying to save the world. After my father died, I was obsessed with stockpiling money to synthesize drugs for the pandemics that I knew were coming. Until that point, I would still have an occasional lady in my bed, but once I had the dream about the change in society, I just didn't have time for sex. I mean, don't it get wrong, I still have stroke sessions with myself, but over the last three years, it's been less often. *Shit, I've become a weird, loner, mountain dweller.*

I need to get out of this shower. Nicole is probably waiting for me.

# CHAPTER 4

# A DECENT MAN

(Nicole)

---

I close and lock the door behind Liam and head to the bathroom. Great, there's a rainfall shower. I've always wanted to try one, but never have. It's too hard to keep my flat-ironed hair straight. Well, I guess I'm taking a bath. I turn on the water and take off my clothes. Looking in the mirror I sigh, "Crap, I look like someone beat me with a roll of quarters. I've cried too much today." I've lost a lot too, my support, my dignity, my faith in my people. My mother and father made sure we grew up to be proud of our Blackness, but here I am, ashamed of how my people constantly reject my child. He's a part of me, and that should be enough.

I know what Liam wants to talk about. He wants me to follow him off somewhere. My head is telling me to run away from him. My heart is telling me he's a decent man. My gut? Well, my gut is telling me that he's my best option for keeping my son safe. I turn off the water and step into the tub.

Liam is tall and built like a god—dark brown hair, deep blue eyes. He's gorgeous, more than gorgeous. He's strong, prepared, and calculating. Yet, it's clear that he's kind and gentle. Five years ago, I would have met him, fallen in love with him, and followed him anywhere. Things are different now. It hurts my heart that my people haven't found a better way. The oppressed oppressing the oppressor, never works. I learned that from one of my favorite philosophers. It's too dangerous to be with Liam. "Oh, Renee. I wish you were here to tell me what to do." I really need my big sister.

I spend a few more minutes in the bath before drying off and heading into the bedroom to throw on some pajamas. Unfortunately, I only had room for something small, so I packed a set with shorts and a cami. I cannot go in there wearing this. Please let there be a robe in this closet. I walk over to the closet and open it. "Yes!" Okay, time to face the music.

# CHAPTER 5
# ALL ROADS LEAD TO YOU
(Liam)

I enter the living room before her, wearing only my boxer briefs because I forgot my robe is in the other bedroom. My other options were the wet, freshly washed clothes I just took off, or my suit I wore to the funeral. I hope she isn't offended. As soon as she comes out, I'll run in and grab my robe. That's when I hear the door open. I look up and there she is standing in my robe. This is bad. I grab the closest decorative pillow on the sofa and place it in my lap to hide my growing erection. There is nothing sexier than a woman, naked, under her man's clothes.

Nervously, I quickly apologize for my nakedness. "Hey, sorry Nicole. I forgot my robe was in your room."

"Oh, I'm sorry, Liam. Here..." She opens the robe to take it off and I see all her bare skin in those skimpy shorts and clingy tank top.

"No, please, you keep it. Just please forgive my bare chest." Though it sounded gentlemanly when I said it, it was really to hide just how un-gentlemanly I was being.

She is just as eager as I am to change the subject. "May I ask you something?"

I look at her with sincerity, "Absolutely."

"How did you come to have a suite in this amazing resort?"

"Can you keep a secret?" She nods. "Well, I used to own this resort. When the racial clash went downhill for people who look like me, I signed it over to my best friend and asked if I could keep this room."

"Wow. May I ask you another question?" I nod. "Not that I'm staring, but what happened to your chest?"

"I was shot." Changing the subject quickly, I ask, "What size shoes do you and Zion wear?"

She takes a deep breath, and I brace myself for the fight that doesn't come. "Seven for me and kids size two for Zion." I guess she notices shock covering my face because she asks, "What?"

Smiling and shaking my head with my hands up, "Nothing."

"You're surprised I'm not fighting you?"

"Well, yes. Give me just a second." I send Thad a text asking him if he can find boots for both of them. Then, I continue, "What made you change your mind?

"Water helps me think; it always has. While I was in the bath, I tried to come up with a feasible plan to find my family while keeping Zion safe."

I already know the answer but need to hear her say it. "And?"

She sighs, "And all roads lead to you. Please tell me you're not one of those men who likes to gloat."

I smile, "Absolutely not. I just want you both to be safe."

"I'm almost afraid to ask, but where are you taking us?"

"I have a home in the mountains. It's a three-day hike. Before I came back to civilization yesterday, I was up there for three years without seeing another person."

"Okay, the mother in me is officially freaked out. You want me to take my seven-year-old child on a three-day hike to a remote location where there are no doctors?"

"Is Zion sick?"

"No, but..."

"Are you sick?"

"Well, no, but..."

"Then what's the problem? Didn't you see that room in there? There are a lot of medical procedures I can perform."

"Are you a doctor?"

I stare at her hoping this conversation won't lead her to changing her mind. "No, I'm not an MD, but I have a PhD in biological sciences in public health."

"Stop talking!" I look at her as if she slapped me in the face. "I'm sorry, but you're giving me an anxiety attack. I only recently started getting them."

As I spring up, the pillow falls out of my lap. Thank goodness my erection went away. Gently, I take her hand and help her sit on the sofa. I sit down in front of her on the coffee table. "I'm guessing you probably aren't taking any medication for these attacks, so just sit here, close your eyes, and take a few, deep cleansing breaths." She does and I watch her breasts rise and fall with each breath. One day, I'm going to hold her in my arms and feel them against me. After a few deep breaths, she slowly opens her eyes. "Better?"

"Yes. Sorry about that. This is hard for me, I used to be so strong and self-assured."

"You still are! What you did today for Zion was one of the bravest things I have ever seen. You, are very strong." I look down and realize I'm still holding her hand. She hadn't noticed either. She begins to pull away, so I gently let go. "We should get some sleep. It's best if we leave under the cover of night. I'm thinking 4 a.m. which means we need to be up by 3:30."

"You sure you don't need to ask me more questions before you take me off into the woods?" She gives me a little smile.

"If I ask you everything I want to know about you now, what will we talk about during our hike for the next three days?" I smirk and stand. She stands too, and I walk her to her room. "Good night, Nicole. It has been my absolute pleasure meeting you today." I turn and go back to the sofa where I'll be sleeping tonight.

CHAPTER 6

# THE REAL ADVENTURE

(Nicole)

---

The night must have flown by because I'm awakened by a soft knock at the door, and then I hear Liam's soothing voice, "Nicole? Nicole, time to wake up." I don't respond right away because I think I'm still dreaming. Then, I hear, "Zion, buddy, are you awake? Wake your mom up please."

I call out to let him know I heard him, "Okay, I'm up."

"Zion, time to wake up, kiddo. We have to go."

"I don't want to leave this bed, Mommy, please. Please, can we stay here?"

"I wish, baby. Do you remember when I told you that the next few weeks were going to be full of exciting adventures?"

"Yes, but I don't like this adventure. It isn't any fun. It's too sad and scary."

My heart breaks to hear him say those words. "Yes, it has been, but now the real adventure begins. We're going with Liam, but we must leave before the sun comes up so no one will see him or you."

Zion sits straight up, "We're going with Liam?"

"Yes, we are, but we need to hurry up and get out of here." We both get out of bed and are ready in fifteen minutes. We head into the living room to find Liam at the dining room table having breakfast.

"Either of you hungry? Thad sent up some eggs, bacon, potatoes, toast, and juice if you're hungry. But you only have a few minutes to eat. And guys, you can't wear those sneakers. The boots over there are for you."

"Okay, you heard him Zion. Put some food in your stomach."

"Nicole, you too. I'm finished. Let me repack for you. I have a backpack for you; that suitcase won't cut it either."

I pout a little because that's my favorite piece of luggage. It's a hard-shell Tinker Bell suitcase. I remember when I got it, but I won't complain. I simply say, "Ok, thank you, Liam." I sit down with Zion to eat.

Liam finishes packing my backpack and calls me over. "I need to ask you something."

"Yes?"

"I saw your tampons. Are you bleeding right now? I ask because there's a certain way you'll need to dispose of them on our hike."

"Oh, no. Not yet, I just always have to be prepared. Crap, Liam, will I be able to get supplies?"

"Don't worry, I got you covered. I'm sure I won't have everything you need or are accustomed to, but we'll figure it all out. I promise. Once we cross into what I call the safe zone, I don't want you to worry anymore."

"When do you think we'll get to that point?"

"This afternoon."

"Hey guys, are we leaving or not?" Zion has put on his boots and jacket and made it to the door.

Liam gives a chuckle and says, "Yes, sir! Let's do this." He walks over to Zion. "How do your boots feel? Comfortable?" Zion smiles and nods. "Nicole, what about you? Are your feet good?"

I stand up after putting them on. "Yeah, they feel good." I turn to Zion, "Zi, don't forget your mask. It's over…" Liam cuts me off.

"About the masks, those are a no go. Those don't provide enough protection." He hands us two masks that he grabbed from the lab. They match his. "These protect against most airborne agents. They also have a red-light indicator that will flash when anything bad is detected. I designed them myself." Handing them to us, he says, "Okay, now we're ready."

Taking a last look at the beautiful suite and my favorite piece of luggage, I wonder what this next chapter of my life will look like. Will I find my family? Will this new place be a place where Zion can thrive and be accepted? Will he be happy? Is Liam who he says he is? Will he make a good role model for Zion? I sigh and turn to Zion and Liam. "I'm ready."

# CHAPTER 7
# I WILL DROP YOU
## (Liam)

---

After grabbing the boots Thad left outside the suite door, I shot him a quick thank you text to let him know we would be leaving soon. Once we all had breakfast and got dressed, it was time to go. As soon as I open the door to head out, I spot Thad leaning on the wall directly in front of the door.

"Wow, okay, I see how it is. You stroll in here off the street, eat my food, use my connections and what, slither out in the middle of the night without saying goodbye? Not cool man."

I pause, not sure if he's actually upset. "I'm sorry, Thad. I just know that it's a crazy hour and you're a married man now, with a kid. I just didn't want to disturb you."

"I'm not mad. I'm hurt. And you are never a disturbance to me. I never sleep when you're here. I know you've gotten used to being alone out there in the wilderness, but I worry about you." Changing the subject quickly, "You must be Nicole." He reaches out and shakes her hand. "Nice to meet you." She nods. "Listen, I know you're probably wondering if you can trust this guy. Let me tell you, you can. We've been friends since grade school, best friends. He's more like the brother I never had." Turning his attention back to me, "I'm sorry again, man, about your mom. Wish I could have been there."

I interrupt him because I don't need Nicole worrying about me or feeling sorry for me. "No, it's all good. I know you would have been there if you could. I love you, brother, but we really need to get going. Since you're here, help me lock up?" We lock up and head out of the building.

As we walk, Thad continues questioning me, "You have everything?"

"Yes, Thad."

"Water?"

"Check."

"The food I packed up?"

"Check."

"Weapons and ammo?"

"Do you not see this big ass rifle on my back?" I laugh. "Check."

Then he whispers, "A fine ass honey to keep you warm at night?"

We both laugh. "Let's not get ahead of ourselves." We reach the utility shed at the edge of the resort. "Okay, until next time?" We hug.

"Until next time. Be careful. I love you, man. Let me know when you make it back."

"Love you too, bro. Will do." I open the shed door with the same key I use for my room. Turning to Nicole, "After you."

Nicole crosses between Thad and me and turns to Thad. "Thank you for everything. I'll try to take care of him." She and Zion head into the Shed.

Thad gives me a wicked grin and a wink as I close the door behind us. "Right this way." Toward the back of the shed is a counter. I reach under it and punch in a code, the floor opens up.

Zion and Nicole gasp. "COOL! Mommy, it's like one of those spy movies!" They head down the stairs and I follow. The floor slides back into lock position. It's dark but there are motion sensor lights which garner another gasp from Zion.

"This tunnel is two hundred feet and will let us out right at the tree line. I'll exit first in case there are any surprises." It's now 4:15 a.m. and we're a bit off schedule so I hurry us through this part. We need to get as far off the beaten path before the sun comes up. I hope Zion can keep up. "Guys we're a little behind schedule so I may need us to pick up the pace for the next two hours." I reach down into my pants leg and pull out a Glock 26 and hand it to Nicole. "Do you know how to use one of these?"

Her eyes widen. "No, not at all! I have a PhD in Anthropology!" She snatches the gun from my hand. "Does this thing have a safety?"

Still moving us at a quick pace. "Not the way you're thinking, but it won't accidentally fire. You have to intentionally pull the trigger. Zion, under no circumstance do you touch any of these guns before I can give you proper instruction. Do you understand?" He nods. "Nicole, if anything happens to me, find your way back to the resort and defend your son. Got it?" She nods. We reach the hatch to exit. "Ready?" They both nod. I take several deep breaths and open the hatch. Rifle pointed up; I climb out of the hole. I reach the top at eye level and scan the area. Everything looks clear. After I climb out, I gesture to them to follow as I stand guard. Once they're out, I close and lock the hatch and cover it up with whatever is covering the surrounding ground. "Okay, let's move." The next five miles are crucial. I need them to stay close and quiet because white people hideout up here trying to stay out of the guards' way. It's far away enough for the guards not to notice, but close enough to have access to supplies. Capture could mean a life of enslavement, or worse, death. These people have nothing and, therefore, have nothing to lose. So, they do what they have to in order to survive including stealing and killing. I hope Nicole will forgive me for springing the gun on her. But if I had tried to give it to her earlier, she may not have come.

Suddenly, I hear a noise coming up behind us that is moving at a different pace. I instinctively spin around and aim my rifle in front of me. Nicole and Zion duck down. *Good instincts.* I don't move. Without shouting I say, "Come out." A young white boy, twelve, maybe thirteen, comes into my view. He could be a decoy. I'm not stupid. I don't lower my gun. "I don't want to hurt you, kid. What do you want?"

With his hands in the air, he says, "Do you have any food, mister?"

That's when I hear the steps approaching behind me. I spin the other way and Nicole draws her weapon on the kid. I say to the two older boys approaching, "We're just passing through. I'm not into hurting kids."

Nicole speaks behind me, "But I will drop you if it comes down to your life or my son's." *Where'd that come from?* I knew she was an amazing woman. I'm actually turned on.

The oldest of the crew, maybe sixteen or seventeen, holds up his hands. "Nice guns. You win. Do you have anything that might keep us from waking up everyone on this hillside?" He tilts his head and raises his eyebrows.

"What will help you out the most?"

"Got any drugs on you?"

"Nope, and if I did, I wouldn't give drugs to a kid."

"Cash?"

I reach into my pants and pull out another wad of ten, hundred-dollar bills and toss it to him. "Are we good?"

A huge smile hits his face. "Yes, mister! Can I come with you? Maybe work for you?"

"No. Just stay out of trouble and share with your crew." He nods and they run off.

I kneel down to check on Zion and Nicole. "You two good?" They nod, yes. "You both handled yourselves great with that. Let's get out of here."

Two hours pass and the sun is up. I see the marker I planted when I came down the mountain two days ago. We're out of the worst of it, but I wait another mile before I tell them. The temperature has dropped slightly, but early spring weather is typically cold out here. Lowering my rifle, I slow our pace. I look over at Nicole. "We're out of harm's way. Every step we take now is safer than the step before it." I start at her shoulder and slide my hand down her arm to her hand and take the gun, putting it back in my ankle holster. "Zion, are you ok?"

"Yes, I'm fine."

"It's safe to take off our masks." I decide to walk next to Nicole so we can get better acquainted. "So, PhD, huh?"

"Yes, but it wasn't all it was cracked up to be. Getting tenure for a Black woman at a predominately white institution was not a walk in the park."

"I have a PhD in biological sciences from Harvard."

"Okay, knock it off. No one is that perfect," she smiles.

"I'm not perfect, far from it."

"You protect women and their kids. You give multimillion-dollar properties to your friends. You ask kids who mean you harm what will help them the most. And you have an advanced degree from Harvard. That's pretty close to perfection in my book." She's impressed.

I smile at the admiration. "That's just the good stuff you know about me. Where did you earn your PhD?"

"USC, nowhere close to Harvard, though they seem to think so. What did you do before all of this stuff started happening?"

"Well, my master's is from USC." I interject to let her know this Havard man respects the prestige of a degree from USC. "As far as what I did before, I was the owner and president of the board for a finance company that has been in my family for four generations. I had a couple of pharmaceutical and communication patents. Then, I had the foresight to get all of my financial affairs in order five years before the chaos happened."

"What? Are you saying that you actually knew the fabric of the country was going to be turned upside down and there would be multiple world pandemics?"

"I guess you think I'm strange, huh?"

Nicole smirks and shrugs her shoulders. "Well, yeah, but not because you can see the future." For the first time, she smiles at me like there is a connection between us.

I smile back before trying to prove to her I'm not a total headcase. "Seeing the pandemics coming was science, seeing the future of my race, that was more mystical, and I haven't experienced anything else like it since."

Zion has been walking in front of us for several miles, just taking in the sights. I've only needed to call him back on the path twice. I love how he's taking it all in. If I ever had a son, I'd want him to be like Zion—smart, fun, inquisitive, and respectful. We've been walking for almost eight hours. They're getting tired and there's a spot I enjoy coming up. It's a clearing with a stream in the distance. I've seen a few deer stop there for water. "I think we need to rest for a bit. Eat and relax. I know a nice spot."

"I'm not tired," Zion says. "I'm ready to get where we're going."

"Well, we're going to have to sleep out here for two nights because where we're going is three days away. Besides, your mom looks like she could use a break, and we all have to take care of each other out here. What do you say?"

"Alright. But just so you know, my mom doesn't like camping. She said she would only go glamping."

"Zion, I would appreciate you not talking about me like I'm not here," she says as she rolls her eyes. They seem to tease each other a lot.

"What's glamping?" I ask.

"I'm terrified of bears and I'm a lady, which means, I need to sleep indoors. And I need running water and electricity."

It's a proud declaration and I laugh hardily at the adorableness of it.

# Chapter 8
# It Already Feels Better
(Nicole)

---

I'm finding that I am really enjoying Liam's company. It's been forever since I've been with a man, and I don't know why my body is responding to Liam this way. I barely know him. Strike that, I don't know him. I've never even had a one-night stand. I don't do casual relationships, never have. Sex without the emotional connection, just never really appealed to me.

He leads us to a small clearing in the woods. There's a huge fallen tree. "Hang on a second. Let me make sure it's safe." He goes and looks around the fallen tree and I hope he's not looking for snakes, but I'm pretty sure he is. Once he checks it out, he gives us the "all clear" and waves us over. "Have a seat," he says. I take his extended hand and he guides me over to sit.

This place is the thing dreams are made of. We're surrounded by trees, and I can hear the stream that's fifty yards in front of us. Liam goes in the extra satchel he's been carrying and hands us each a turkey sub. "Thanks. And, by the way, this scenery is absolutely beautiful. I have only imagined that such a place exists. How did you find it?"

"I've gotten to know these woods pretty well over the last five years." Liam smirks and teases Zion. "Zion, you're eating pretty quickly for someone who isn't hungry."

"I'm just trying to hurry up so we can start back walking."

"There's no rush now, buddy. You can take your time eating and we can take our time getting where we're going. It's a slower pace up here." Liam turns his attention from Zion to me. "Almost as if time itself has slowed down." Though I've been looking at him all day, I really take him in without any distractions for the first time. Now that he's in his element, I can see there's so much more to him than the warrior he projects. He's gentle, and there's something very vulnerable behind his eyes.

Caught in the gaze of his eyes, I respond. "Yeah, I can see that. So, there's no one else where we're going?" He shakes his head. "Doesn't that get lonely?"

He nods and tries to downplay it. "Yes, but I've gotten used to it. It will be nice to have company for a change." He looks away from me, staring out into the distance, and says, "It already feels better."

My impetuous son unknowingly ruins the moment. "Finished!"

"Zion! That was too fast! Make sure you drink some water, son."

"I'm fine, Mommy. Just hurry up, please." He looks at Liam and says, "Is it safe for me to explore?"

Looking around, Liam says, "No, not really. It's safe from people, but I have seen bears up here. Even though you're a big boy, you're still just a tiny morsel to a bear. Why don't you explore right around here? Stay within a few feet of us."

"Please." I add to let Zion know that I agree with Liam. Once Zion is far enough away, I decide to ask Liam a question I think I already know the answer to. "Why did you come down from your mountain now?"

He balls up his paper and puts the trash back into the resealable bag in his satchel. It takes him several moments to respond, but I wait patiently. "My mom passed away. Yesterday was her funeral." He blinks hard and turns away from me, resting his elbows on his lap. Whispering, "My mom was an amazing mother. Much like you with Zion, she always put me before herself when I was growing up, even though I didn't live with her."

Scooting over to be closer to him, I take his large hand into mine to let him know it is okay to feel what he's feeling. "I'm so sorry. Why didn't she live with you, if that's okay to ask?

"It's fine. Really, it's a huge part of who I am and if we're going to be friends, you should know." Sitting up straight to face me, he continues. "My father was an abusive racist. He beat my mother and threatened to kill her if she ever came around me. She would meet me at the park when my various nannies took me. All of my nannies were women of color, and my father would call them any and all racial slurs you can imagine. But my mom and all of my nannies taught me love, kindness, and compassion. I hated my father, and I was glad when he dropped dead."

I squeeze his hand. "You're right. That explains a lot. I'm glad you had good nurturers. I am a firm believer that a man who has a good relationship with his mother, or mother figure, grows up to be a great husband and father." I smile nervously, not sure if I should have said that last part. "So, did you have a favorite nanny?"

His mood lightens, and he smiles, looking at our intertwined fingers. His hands dwarf mine in size. "Yes, Ms. Cassie. Ms. Cassie was basically my grandmother. She was the only one who really got to know my mom. She took care of both of us."

Now that he is sounding like himself again, I begin slowly withdrawing my hand, but to my surprise, he tightens his grip. He raises one finger to his mouth for me to be quiet, and then he looks around for Zion. Zion has already put his attention on the deer that is just a few feet in front of us, heading toward the stream.

Liam smiles and whispers, "I was hoping we would see at least one while we were here." He gazes at me as my eyes fill with amazement. I meet his gaze and for the first time, I don't deny the attraction. I blush and he smiles softly. The doe laps up the water until she has her fill and then quickly runs back into the safety of the trees.

Zion jumps up from where he'd been playing with a lizard and runs over to us, the action breaks up our interaction. "Mommy, did you see that? That was freakin' awesome!"

"Yes, it was! How about you pack up? I think I'm rested."

We all stand, and Liam takes our trash to dispose of it properly later. We walk and talk, getting to know each other for a few more hours until it starts to get dark.

CHAPTER 9

# A FEAST OF TALES

(Liam)

---

"Alright you two, ready for your first night of camping?"

"YES!" Zion shouts with excitement.

Nicole says, "Absolutely not." But she giggles anyway. I pull the tent out of my backpack and begin setting it up. "What do you want us to do? How can we help?"

"I'm so used to doing everything by myself. Some help would be great. Zion, look around this area and find as many sticks and stones as you can. We need to make a fire so we can heat dinner. Nicole, why don't you just stand there and look pretty." I flash her a smile and a wink.

She blushes, as she's been doing every time I compliment her, and says, "I can do something else. I'm capable."

Zion walks past her and says, "See Mommy, I told you, you really are pretty."

I chuckle at the exchange. "Okay, pretty lady, if you want something to do, look in my satchel and decide what we're eating for dinner. What you don't pick, we'll eat for lunch tomorrow. Tomorrow night's dinner will be a surprise."

She stops in her tracks and turns to me, "Does that mean we have to catch dinner tomorrow?"

I brush pass her and poke her in the side, "Shhh! Come on, don't ruin the surprise!"

Laughing she says, "Um, I call standing around looking pretty for my job duties tomorrow."

The two-person tent was quick to set up. I swapped out the single for this one back at the resort, but I didn't have anything bigger. For dinner, Nicole pulled out chili and three bags of corn chips. "What does a rich white boy know about chili and corn chips?"

"Oh, okay, I see you have jokes."

She pokes her tongue out at me and for the first time, I allow myself to acknowledge my growing desire to pursue her romantically. Bringing her out here away from the madness has been worth it. I wonder why she's not married and where Zion's father is. Hopefully, we'll get to talk later.

I call Zion over to show him the safe way to build a fire in the forest. Once dinner is done, we play *charades* and *would you rather* before Zion begins to fall asleep. Nicole helps him into the tent, and he's out in a matter of seconds. I'm not sure if she will come back out, but I hope she does. Just as the thought crosses my mind, I see her backing out of the tent. She must be enjoying my company as much as I'm enjoying hers. Nicole sits on the other side of the fire, and

I frown a little. She smiles and gets up to come sit closer to where I'm leaning against a tree.

"Nicole, why aren't you married? I can't imagine a man not wanting to be with you. You're beautiful, smart, funny, sexy."

Smiling but looking away, "Thank you. I was married." She drops her head, embarrassed to share with me. "He was a jerk, not like your father, but a jerk none the less. He never hit me, but he never stopped cheating on me." Shaking her head, "I was so stupid. I just kept forgiving him, even though it broke my heart every time."

"Why did you forgive him?"

"I know it's dumb, but I didn't want to admit that I had failed. I failed at something as simple as being a wife." She looks down and shrugs.

"I haven't been married, but I hardly believe that being a wife is simple." She nods and shrugs, acknowledging that I have a point. "How did you fail?"

"For the longest time, I wasn't sure. I was supportive in every sense of the word, or so I thought. I supported him in everything: his work, his hobbies. And when he lost his job, I paid for everything. Turns out, what I saw as support, he saw as me pushing him out of his comfort zone."

"What about in the bedroom? If that's not too private to share."

"I tried. I really did. I was willing to try 95 percent of anything he wanted, but in the end, our sex life was non-existent."

"How do you mean?"

"He said he cheated because you can't fuck a wife, excuse my language." She looks up as I smile, letting her know that I'm not offended. "I asked him to explain. He said a wife should be made love to and not fucked." She shyly lowered her head, embarrassed by what she has just admitted. "Well, for the record, he wasn't making love to me either."

"Nicole, you know that was an excuse for him to keep sleeping around, right? He wanted to make it seem like he was being respectful, but that was total bullshit. Yes, a woman should be made love to, but there's nothing wrong with fucking your woman, your wife, from time to time. For instance, if I was your man, I'd want to share every physical expression of my emotional and physical self with you. I would want to explore your entire body and how it responds to my touch. I'd tenderly make love to you as often as I could, but sometimes I would want to remind you of my carnal desire for you by fucking you so deep and hard that my name becomes the only word in your vocabulary. But maybe that's just me."

She gasps, and her eyes grow even bigger, like a doe caught in the headlights. Squirming, she averts her eyes as her breathing becomes shallow. Very subtly squeezing her thighs together, brushing a few stray hairs behind her ear, she exhales slowly. It's a feast of tales to hide the truth of how turned on she is by my words. Finally, she manages a response, "Well, damn. Good to know." Blushing, she slowly caresses her bottom lip with her thumb.

Getting back on topic before I succumb to my desires, "What did he say when you took Zion?"

The question interrupts whatever is going on in her mind. "Oh, no, Zion isn't his. I was married to a Black man. I was artificially inseminated with Zion after our divorce. I figured I was an educated, gainfully employed woman and I could do it on my own. Unlike you, I didn't anticipate the impending changes in society because I definitely would not have selected a white donor. Plus, I didn't feel like getting back into the dating game."

"Well, that was not the answer I was expecting. You're amazing. So, you went through your pregnancy, labor, and delivery, everything all alone?"

"I wasn't alone. I had my sister and my mom. My sister, Renee, is my best friend. I miss her. She is my biggest cheerleader. She's a nurse and was with me in the OR when I had my emergency C-section." She sighs, "I wonder what she's doing right now." She gazes up at the stars.

"Hey, she's probably thinking about you, too. I'm going to help you find her."

"So, you've said. I believe you will try, but it still makes me sad. Anyway, what about you?"

"Women?" I should have known reciprocation would be required in this conversation. Not that I don't want to be honest with her, I just don't want to come off as a weird, sex deprived, recluse.

"Yeah. Come on, Liam. I tell, you tell."

I shrug and look down at the grass I've been plucking with my hand while we've been talking. "Not much to tell. I've never been married, and I haven't been with anyone in five years."

"What, like no sex?" The look on her face is one of total shock.

Chuckling at how it sounds now that I've said it out loud, "Nope."

"Get out of here with that. Really? I don't believe it. A gorgeous, confident man like you?"

I smile, nod, and shrug at the compliment. "Really. What about you? How long has it been for you?"

She raises an eyebrow, "Almost a decade."

"Why? I'm certain men must flock to you."

"Because between work and Zion, I just never made time for myself. And you're just as bad as I am, so stop judging me."

I smile devilishly, "So…"

"Let me stop you right there, Mr. Charisma. I know there's an attraction brewing here, but I'm not into one-night stands. And I'm not sure how to get back to civilization if it doesn't work out. So, no."

"Now, let me stop you, pretty lady. I never said anything about a one-night stand. I know we just met, but I'm enjoying getting to know you. Out here, we have nothing but time. I'm not in a rush and I'm not going anywhere. Let's just keep getting to know each other and if anything happens between us, we'll deal with it. But you need to know that I recognize you are not the kind of woman to use for a one-night stand." I pause and look down, not wanting to look into her eyes, fearing that they are filled with rejection. "You're the kind you keep and marry." I pull up my pant leg, hand her the gun and show her the bear spray behind us.

Nicole grabs my arm as I get up. "Liam, are you ok? I didn't mean to upset you. I'm just scared. My life has changed so much over the last two days."

"No, Nicole, I'm not upset. I just need a little physical distance between us. I just promised you I'll wait, but I'm also very attracted to you. If I stay here any longer, I might just have to have you and I don't want to rush you."

"Maybe we can find a happy medium. We've both been through a lot, lost a lot. Maybe we can just take things slowly. Like right now, I really don't want you to leave."

"No?"

She smiles tenderly while looking up at me with those big, beautiful, brown eyes, as the light from the fire accentuates her delicate features, "No."

"What do you want me to do?"

"Will you just hold me for a little while? It's been forever and a day since I've been held, or comforted."

"Yes." I put my back up against the tree trunk and pull her in close to me, wrapping one arm around her. With my free hand, I grab the blanket I planned to sleep under and spread it over our legs. "This good?" She nods her head against my chest. "Nicole, my mom always told me that one day I would meet someone special and that my heart would know it before my head would. She said that it would happen in the blink of an eye. I never understood what she meant until yesterday. I think it's significant that I met you on the day I laid her to rest. It was like she guided me right to you." Nicole tilts her head up to look at me. It's an image I plan to hold on to for the rest of my life. Needing more contact, I ask her, "May I kiss you?" She nods. I lower my head and our lips meet. Her lips are soft and warm; there is a sweetness to them. I kiss her slowly and softly. Each kiss flows through different parts of me, like life itself is being restored throughout my body. I didn't realize I needed to be restored. She touches my chest and then my face encouraging me to escalate things, so I part her lips with mine. She doesn't resist me as I dip my tongue into her mouth. Her tongue welcomes mine into an erotic dance. Running her fingers through my hair, pulling me in closer, our breaths become heavy with passion. I need to pull away because my cock is rubbing against the zipper of my jeans. It's becoming uncomfortable. I have to stop kissing her before I need to pull it out to relieve the pressure. I place a last few soft kisses on her lips and press her head back to my chest. "Best first kiss ever," I whisper. She nods her head against my chest in agreement. We sleep in this position until the sun comes up.

# CHAPTER 10
# UNDER THE STARS
## (Nicole)

Today we got moving early. Liam said that we made great time. We made it to our overnight site two hours early. Apparently, we're only six hours away from our destination. Normally, the thought of a six-hour hike would be daunting, but after the last two days, six more hours sounds great. And once again, our campsite looks like paradise to me. It's at the bottom of a small waterfall that pours into a beautiful pond surrounded by lush green grass and trees. Liam says that he's never seen bears this high up, but he always assumes they're around.

"This is stunning." He brushes pass me, grazing my arm with his and it sends a shiver up my spine. We've been careful to keep our distance today around Zion, but he's already taken off toward the water, so he didn't see the exchange.

Liam leans in close and says, "I'm glad you like it." He turns and calls out to Zion, "Hey buddy, we need to work before we play. Where's our firewood?"

"Ah man, Liam! There aren't as many sticks around here." Zion comes back to us sulking.

"I know, that's why I'm going to go with you right over there where those trees are and help you look. Plus, since I use this site often, there's already a fire pit." He winks at me. "Will you make our site cozy? You know, put your woman's touch on it. I'll set up the tent when I come back, just spread out everything, please."

I watch Liam and Zion walk off together, discussing some Obby on Roblox. The image of them together warms my heart. Did it really take all of this for me to find Mr. Right? He's going to disappoint me in some way. But for now, for once, I'm going to do something for me. Last night was amazing, and all we did was kiss a little. I continue to set up camp by pulling out the tent and laying it out without attempting to put it up. I pull out the blanket I found in my backpack this morning when I changed clothes. Liam must have stuck it in there when he repacked it. I look up and see the guys heading back, each carrying a bundle of sticks. They drop them into the fire pit in the center of where I set up.

"Zion, I will get the tent setup and then we can play for a bit. You're a great helper." I like how Liam talks with Zion and encourages him.

"Mommy, do you think we can go swimming?"

"I don't know. Ask Liam."

"Ask Liam? Is Liam going to be my daddy?"

My heart begins to pound. I can't believe this child is embarrassing me like this. The last thing I need is for Liam to think I'm trying to saddle him with being responsible for my son. "Zion! Please keep your voice down and stop asking me questions like that."

"Too late, I already heard it." Liam looks over at Zion and smiles. "I wouldn't mind if you thought of me as a father figure, if that's alright with your mom."

"Cool! Can I call you daddy?"

Clearly agitated and embarrassed, I yell at my child, "OH MY GOD, ZION! That's enough. No, you can't call him daddy. His name is Liam and if anything changes, I will let you know."

I feel Liam's large arm wrap around my waist from the front as he faces the pond and I face the tree line; he whispers to me, "That's enough." I look up at him. There is no anger, embarrassment, nor judgment in his eyes. I take a deep breath and nod.

"You know, Zi, I think you're right. Let's go for a swim," Liam calls out to Zion. I watch them race to the water. Liam takes off his shirt while running. His back is just as amazing as his chest, broad and muscular. Just before they run in, they stop to take off their boots and socks. Both strip down to their underwear. I giggle and shake my head at the image and prospect that maybe Liam wanted the role of father in my kid's life. Liam's voice pulls me out of my thoughts. "Hey, pretty lady, are you coming?"

Walking toward the water, I decide I'm going to keep my shirt on and I'm grateful that I threw on my boy-cut panties for comfort. Zion has seen me in a swimsuit before, but it just doesn't seem appropriate to let him see me wearing nothing but underwear in front of Liam. I take off my boots, socks, and jeans, and walk into the cool waters of early spring. They both splash me. Zion's splashes hit me no higher than my waist. As I bend down to gather water to splash him back, I get hit with a wave of water that hits my face and hair. I freeze in shock. Both of the guys freeze too.

"Ooh, Liam, you are in big trouble! Mommy does not like getting her hair wet."

"Shoot, Nicole, I am so sorry. Are you mad?"

I look at Zion first, and then I look at Liam. I calmly reach up to take my ponytail holder off and undo my braid. My hair drops down my back to my waist. I never cut my hair, but I like to keep it flat ironed. I look at both of them before I flash a wicked smile. "Oh, no, you're both in trouble!" Zion giggles hysterically as we all splash each other. Liam lifts Zion and spins him like a helicopter before he tosses him a short distance. He hasn't had this much fun since we left our home over a month ago. Yeah, this is going to be good for him, for us. We play for a bit longer before Liam decides they should work on trying to catch dinner.

As I find a spot to dry off in, I braid my now curly hair into two cornrows while watching Liam walk Zion over to a different area of the pond. He points to different spots of the pond and instructs Zion. Then I see him reach down with his hands. *Is he fishing with just his bare hands? We're going to starve tonight.* But after only the second try, he comes up with a sizable fish. I'm impressed. Then Zion tries. Liam is very patient with him, which makes him be patient with himself. After a dozen tries, Zion finally catches one. It's smaller than the one Liam caught, but he's thrilled, nonetheless. I can hear him squealing with excitement. I jump up and run to my backpack to see if I can find my phone. It's been off since we left the resort, no need for it without signal or a way to charge it, but I want to take a picture of them when they get over here.

"Mommy, mommy, did you see that?"

"I sure did. That was awesome! You did such a great job!"

"Liam said the first time he tried, it took him a whole hour before he got one."

"Ok, can I get a picture of you two with these fish?" They pose in their boxer briefs and boots holding up the fish. It is the most adorable sight I've seen in a long time.

Liam cleaned and cooked both fish and we ate right around nightfall. Tonight, it's singing under the stars. I've never liked my singing voice, but Zion loves when I sing to him; Liam doesn't seem to mind either. Then, Liam totally surprises me with his rendition of Joe's "I Wanna Know." In my head I thank whoever versed him in R&B. I thought it was very sweet and sexy. Thank goodness my child has lost interest and fallen asleep because my panties are now soaked. "Liam, will you please carry him to the tent?"

"Absolutely." He picks up an exhausted Zion and carries him to bed. He gets Zion comfortable and zips the tent.

Standing up, Liam turns to me with desire in his eyes. He comes over, drops to his knees in front of me and leans back on his haunches. "I have wanted to kiss you all day, pretty lady." I lift myself to my knees, to get as close as I can to eye level with him. I gaze into his deep blue eyes. *I think I want to spend the rest of life getting lost in these deep blues.* We quietly stare at each other for a few moments like we're memorizing each other's face. He leans in and kisses my waiting lips. He places his arm down the length of my spine for support. With his other hand, he pulls my legs from under me and wraps them around his waist forcing me to straddle him. Then, he twists us around so that he's in a seated position facing the tent with my back to it.

He grunts against my lips, "Nicole, I want you so fucking bad."

Panting, I tell him, "I want you too, Liam, but I just can't with Zion so close."

"Yeah, I know, and I wouldn't put you in that situation. That's why your back is to the tent. I'll keep watch while I touch you and make you come. May I touch you, Nicole?"

Breathlessly I beg, "Please."

He unbuttons and unzips my jeans. He slides his large hand into my panties. "Will you come for me, Nicole?"

"Yes."

He holds my gaze as his fingers separate my wet folds and he begins to massage my clit. "Hmmm, you're so wet. Is this all for me?" I nod. He grunts and devours my mouth. I can feel how hard he is. He takes his other hand and puts it under my shirt. He frees my right breast and squeezes my hardened nipple. I moan against his mouth. He releases my mouth so he can devour my breast. "Hmmm, I love your breasts, they're so big." He flicks my nipple with his tongue before sucking it into his mouth. Liam slides one of his long, thick fingers into my pussy. He grunts again and comes up from my breast. "Damn, you're tight. Nine years is a long time. I promise you'll never go without again." He watches my expressions. "Hmm, I wish I could be inside you." Then, he adds another finger. My eyes widened and I grimace just slightly. "Hmm, yeah, I'm going to have to go slow our first time to stretch you." Then he uses his thumb to stroke my clit, and I start to relax around his fingers allowing them to slide in and out of me more freely. Breathing heavily, my head drops back. "Yes, Nicole, let me pleasure you. Don't fear this; don't fear us."

"Oh, Liam, it feels so good. Mmm." I lick my lips and roll my hips against his hand as he fingers me. Feeling my stomach clinch and my pussy spasm, we squeeze each other tightly, bracing for my climax. I moan his name as I come.

We stare into each other's eyes as he slowly pulls his fingers out of me. I miss them immediately, but they've left behind an echo inside of me. As he pulls his hand out my panties, he keeps his eyes on me to make sure I watch him lick my wetness from his fingers. "Mmm, you feel good and taste good. I can't wait to be inside of you."

"I'm looking forward to it." We kiss and cuddle until we fall asleep under the stars. Yes, I can get used to this.

# CHAPTER 11
# WELCOME HOME
## (Liam)

---

Nicole and Zion are both worn out today. I try to encourage them to get up by reminding them of just how close to home we are. I whisper in Nicole's ear, "Come on, pretty lady, we're just six hours away from me being able to make love to you properly."

She stretches, moans, and smiles. "Mmm, that'll do it. I'm up!"

I give her a little peck on the lips, "Good." Heading over to the tent, I call out to Zi. "Zion, buddy, it's time to get up so we can get moving. There are so many fun things to do when we get home, and you can sleep as long as you want."

"It's barely daytime. I'm tired of walking, Liam. Where's my mommy?"

"Nicole..."

"I'm already here. Let me squeeze in." She squeezes into the tent with us. She sits down and pulls Zion into her lap. Once she has him cradled in her arms, she says:

My dear, Zion,

you can't be like a lion.

Please don't lie around,

let your feet hit the ground.

There's so much to see and do,

the whole world's waiting for you.

She kisses him, and he smiles big, "I love you son. Today, we finally get to see where Liam is taking us. Aren't you excited?"

"Yes, I'm just tired. I'm up now. Thank you for the poem, Mommy. I love you."

Kissing him all over his face and tickling him, Nicole tells Zion, "Get dressed, please."

I exit the tent first and help her out. "You're a great mom."

Today I let them set the pace. It takes eight hours instead of six to reach my border. When we arrive at the mountain wall facade I had built, Nicole looks at me and asks if I'm lost. We follow the wall to the patch of vines and trees that cover the opening. I smile at them and say, "Welcome home!" I push back the brush as they walk through. Once we clear the tunnel of the facade, the entire compound becomes visible as we stand atop the forest ridge. The thick trees provide excellent cover from any view above. There's a waterfall at the opposite end of the ridge that spills into a tranquil pond. Pointing at the waterfall, I explain the design. "I had some of the water re-routed from a nearby natural water source, but I also have dam doors that will cut it off if needed to prevent flooding. So far, I've built a dozen large, luxury cabins, but they're all empty as I haven't been able to get anyone to join me up here." I look down at Nicole as she takes it all in. "So, what do you think?"

Zion jumps up and down. "I love it! Mommy, we're going to live in a house and not a condo! Can I pick which one we live in?"

Nicole is speechless but mouths, "What the hell!" She covers her mouth quickly. "I'm sorry. I mean, wow. You've been busy. You're really the only one up here?"

"Yes."

"Which cabin is yours?"

"None. Come on, I'll show you my place. Zion, is it ok if you stay with me for a while? It would be doing me a big favor."

Probably not quite comfortable with the living arrangement I just proposed, Nicole asks, "Do you have enough room for us?"

"Actually, my place has four bedrooms. And since it snows up here, I have a lot of indoor activities, a heated indoor swimming pool, a track, a basketball court, bowling alley, and a skateboard park. I even have a movie theater."

"Wow! Okay, I'm all in!" Nicole grins from ear to ear with excitement.

"Me too, Liam!"

We arrive at the entrance. I punch in the code and say it out loud so they can hear me. "8873216452—you guys got that?" They both shake their heads no. I chuckle. "We'll work on it. Come on in. It's going to be nice to have people here with me."

"This is the main level. The bedrooms, kitchen, dining room, living room, and theater are all on this floor. The floor above is my medical lab and communication center. The floor below is all the sport activities. To be safe, Zion, I don't want you down there alone yet. Okay?" He nods. "The level below that is supplies, food, artillery, a shooting range, and day-to-day items; think of it as the compound's store. And the lowest level is the power grid that powers the entire compound." I don't want to tell Zion that he can pick his own room without his mom's permission, so I say, "Nicole, do you want to help Zion pick out a room?"

"Sure. I don't want him too far from me. Where's your room, Liam?"

*Did she just?* ... It's impossible to contain my smile, "Come on, I'll show you. My room is the one at the end of the hall."

"Cool. Okay, Zion, you and I will take these two rooms. You can pick which one you want."

"I'll take the one in the middle so you can both protect me."

His concern breaks my heart. "Zion, you're safe here. You won't need protection while you're here. I need you to know that you're safe." His choice is a good one and there's sound reasoning behind it. Like his mom, I have decided to protect him with my very life, and I want him to know it. However, I caught Nicole's expression, so I try to put her at ease and say, "When I had the place built, I'd hoped that I might have kids one day." I give her a subtle wink.

She smiles. "I really hate to do this to you both, but is it okay if I lie down? I'm exhausted and my back is aching."

"Sure. Are you okay?"

"I'm fine. Zion, please unpack and listen to Liam. Come sit with me if Liam needs a break, okay?"

Zion was about to respond, but I cut in. "We're fine. We'll hang out and get some dinner started. I'll get him settled into his room. And maybe we'll play some games. We'll wake you up when dinner is ready." She just nods at me. I'm concerned about Nicole. I hope she isn't having second thoughts about being here, maybe she's still sad about her sister. "Hey, before you lie down, will you please give me your phone? I need to let Thad know we made it home safely, but I also want to send a picture of your sister to my contact. Zion can help me select a picture to send."

"Actually, we took pictures for this very reason before we left home. I have pictures of my whole family. Here you go. And thank you for watching Zion. I'll make it up to you."

"Come on buddy. Let's go do some manly stuff!" Zion giggles as we walk out of the room together.

## CHAPTER 12
# I HAVE A CURE FOR THAT
(Liam)

I'm able to accomplish everything I needed to do in just a couple of hours. Zi helps me set the table for dinner and I head off to go wake up Nicole. She's still asleep when I get to her room, so I sit on her bed, and gently rub her cheek. "Nicole, dinner is ready. Nicole?" She opens her eyes and then she doubles over in pain. "What is it? What's wrong?"

"Excuse me, Liam, I need to get up." Once she stands up, I see the blood.

"Nicole, you're bleeding."

"Crap! I'm sorry. Did I ruin your sheets? I thought my lower back pain earlier may have been from the backpack, but I had a feeling it was more than that. Let me get cleaned up and I'll join you guys for dinner." She takes one step and falls down. I rush to her and pick her up and carry her into the bathroom. I run her a warm bath, help her take off her clothes and avoid looking at her body to be respectful. "Liam, I'm so embarrassed and I know I'm bleeding all over you."

"It's fine, pretty lady. I'm going to take care of you, but I have to ask, is this normal?" She nods. "Do you have fibroids?" She looks at me in shock like she didn't expect me to know about the female reproductive system. I help her into the bathtub.

"Yes, but I don't really want to talk about it."

I let it go for the moment. "Will you be ok if I go make Zion's plate so he can eat dinner? You're not going to pass out on me, are you?"

"No, the pain brought to me to my knees. I wasn't going to pass out, though I do feel weak. Thank you for this and taking care of my kid, and everything you've done for me."

I lean down and kiss her on the forehead. "I'll be right back." I run down the long hallway and into the dining room on the other side of the floor. "Buddy, I'm going to make your plate. Your mom isn't feeling well, and I need to help her. Do you think you can eat dinner on your own?"

"Yes. May I take my plate to my room and play some video games and watch YouTube?" I nod. "What's wrong with my mommy? Is it her fibroids?"

"Yes, it is. You know about her fibroids?"

"Yeah, she told me all about it because I saw blood one day. She gets like this sometimes and she stays in bed for two or three days. I help take care of her and keep her company. We keep microwavable food in the freezer so I can heat stuff up when she's sick."

"You're a good kid. Well, how about this time, I take care of her? I'm even going to make those fibroids go away. So, you're off this time. Just stay out of trouble."

I head back to Nicole who is getting out of the tub. "No, ma'am. Please sit back down. I want the warm water to soothe your back muscles. I'm going to take you upstairs and give you some medication."

I sit on the tub to talk to her. "I talked to Zion, and he told me all about your battle with fibroids. I have a cure for that. I'm going to make you all better."

Huffing at my persistence, "That boy talks too much." She tilts her head to the side and asks, "You can do that?"

"Pretty lady, I never make idle promises. Come on, let me take you upstairs." She stands and I help her out of the tub. I dry her off and step out of the room so she can put on one of my large t-shirts. I pick her up, stop at Zion's door to make sure he's settled in, and then head upstairs. "I hoped to ease you into this side of my life, but now you get to see how truly imperfect I am."

With her arms wrapped around my shoulders, she looks up at me. "Should I be afraid?"

"You should never fear me. I will never hurt you or Zion, but what I'm getting ready to share with you may scare you and it will probably make you angry." I get to the lab and open it with my retinal scan. The lab expands as far as the eye can see.

"You're right. What the hell is all this, Liam?"

"Relax, and I will tell you while we work. Shoot, I forgot to grab dinner. Just lie here and don't get up please. I don't want you hurting yourself." I run out of the lab, down the stairs, grab two plates and hurry back up to her. "I need you to eat so the meds don't upset your stomach. Lean back and let me do a quick scan of your body."

"What are you looking for?"

"Your fibroids. But since we're scanning, let's just check everything."

"Well, you're going to know me a whole lot more than I know you."

"I would gladly let you scan my body." I give her a devilish grin.

*"Scan complete."*

Nicole pops up on the examining table. "Let me guess, your girlfriend? She's not going try to kill me, is she? I've seen way too many sci-fi movies to be ok with this scenario."

I laugh. "No, she won't try to kill you. She's confined to this floor in the lab and communication center unless I access her from another room. But yes, she is AI and has been my main companion for the last three years."

"Gisele?"

*"Yes, Dr. Sinclair."*

"This is Dr. Simmons. She just moved in."

*"Hello, Dr. Simmons. It is nice to meet you. It appears you have four benign masses in your uterus."*

"Um, hi, Gisele." Nicole shrugs and squints at me. "Thank you? And please call me Professor Simmons instead." She grabs my hand and holds a look of disbelief on her face.

"Nicole, it's fine. Do you remember when I told you I had patents for medications?" She nods. "Well, I discovered a cure for fibroids, but I am unable to share it with the world."

"What do you mean by unable?"

"I mean the last time I tried to share a cure for something that would have put a lot of people out of business, someone tried to have me executed. I was shot twice in the chest. So, while I haven't stopped finding cures, I've definitely stopped trying to make them available to everyone. I will help who I can, but I won't put myself out like that again."

"Liam…"

"Do you want something to knock you out while this works or do you want to be alert?"

"I'm a mother, I need to be alert. Talk me through this, what are you giving me?"

"This is just a muscle relaxer. This is for pain, and this… This is the pill that is going to dissolve the fibroids. You may be uncomfortable the next couple of days while they dissolve and pass out of you. I've worked pretty hard to find a mixture that minimizes the pain. The way I see it, women who have fibroids have endured enough pain." Nicole nods in agreement. Sighing with the slightest hint of annoyance, I continue. "And finally, unfortunately for me, you shouldn't have sex for the next four weeks…" I wink at her, "but you're worth the wait." She smiles and gives my hand a little squeeze. "Also, no tampons so if you're wearing one take it out, please."

"In front of you? Um, ew."

"Nicole, I have period blood on my jeans right now. We're well beyond the ick factor."

"Okay, fine, turn around. And Liam, this conversation isn't over."

I turn around as she requested. "I figured." With my back to her, I hand her the pills. "Take these, we'll eat and talk about whatever you want to talk about."

She takes the pills and I pull over a tray for us to eat on. She begins the conversation that may change her opinion of who I am. "Liam, Lee, you're clearly a genius. Are you the good kind of genius looking to save the world? Or are you an evil genius like Brain looking to take over the world?"

I laugh at her *Pinky and the Brain* reference. "Well Nicole, you've been in my presence for a full ninety-six hours. What do you think?"

"Well, of course I want you to be the kind that saves the world, but with this lab... Do you have anything in here that could cause a pandemic?"

"No, but I monitor labs all over the world. And when I see a new strain of something that they're studying pop-up, I go into their system and snag the data to work on the antidote. But all of my synthesizing is computer generated so the actual viruses are not here."

"If you can retrieve data, can't you put data in? You know, like the data for a cure?"

"Sure. Companies look at what's going out, but they closely monitor what's coming in from the outside. I have a very sophisticated system that is connected to an unsanctioned satellite that I was able to launch through a friend in the space program. It's how I communicate with the outside world. If my signal gets traced back to that satellite, it could inadvertently jeopardize hundreds of thousands of lives. If that happens, the pendulum may swing back in the wrong direction. As bad as things are, I think in the next couple of years, America will be in a better place. We just need to be patient and ride this out."

"Interesting." Her facial expression tells me she is analyzing the information I just gave her, but she's not prepared to dig any deeper. "Hey, do I have to stay in here all night? Zion is mature for his age, but he is still just a little kid. He's already been too far away from me for too long."

"No, I can take you back downstairs. I'm sorry, this whole parenting thing is new to me."

"Excuse me? Parenting thing? I see you two are set on being father and son, huh?"

"He's an amazing kid and he should have a dad. I think we have a really great connection, but if you want me to back off, I will."

"I think, like with our budding relationship, you should probably take it slowly."

I pick her up off the examining table. "Nicole, will you sleep in my room tonight so I can keep an eye on you?"

"No, I think I've already bled in enough rooms for one night, but you are welcome to sleep in my room."

"Done."

When we get downstairs, she asks to stop at Zion's room. His door is opened, and he's fallen asleep next to his plate with a Roblox story game up on the screen of the tablet I gave him earlier. I sit Nicole down on the bed and pick Zion up off the floor. Feeling Nicole's eyes on me, "Yes, I know he can't play video games all the time, but from what I've been told, he hasn't had much time with electronics in the last month. I thought he could use some fun time."

Rolling her eyes, "Yeah, sure, that's what it is. You're just a big softy. You know, if you really want to be a parent, you have to understand that sometimes you'll have to be the bad guy."

I hold Zion down in front of her so she can kiss him goodnight and then I place him in the center of the huge bed. And for the first time, I place a kiss on his forehead. I look up at Nicole smiling on the other side of the bed. "What are you smiling at?" She just shrugs. "And yes, I understand there's more to parenting than games. I plan to teach him everything I know. Everything." I walk back to her and pick her back up. "Come on, let's get you to bed."

We walk into her room, and I see the bloodstained sheets. "Damn it, I'm sorry, Nicole, I forgot I need to change the sheets. Can you sit up for a few minutes while I take care of this?"

"You've done enough, Liam. Just tell me where the clean sheets are, and I can do it."

"Like hell you will!" I sit her on the chaise that's in the room. Shaking my head, "You really have no idea how to let someone take care you. You're going to sit here, not move, and look pretty in my shirt while I change these sheets." She gives me a little smile. "Nicole, I need you to think of this as an actual post-op. I didn't cut into you, but your body is going through a major transformation, even as we speak. I need you to stay in bed for two of the four weeks."

The way she scolds me with her eyes lets me know how unpleased she is with the directive. "I thought you said it would only take three days."

"I did. It will, but you should allow your body enough time to recover. If you had a job to get back to, maybe you could be back on your feet sooner, but I want you to heal completely."

"We were supposed to be sharing a bed tonight for a different reason. I'm sorry."

"Pretty lady, please don't apologize for something completely out of your control. We have plenty of time to work on that. Think of this as an opportunity to slow things down like you wanted, more time to get to know me." I finish the bed and place a few of my t-shirts where I'm going to lay her to catch the blood. It's no big deal; I've got about a thousand of them. I place her on the t-shirts and push a button over the bed to turn the lights off. "I'm going to go take a quick shower. I'll be back to check on you."

"Check on me? I thought you were keeping me company tonight."

I smile, glad that she wants me around. "I will. I'll be back."

I shower and change in my room. Usually, I sleep naked, but tonight I throw on some shorts over my boxer briefs. Hopefully, that will help contain my morning wood. I head back to Nicole's room. I figured she might be asleep by now, but she isn't. "Nicole, are you alright? Do you need me to get you anything?"

"I'm ok. I guess I'm just nervously waiting for the 'discomfort' to kick in."

"Don't be nervous. I'll be here for whatever you may need. Plus, the pain killer I gave you should last until morning. It's a little something I designed myself." I get into the bed with her. "May I hold you?" She nods. I spoon her and wrap my arms around her waist lacing my fingers right over her lower abdomen where her uterus is. "Is this ok?"

"It's perfect. You're… perfect."

I kiss her on the cheek. "I'm going to place an order in the morning for clothes and supplies for you and Zion."

"What? Like from Amazon? You can do that?"

"No, Amazon is a bit too public. Like everything else, I know a guy." I chuckle and seductively say, "Tell me what you need, what you like."

"Alright now, Dr. Sinclair, don't start anything we can't finish."

"What?" We both laugh. She rattles off some things and we talk for another couple of hours until she drifts off to sleep in my arms.

# CHAPTER 13
# LOVE EYES

(Liam)

I wake up early the next morning, check on Nicole, and start my day. Peeking in on Zion, I'm happy to see he's still asleep. It warms my heart to know that I've provided him a space where he's comfortable and safe. I'll come wake him up after I get off the call with Chris. I head into my communication center, and everything powers up.

*"Good morning, Dr. Sinclair. How may I assist you?"*

"Good morning, Gisele. Will you please connect me to Chris Ito?"

*"Yes, sir. I will let you know when the connection is made. While we wait, sir, how is Professor Simmons this morning?"*

"Professor Simmons is fine. Speaking of Professor Simmons, will you please get me her measurements from her scan?"

*"I am sorry, sir, I don't understand your request."*

"I am placing an order for clothing…"

*"Sorry to interrupt, sir, but Mr. Ito is on the comm."*

I turn around to the large screen covering the wall from floor to ceiling and see my friend, Chris. Chis is three inches taller than me at 6'5" and built like a brick wall, half Black, half Japanese, always popular with the ladies. We met freshman year of undergrad. I always teased him that girls only liked him for his dimples. "Lee, my man! What a nice surprise! How are you? Sorry to hear about your mom."

"I see you've been talking to Thad."

"No, Sergio told me. I haven't spoken to Thad in over two years. He doesn't fuck with me anymore. Not since the incident."

"Yeah, well man, can you blame him? That was fucked up. Why would you send that woman over there? Alicia was pissed."

"It's not my fault Thad likes crazy women. That bitch fucked up two of my stakeouts looking for him. I told her crazy ass that Thad never worked for me. She said she was going to keep showing up until I gave up Thad. So, you know what the fuck I did? I gave up Thad. The shit was getting ready to fuck up my money."

I give off a deep belly laugh. "Yeah well, you know Alicia didn't deserve that. Word has it that Alicia handled her, but Thad was still in the doghouse for a while."

"But he messed around with her before things got serious with Alicia. I wouldn't have sent her there if I wasn't sure that Thad would never cheat on Alicia."

"Well, Alicia was still upset."

"Anyway man, what's up?"

"I need to place an order."

"That's not like you. You usually place an order every seven months or so. It's only been four. Are you alright out there?"

"I just sent you the list."

Chris opens the document on his end. "Um, did you grow a vagina and shrink?"

Shaking my head, "Nice. I met someone."

"Looks like you met two 'someones.' And what the fuck man! You are still a weirdo. Who pulls a woman's measurements from a bio-scan?" Shaking his head and laughing at the odd situation, he asks, "So, are you going to tell me about the woman who was crazy enough to follow your ass, with her kid, into the mountains?"

"It depends. Are you done?" He shrugs. "Her name is Nicole. She's not feeling well right now. I'll introduce you to her once she's feeling better. She has a seven-year-old son; he's an awesome kid. He's biracial, closer to me in skin color than his mom. She was artificially inseminated, so there's no man in their lives. That's the short version."

"Wait, she's Black? Do you like her?"

"Yes, she's Black. And yes, I like her. Chris, man, I think she's the one."

"Again, wait. Not that I'm not happy for you, because I am. And you know, I think you've been alone for far too long, but how long have you known this woman? How did you meet?"

"Okay, Chris, calm down! I'll tell you everything." I appreciate Chris looking out for me, but Nicole means me no harm. He's paranoid when it comes to my safety. "I met her five days ago outside of Thad's place. She and her son had just had a run-in with the guards. They got separated from the rest of their family because she is a Black woman with a biracial child."

"Oh, is that who you have Sergio looking for?"

"I sure hope Sergio is only telling you about my life because we're all boys. Hey, anyone heard from Jimmy and Eddie?" James and Edward are the British twins in our crew. Though identical, they are easy to tell apart. Eddie went through a rebellious phase and has an edgy style. They hated their father as much as I hated mine. The Bennett fortune makes the Sinclair fortune look like peanuts. They have old money and are very well-connected throughout Europe.

"Jimmy checks in every few months. They're fine. Still in London running things."

"Okay good. Listen, in addition to that list, do you think you might be able to throw in three or four nice dresses for Nicole? I might want to pretend to take her on a date."

"You know I got you, Lee. Listen, it will take me a few days to get the order together. And yes, I will personally make the drop."

"Thanks, Chris. Let me know when to expect you."

"Will do. And Lee, good luck with Nicole."

---

Six days later, on the day of the drop, I ease out of Nicole's bed at 4 a.m. so I can be in position at 5 a.m. It isn't safe to make the drop inside of the compound, so I need to go to the drop point and transport the supplies back inside. I don't even make it 200 feet before I hear his footsteps. Stopping and without turning around I say, "Zi, what are you doing here?"

"You said you would teach me everything you know. You've shown me how to fish, shoot a gun, chop wood, install a toilet, and how to send secured messages. Why can't I do this with you?"

I sigh. "Did you leave your mother a note?"

He runs up beside me. "Yes."

"We might not get finished until late this afternoon." I tell him to give him the opportunity to go back inside. He shrugs. "Okay, fine, come on. But if something happens to you, your mother is going to kill me." Truth is, I love having him around and I welcome his company.

He giggles. "Liam, may I ask you a question?"

"You know you can ask me anything. What's up?" He's so inquisitive. Our conversations always keep me on my toes. I wonder what the topic will be this morning.

"Do you like my mommy?"

*Oh, shit. I need to be cool.* "Of course, I do."

"I know you like her but, do you like her, like her? Like boyfriend and girlfriend like her. Mommy says there are three different kinds of love, love for your family, love for your friends and romantic love."

"Well, I would agree with her."

"Well, which one?"

95

"I'm not sure I should be having this conversation with you. Why are you asking?" I want him to always feel like he can talk to me, but I don't want Nicole to be upset.

"Because you sleep in the bed with mommy, and you always look at her with love eyes."

"Love eyes?" I want to laugh, but I don't want him to think I'm laughing at him, so I keep my laughter inside.

"Yeah, you know how in the movies right before people kiss, they look at each other? Those are love eyes. You look at my mom like that."

This time I laugh, but I see the seriousness in his eyes. "Yes, Zion. I like your mom a lot. Like a girlfriend, maybe more."

"I think that's good. So, if you maybe love my mom, do you love me too?"

This time, I stop and kneel down next to him. "Zi, I love you buddy. No matter what happens between your mom and me, I will always love you like a son."

"That's cool, but..." He pauses, unsure if he should finish his thought.

"It's ok, Zion, you can tell me."

"Can you take out the 'like' part? I always wanted a dad, but I never had one. Mommy always said that we are grateful to my father for helping us become a family, but that he will never be a part of our family. I want you and mommy to get married so you can be my daddy."

"Buddy, there's a lot more to two people getting married. They both have to want it. Your mom and I are still getting to know each other. We haven't talked about marriage. She knows I like her, and I think she likes me too, but that's it for right now." I stand, knowing that we've probably discussed more than Nicole would be comfortable with. "Let's get moving." We reach the border facade in fifteen minutes and the drop point five minutes after that. The drop zone is a clearing fifty yards from the tree line. "Zion, it is important that when you get to the tree line, you always survey the area. Do you have your binoculars?"

"Yes, the ones with night vision and heat sensor."

"That's my boy! You're a quick learner. Now scan the area and let me know if you see anything."

"Nothing but that bunny at, uh... uh... nine o'clock."

"Good job." I gave him the high-tech binoculars a couple of nights ago and brought him outside to test them. I'm learning that he's great with technology.

"Da..." He hesitates, but continues with my name. "Liam, what's that sound?"

Patting him on the back, I nod and give him permission to address me in the way he feels most comfortable with. "It's ok, you can say it." He nods, but I but I don't want it to feel forced now, so I talk over him. "Good ear by the way. That's Chris' plane in the distance."

"It sounds huge!"

"Just you wait. My friend, Chris, purchased a large cargo plane when he started running humanitarian drops. It is huge. Now let's be really quiet so we can hear the cargo doors open and then we will go out and give him a wave when he makes the drop." We hear the sound of the doors opening just a few moments later. We step out into the clearing.

Zion grabs my arm and pulls it. "Daddy, wait! What if the supplies hit us when they come down?"

Hearing him call me daddy for the first time makes me feel like a superhero. "No, son, the pallets have parachutes and are guided by GPS. We're fine. He's making the drop. Let's wave to Chris." As I look up to watch the drop, I notice something is amiss. "Zion, how many chutes do you see?"

"Three."

"Me too. There were supposed to be only two. Chris, what did you do?" Walking across the clearing, we reach two large crates and one huge crate. I'm going to have to break these crates down. I'll try to find a way to repurpose the wood. I try not to produce much waste out here. I take the butt of my rifle and hit the closure, slowly pulling the door open.

"THAT IS SO COOL, DADDY! I WANT TO RIDE IN IT! CAN I? CAN I? CAN I? PLEEEEEASE!"

I try to stay calm, but I'm with Zion. "Yep buddy, this is super cool!" Chris really came through. Not that I needed an ATV, but it could be useful. I wave Zion into the crate first and then I follow. We get in. The key is in the ignition; I'll have to change that to a palm scanner. It's surprisingly quiet. I drive it out of the crate, and boy is she a beauty. While inspecting the machine, I see an envelope on the dash. I open it and there is a note inside.

> Lee,
>
> I am so happy that you found someone to share your world with. Please accept this as a wedding/kid shower gift. LMAO and fuck you too!
>
> -Chris

Laughing out loud. *Thanks, buddy.*

This thing is fully enclosed, electric, has four seats, is all-terrain, has a front winch, towing capabilities, and a cargo area in the back. This will make my time out of the compound quicker when I need to hunt and gather. "Zion, this is going to help us get all of this stuff inside faster." I break down the crates and have Zion keep watch, even though I know there's no one this far up the mountain. But this stuff is heavy, and it gives him a job. The ATV turns an eight-hour job into a three-hour job. We're able to drive the vehicle through the bay door that's hidden in the facade wall that follows a tunnel directly to the basement store-room. I decide to unload and take inventory later. Nicole should be awake, and I want to check on her.

# CHAPTER 14
# I CAN WALK
## (Nicole)

I felt Liam leave the bed early this morning, and I missed the comfort of his arms the moment he left. It's amazing how quickly I've grown accustomed to his presence. I feel safe and loved; strong and beautiful. He's attentive and kind; strong but gentle. He has bonded with my son in a way that no man has. The truth is, in my heart, I already know that I'm his and he's mine. I just need my mind to stop telling me that my feelings can't be valid because of the short time I've known him. Liam is everything I've ever wanted in a man. It's like he walked into my life straight out of my dreams. And with that, my heart told my head to shut up.

"Mommy, Mommy, Mommy!" I hear Zion running down the hallway. He gets to the room first. Liam follows just a few seconds behind. Zion jumps onto the bed, hugging and kissing me. "Mommy, Daddy's friend... I mean Lee's..."

Liam jumps in, "Nicole, I'm..."

"Calm down, both of you. If you two mutually agreed that that's what you want, I am 100 percent onboard with it." Both of their grins touch my soul in a way that it has never been touched. I know instantly that Liam is officially a part of us, and we are now a family of three. "So, go ahead, what did daddy's friend do?"

"Daddy's friend gave us a cool ATV. It's awesome!"

Liam leans down and kisses me on the lips, "Good morning, pretty lady." My eyes grow with surprise as it's the first time he has kissed me in front of Zion. "What? It's been a long morning that included informing a very protective seven-year-old of my intentions for his mother."

I giggle. "Sounds like an interesting day." I watch them as they both beam with joy from their newly defined relationship.

"Mommy, when can you get up, so we go look at all the stuff daddy got for us?"

"Hey buddy, why don't we give mommy some time. Actually, I'm hoping to get you into the lab today for an updated scan. I'd like to check your progress; see how you're healing."

"Gee, I don't know if I can find time in my busy schedule to let you carry me to the lab. You know, I can walk," I stick my tongue out at Liam.

Liam shakes his head at me in disapproval. "Yes, I can see that since you disobeyed me and got dressed on your own."

"Why, yes Lee, my shower was absolutely glorious, thanks for asking."

"Okay, smarty pants. Shall we go now?"

"Daddy, can I come upstairs and play in the comm room? I like all the screens. It makes it seem like I'm inside the game."

"Sure, just remember to login with the scrambled signal."

It's like these two have their own language. Once in Liam's strong arms, I kiss him on the cheek and lay my head on his shoulder. I whisper in his ear, "Thank you for accepting the role." Zion uses his own hand scan to enter the comm room. I gasp, "Well, that's not fair. I want one!" Zion giggles and closes the door. Liam takes my hand and places it on the screen, the lab door opens. I smile from ear to ear like he just gave me an unexpected gift.

He looks at me and smiles. "You're such a brat! I took your handprint from your bio scan," he shrugs.

*"Good morning, Professor Simmons and Dr. Sinclair."*

"Good morning, Gisele." We say in unison.

Liam lays me on the examining table. "Gisele, please scan Professor Simmons for an update on her fibroids." He rubs my cheek as I look up at him, trying to draw courage from him. His eyes are filled with tenderness and concern. Everything in me wants him to rip off my clothes and take me right now, but I know he won't even though I stopped bleeding already.

*"Scan complete. There is no trace of fibroids in the uterus."*

With our eyes still locked on each other, we both smile with relief. "Gisele, am I still able to conceive and carry a child?" Liam's eyes change to dread and worry. I squeeze his hand a little.

*"Your uterus is intact and there are no biological barriers to conception."*

"Thank you, Gisele. Please go into sleep mode." The comm goes silent. "Nicole, that's great news. Are you interested in having another child?"

I look away, not sure how to interpret his expression, "I just wanted to know." I feel his hand releasing mine. I look back at him and see a look of disappointment. Tightening my grip on his hand, I attempt to read his reaction. "I wanted to know because I love it here and it's an amazing place to raise a family. And Zion should have a sibling or two. Besides, I'm not getting any younger."

"We've been so busy with this and just trying to get settled in. I feel like we've talked about everything except what a future together would look like."

"Why do you think we've avoided it?" He shrugs. "Come on Mr. Genius, you can do better than that."

"Fear?" I nod at him. He continues, "I guess I'm afraid of rushing you, but since we're on the subject, would you consider a future with me?"

"Liam, I've had nothing but time recently. And, yes, I can see a future with you. I've been afraid to admit that even to myself, to allow myself to hope or believe we could be together. And I don't want to pressure you either."

"How about this, Nicole... Let's agree to kick fear out of this relationship." I nod at him in agreement. "I promise to be honest with you about my feelings, desires, and my needs."

"I promise you the same, Liam. So, I'll start. Right now, I really want you to kiss me." He leans in and passionately kisses me. He pulls me up into a sitting position. His kisses are hard and full of lust. He grabs my left breast and squeezes hard. Breathless, I say, "Do we really have to wait another two weeks?"

He abruptly pulls away, "I'm sorry, yes, we really need to wait." He sees me pout. "Hey, I really want to bend you over that table and fill you up with my seed right now. And that's why we really need to get out of this room."

I raise my eyebrow and point to the huge bulge in his jeans, "Um, we can't go anywhere yet." I smile but keep staring at his erection. Trying to change the subject quickly, I blurt out. "So, what's in the shipment we need to unpack?" I bite my bottom lip.

"Nicole, it isn't going to go down with you watching it. And you biting your lip certainly isn't helping." I hop down off the table. "HEY! What do you think you're doing? Get back on that table, please." He heads towards me.

I move quickly behind the table I just jumped off. "Nope! I can walk."

"Absolutely not." He glares at me trying to anticipate my next move.

I stand on my tippy toes to look over the table. "Ha!" I point at his crotch. "I guess little Lee-Lee went nite-nite. Let's go downstairs." I smirk calmly and walk from around the table. Keeping my eyes on Liam's annoyed expression, I head towards the door.

"You're not walking there."

"Wanna bet?" I beat him to the door, but he snatches me up before I can open it.

"Let me explain something to you. I'm an entire foot taller than you and I outweigh you by nearly one hundred pounds. I will throw you over my shoulder and spank you."

"Ooh, Daddy! Is that a threat?"

Smiling and shaking his head, "No, it's a promise. I want you fully healed. Plus, I don't want to risk any setbacks. Besides, the longer it takes for you to heal, the longer I have to wait to be inside you. Now knock off this independent, superwoman bullshit and let me take care of you."

Sighing and rolling my eyes, "Well, okay, when you put it like that."

# CHAPTER 15
# THEY'RE MY FAMILY
## (Liam)

We spent a few hours checking out our shipment. Nicole and Zion loved their clothes. Nicole was thrilled to see the dresses, heels, makeup, hot comb and flat-iron. I'm so going to miss her waves and curls. Even though she is the most beautiful woman I've ever seen, she needs to be able to feel beautiful in her own way. But I feel like I have to say it. "Nicole, I know you asked me to order you that stuff so you can straighten your hair, but I like it natural. Will you still wear it this way sometimes?"

"Yeah, the natural look is growing on me too, but I'm not totally ready to give up my heat yet." She gives me a flirty smile.

"Daddy, I love all the video games, but did you have to buy the books?"

"Absolutely. No son of ours is going to be a knucklehead."

"Hey, Mommy says that too!"

"See?" I nod to Nicole, and she winks at me in approval. "Mom will teach you English, history, and social studies. I will teach math, science, and technology. Unless Mom wants to teach math."

"NO!" They both say and laugh.

"Mommy gets frustrated with me when she helps me with my math. She thinks it's easy, but sometimes I don't understand."

"I will be patient and come up with fun ways to learn. You have three more weeks to just have fun without any schoolwork. Then, we hit the books."

"Okay, Dad."

"I'm going to go get dinner started. Call me when you guys are ready to come up. Zion, use the intercom. Do not let mommy trick you into letting her walk up the stairs or even to the elevator." As I walk by her to leave, she once again sticks her tongue out at me. I playfully smack her on the butt and tell her, "I saw that." She gasps and Zion giggles.

While cooking dinner I hear the intercom chime and I expect to hear Zion, but it's Gisele. *"Please excuse the intrusion, but Mr. Sergio Bautista is trying to get you on the line."*

"Thanks, Gisele. I'll be up in a minute." The food is ready, so I turn everything off and head up. Gisele gets me connected to Sergio. Thad met Sergio in a communications class during sophomore year and introduced him to Chris and me. He was our private investigator when the crew came together. Sergio could find out anything about anyone. It is a very useful skill. Now he runs an entire town. He's essentially the mayor. Serg is Filipino-American, and the town is predominately people of color. It's a nice place that the port guards won't allow white people to go, but a few have made it there using alternate routes. Sergio makes sure that everyone is treated fairly. He's a family guy, married to his wife Ophelia, and they have four kids. Hate is not something he will tolerate in his home or his town. While Serg stands at 5'8", his heart and role as a protector makes him a giant.

"Hey, Lee. I found your lost cargo." He beckons someone over. I see Renee and her three kids. "Lee this is Renee, Justice, Journey, and Joy."

"Oh, my God, Sergio! Can you guys hold on for like three minutes?" Sergio nods.

I run out of the comm room and down three flights of stairs. I fling the door open to the storage area and startle Nicole and Zion.

"What's going on?" Nicole screeches.

"I need you both right now." I pick up Nicole and Zion follows. "Zi, get the elevator. We're going to the comm room." We make it to the top floor in no time. Zion opens and holds the door for us. Once in, Nicole and Renee scream with joy. Tears flow down both of their faces. The kids are excited. Renee's children are older than Zion. Justice and Journey look to be young men in their early twenties and Joy looks about sixteen. I sit Nicole down in front of the screen and step away.

"Where are you guys? I'm so happy to see you. Are you ok?" Renee asks her little sister.

"I can't tell you exactly where we are, but it is beautiful and we're safe. Liam, baby, come here. Renee, this is Liam Sinclair. He rescued us less than an hour after we got separated from you. Are you guys somewhere safe?"

"Yes, we met Sergio and his family. They've been very kind. But hold up, 'baby'?"

"Tee-tee this is my new daddy!" Zion squeals.

"Really, Nicole?" Renee says in a protective, big sister tone. "And are you hurt? Why was he carrying you?"

"It's a long story, but you remember that health issue I had?" Renee nods. "Well, thanks to him, I don't have it anymore. I have so much to tell you. And look at my babies all rested and safe. I love you guys!" Justice, Journey, and Joy beam with happiness as their aunt dotes on them.

Renee turns her attention to me. "Liam, is it?" I nod, "I don't know you, but I know my sister. She looks happy right now. Thank you for rescuing them, taking care of them, and clearly, loving them."

"Finding them has been the greatest gift I have ever been given," I say as I feel myself becoming emotional. "Can you get Sergio back? I don't mean to break up the reunion, but I don't want to jeopardize the security of this connection." Really, I'm not ready to share my true feelings with the world. I haven't even said the words out loud to Nicole.

Sergio comes back into view. "I already know what you're going to say, and I've already given them the best accommodations. I'm working on getting them each a dedicated, secured device they can communicate on."

109

"Thank you, man. I'll wire some money. Anything they need make it happen and send me the bill. Sergio, they are my family now." Nicole hugs my arm.

"Sergio, thank you for your help," Nicole says. "Guys, I wish I could hug all of you."

"We love and miss you guys, too. I hope we get to talk again soon. Thanks again, Sergio and Liam for helping my little sister. Bye, for now, you guys."

"Bye, guys!" The line goes dead, and she jumps up into my arms, planting kisses all over my face like I've seen her do with Zion. "Thank you for everything!"

After dinner and getting Zion to bed, we head to Nicole's room, but she stops me. "Liam, can we sleep in your room tonight?"

Until this point, she hasn't wanted to sleep in there. "Nicole, are you sure? I need you to be sure because once we go in there, it becomes official. That will be our room."

"Yes, I know we've only known each other two weeks, but I'm sure. I've never been surer of anything."

I walk her to our room, lay her on the bed, and walk across the room to get some space between us. As I go close and lock the door, trepidation kicks in because I thought I had more time before we would share this bed. The bed where I will make love to her for the rest of our lives. That thought makes my cock stiffen. It's going to be a long night. Standing in an awkward daze, I hear Nicole's voice.

"Liam, please come to bed." I walk over to the bed and sit next to her. I can't look at her. She reaches up and takes my face into her hands. "Look at me." I lift my eyes and face her. She kisses me, but I pull away. "Please don't pull away." I'll never deny her; so, I kiss her back. She scoots back on the bed as we continue to kiss and I hover over her, using my knee to spread her legs. She grabs the bottom of my shirt and pulls it up over my head and off.

"Damn, Nicole." I can hear my heart pounding with erotic excitement as I pull her shirt off and unhook her bra. She pulls her arms out and flings her bra across the room. I waste no time getting her big breasts into my mouth. I use my large hands to squeeze them together, so I can drag my tongue back and forth across her hard nipples before I suck intensely on one. With her nipple in my mouth, I grind down on her. She lets out a little moan. I undo my jeans, trying to free myself. Grunting, I let go of her nipple, "Can I taste you?"

"Mmm, please."

I sit up and remove her jeans but leave her panties on, as a reminder to myself not to slide into her. I remove my jeans but leave on my boxer briefs. Crawling back onto the bed and between her legs, I trail kisses along her inner thigh. She shivers with pleasure. I turn my head to the other thigh, but this time I lick her from mid-thigh up to her sex and then I gently bite. I look up at her as she eagerly anticipates my next move. Gently draping each of her legs over my shoulders and keeping my eyes locked on hers, I slide her panties to the side and lick her juicy lips. She lets out a moan. "Mmm, so soft and smooth. How did you pull this off before opening the shipment?"

"I used your razor this morning while you were out. I hope you don't mind."

I break our gaze because I need to see her, I've been waiting for this moment. "The pretty lady has a pretty pussy. I don't mind one bit." I use my fingers to spread her lips. She's so wet and ready for me. "Fuck," I whisper. I lick her swollen clit. I love how it pulsates against my tongue. I want to thrust my tongue inside her, but I know I shouldn't. I grip her thighs from underneath and lift her slightly so I can lick her anus. The action catches her by surprise, and she grabs my forearms. I stop only long enough to tell her, "Relax, baby, let me explore you." I get a better grip that opens her up more, so I swirl my tongue around it. Her hole is puckered tight, so tight I probably can't even get a finger in, but we'll save that for another time. I feel her body relax as she begins to allow herself to enjoy it. She pants my name. I lower her and return to her clit. With her legs over my shoulders, I wrap my arms around her thighs and pull her down, pinning her pussy to my mouth. I assault her, twirling and flicking my tongue on her clit. She grabs the back of my head.

"Oh, Liam!" She arches her back. "Oh my God! Lee!" I feel little tremors traveling through her body. I continue to work my tongue. Words have left her. Now there are only sounds of pleasure. Her body tenses and she moans loudly in pure delight. She trembles as she comes hard against my mouth. She writhes in my grip as wave after wave of ecstasy takes over her. I slowly loosen my hold on her only as she calms from her climax.

I am so hard and close to my own release. I try to calm my body by kissing my way up her body. To my surprise, she pushes me off and guides me up to the head of the bed.

"Oh, shit." I lie back on the pillow, placing one arm under my head. She grips my boxer briefs at the waist and pulls them down and off, freeing my rock, hard cock.

Her eyes grow big as she lets out a gasp. "Damn, Liam. I guess I underestimated."

"Don't worry." I give her a devilish smile. "I believe in you."

Smiling back at me as if I had challenged her, "I've never backed down from a challenge when it was something I really wanted." Like a confident sex warrior preparing for battle, Nicole angles her body so that I have a view of her sucking me and of her beautiful, round ass. I grunt with approval. She grips my cock with both hands. She swirls my pre-cum with her tongue, spreading it all over my mushroom head. And then opening her mouth as wide as she can, she takes as much of me as possible deep in her mouth. "Mmm." I moan as I reach out and grip her ass firmly. She bobs her head up and down my shaft. It feels so fucking good. Her mouth is wet and hot. The sound of her slurping as her mouth slides up my shaft is almost too much for me to maintain control. I grit my teeth trying not to yell out like a virgin, but it feels so damn good. She gags a little as my tip hits the back of her throat, but she keeps sucking me. "Sorry, baby. Are you okay?" She grunts in approval. My breath catches, my balls tighten. I slowly and gently thrust the tip of my cock into her mouth, hitting the back of her throat a few more times before grunting loudly as I release my hot cum into her mouth. She drinks all of me and then licks me clean.

"That was amazing, Nicole. Thank you, baby."

"Thank you? No thanks required. My man satisfied me, and it was my pleasure to satisfy him." Nestling in my arms, with her head on my chest, she looks up at me, "Liam, you make me happy."

Gently, I kiss her on the lips and confess, "I love you, Nicole. I never want to live without you again. You don't have to say anything. I just need you to know that I plan on spending the rest of my life making you happy."

She squeezes me tightly, "I love you too, Liam Sinclair."

## CHAPTER 16

# TONIGHT IS THE NIGHT

(Nicole)

---

O ver the last week, Liam has given me some space and even allowed me to exercise. It's three days past his "six-weeks without sex" imposed rule for my healing. Three days and I find myself still in my drought. I know I should never swim alone, but I just need to work off this pent-up energy. Swimming has been my escape since I started teaching. Front crawl, backstroke, and butterfly are my most comfortable strokes. One of the swim coaches on campus once told me that my backstroke was textbook. He also said it was a shame I hadn't picked the sport up at an earlier age.

As I wrap-up a few laps of the butterfly stroke, I catch a glimpse of Liam standing by my lane. *Great, now I have to hear about how I shouldn't push it. I'm so not in the mood for one of his lectures.* I stop at the wall and lift my goggles.

"Good morning, pretty lady."

"Good morning. What's up?"

"You left out of bed without saying anything. I'm heading to the house next door to wrap-up a project that I've been working on. I was hoping that tonight, maybe, we could dress up for dinner."

"Sure. Dress up. Okay. May I get back to my workout?"

"Are you okay?"

"Fine. Just needed to clear my head."

"From?"

"Nothing, Lee. You know what? I'm done with my workout. I am going to go check on Zion and maybe go for a hike." I pull myself out of the water and try to move past him, but he catches me by the wrist.

"Nicole, don't do that. I promise I'll make it up to you tonight. Give me a few hours and I promise to give you a night that you will never forget." Though I'm dripping wet in my Speedo razer back and swimming cap, he pulls me in and gives me the most amazing kiss. "Be ready for seven o'clock, pretty lady." He places one last kiss on the tip of my nose. "I love you." He leaves me standing dripping wet and breathless, and not from my workout.

Great, now I feel silly for being upset with him. He's been trying to plan the perfect night. I grab my towel and dry off and go upstairs to shower and start my day. Once upstairs, I peek in on Zion. Surprisingly, he's still in bed.

"Zion, hey kiddo, wake up." He stretches and rubs his eyes. "Are you ok?"

"Yes, Mommy. I stayed up late talking to Journey and Joy. Please don't be mad."

"Oh sweetheart, I'm not mad at all. Your cousins have always been a huge part of our lives. Go back to sleep and sleep as long as you like." I kiss him and rub his head until he falls back asleep. I go to the kitchen, and see breakfast is on the countertop for Zion and me. In that moment, I promise myself to never sweat the small stuff again with Liam. He is a terrific man and I'm grateful to the universe for crossing our paths.

I have a big night in front of me. It's time to shed these mountain man clothes. Using the spa bath in what was supposed to be my room, I wash my hair and pamper myself with all my girly routines I used to do before a big date. Renee would usually hang out with me and give me her opinions on outfits, hair, and makeup. Thanks to Liam and Sergio, I can have her here with me. I grab my personal comm screen and pull up a connection to my sister.

Renee answers the comm just before I hang up. "Hey, little sister! I heard this thing going off, but I didn't know what or where it was. How are you?"

"I'm good. I need your help."

"What's up?"

"Liam is planning a special night for us tonight and I need help selecting an outfit."

"A special night? Sergio told me that you're up in the mountains somewhere in some cave."

"It's not just some cave, it's a luxury cave. Thank you very much. I don't know what he has planned, but he told me to dress up. One of his other friends had a few dresses delivered to me."

"Okay, missy, get to the good stuff. Have you slept with him, or is tonight the night?"

"Slept with him, yes, if you mean sleeping in his arms every night. Intimacy, yes, if you mean kissing, touching, and sucking."

"EW! HEEEEY! LA-La-la-la-la-la!"

"WHAT? You asked." We both laugh.

"A simple, tonight is the night would have sufficed. What has it been, like nine years? Y'all have lubricant? You sure you haven't dried up?"

"Now who's being nasty? Come on, Ree-ree! Help me." I give her my best pouty face.

"Okay, crybaby. Let's see your options."

I carry the screen over to the dresses. "There's light blue, navy blue, red, and two black dresses. I was kind of thinking about this blue one."

"No, not tonight. That black one. It's perfect. What about your hair? I see you're rocking the natural look. It's cute, sassy. Sorry, I'm not there to flatiron your hair."

"I want to flatiron it, but I know Lee likes it natural."

"I know I'm your big sister and I'm supposed to say this, but you look beautiful with your hair natural." She shrugs. "I think you should wear it whichever way will make you feel the sexiest. So where is my nephew going to be while you're having adult fun?"

"Yeah, I wish you were around. I could just drop him off to you. There are like a dozen empty cottages up here. Do you think you guys are going to join us?"

"Maybe after winter. Hey, what do you think about me virtually babysitting?"

"That's like eight to nine months away!"

"Well, you don't want your big sister and nephews and niece to get caught in some random snowstorm and freeze to death, right?" I shake my head, no. "So, do I get to watch my nephew tonight?"

"This luxury cave of ours is huge and we'll be in a different building altogether. I don't know."

I didn't hear the door open, but I hear Zion screeching in the room. "Tee-tee! Hi, Tee-tee! I want Tee-tee to watch me."

The looks on their faces is so endearing, but I'm still hesitant. "Guys, I don't know."

"We'll use Zion's screen, and you take yours with you on your date. If anything happens. We'll call you on it." Renee tries to put me at ease.

Though I'm not convinced, "Oh, okay. We'll see. Ree-ree, I need to go hang out with Zion for a bit, make his dinner, and get dressed. Love you much!"

Zion and I race to the kitchen, and I make grilled cheese sandwiches and tomato bisque soup for lunch. We haven't had a chance to use the bowling alley, so we take our lunch downstairs. Once we make it to the bowling alley, I realize that I have to figure out how to get this thing going. I probably should have thought about that before getting my kid excited about it.

"Nicole? Zion? Are you guys down here?" *This man always shows up when I need him.*

"Yeah, babe, we're trying to bowl."

119

Liam chuckles as he enters the room. "Why trying?"

Shoving half of my sandwich into his mouth, "Don't mock me. How do we turn this thing on?"

Half laughing, half chewing, "I've got it. Great idea, by the way. Sandwich is great too. Reminds me of old times with my mom and Ms. Cassie." The whirling of the machine starts. "I'm glad I came back when I did." He kisses me. "I wouldn't have wanted to miss this." We spend the next few hours having a great family, fun-filled afternoon.

## Chapter 17

# A New Gear

(Liam)

Bowling with Zion and Nicole has been so much fun, and I hope we have many years ahead of us. I love hearing Zion laugh and call me daddy. We even have our own father and son victory dance now. I watch Nicole as she watches us, and she beams with joy. I love making her smile. Thinking about the night I have planned for us, I look at her and tap my watch. Not that we have reservations, but I'm eager to get our evening started. She nods and smiles. I still haven't quite figured out how we're going to do a romantic dinner with Zion. Right now, I have an activity room setup for him in the house, but he'll still be in the house. "Hey, buddy, did Mommy tell you I'm taking her on a date tonight?" Nicole raises an eyebrow at me, not sure where this conversation is going.

"Yes, my Tee-tee is going to watch me! We're going to have fun!"

Confusion must cover my face because Nicole begins to explain, "My sister offered to watch him for us."

"What, here? You're okay with that?"

"Not really."

"It isn't a bad idea." I shrug and smile. "I mean, I designed this place to be impeccably secure from the outside and safe on the inside. No one is getting in here. We can take a comm screen with us and I can activate the cameras."

"My sister said she could alert me if he needs me."

"I think we have a plan." This is good news. I know it's incredibly selfish, but I want Nicole all to myself tonight.

Nicole interrupts my thoughts with her practicality. "Just how far away is this house? That's my baby and there's only one of him."

I take her by the shoulders and look into her eyes. "Nicole, I know that. And I would die if anything bad ever happened to Zion. I will never put him in harm's way."

"Come on, Mom! I'm not a baby and I'm not scared. I will stay in my room the whole time and I'll keep both feet on the ground. Pleeease!"

"Okay, but you have to promise me you won't do anything dangerous."

"Promise!" Zion vows to his mother.

Trying not to let my full excitement show, I keep my celebration to a nod in approval. "Now that we've settled that, Nicole, please go get ready. Zion, you're with me."

After I get Zion setup in his room with his dinner and bring in an extra-large screen, I head off to get ready for my romantic evening. I shower, shave, trim my goatee and dress. Tonight, I decide on my tailored, navy, 3-piece suit with a white shirt, navy tie, and platinum monogram cufflinks. I had a few suits sent up when I first moved up here hoping I would have an opportunity to go to D.C. and speak before congress on the subject of pandemics and pharmaceuticals, but it hasn't happened. For the final touch, I slide on my black wingtips.

I wander down the hallway to Zion's room to check on him and help him get setup with his aunt. Once connected, I'm greeted with a catcall from Renee. I shake my head and laugh, but playfully spin around so she can see the whole suit. "Thank you for watching Zion tonight." I hear the door open next door and Nicole appears in the doorway wearing a fitted, black lace, knee-length dress, and black stilettoes. She kept her hair natural, but instead of her bun she wears at the top of head, she has it out. Her wavy coils fall beautifully around her face. She is the most beautiful vision I have ever beheld. She steps inside the room to compliments from Zion and Renee.

"Thanks. You really think I look alright?" She asks Renee.

"Don't take my word for it. Turn around and look at your man's face."

I realize at that moment that her beauty has rendered me speechless. When she turns to look at me, she turns her back to her sister. The dress has a low back that goes all the way down to the small of her back.

"Don't hurt him now, little sis." She flashes her sister a devilish grin over her shoulder. "Wait, I need a picture. Seriously. JUSTICE, COME HELP ME!" Justice, Journey, and Joy all come rushing onto the screen, gushing over their aunt. "How can I take a picture of them?"

"I got it," Journey says. "Can you guys get together? You look great, Auntie Nicole."

I pull her in close to me and inhale her soft, sweet fragrance. It's intoxicating. I need to wrap this up so we can get out of here. "You get it, Journey?"

Probably sensing my need to wrap this up, Journey smiles and winks. "Yup, I'll send you a copy."

"You two go ahead and get to your date. We're good," Renee says.

"Thanks," we both say and then give hugs and kisses to Zion before heading out. Instead of leading her out of the doors on this level, I guide her to the elevator.

Curious, she asks. "Change of venue?"

"No. There's just no way I'm letting you walk in those heels through the forest. I don't care if it is only a hundred yards away. And by the way, you look absolutely stunning."

"Thank you. You look great too." Her smile is enough to brighten any room.

The elevator doors open, and we step in. As soon as the doors close, I pull her to me and kiss her hard. My hands caress her bare back as our kiss deepens. I slide my hands down to her ass and squeeze. She moans softly against my mouth. I grunt, wishing I could rip her clothes off right here and fuck her harder that she's ever been fucked, but I know

I need to be gentle with her the first time. The elevator stops on the bottom floor and the doors open. I'm already so damn hard and we haven't even set foot into the house. I break our kiss and take her by the hand. Leading her to the ATV.

"Wow, my first time in your new ride." She shimmies her shoulders with flirty excitement.

"It's proving to be useful tonight."

I open the door for her and help her in. Walking around the back of the vehicle and getting in on the other side, I see her looking at me, her eyes filled with longing. My pants tighten from my erection. She reaches across to stroke me, but I grab her hand and stop her. "Not yet, pretty lady. I want to feed you first." She seductively licks her lips. "Not like that," I say with a smile. I start the ATV and pull out using the short driveway that has compound access instead of delivery access from beyond the wall. Two minutes across the rough terrain and we arrive at the house next door. "Will you please stay here for a couple of minutes? I need to put on lights." I run in taking less than two minutes and run back out to her. I offer her my hand and lead her into the house.

As soon as she crosses the threshold, she gasps, "Liam, this is beautiful!"

Instead of working on plumbing in the other houses over the past three weeks, I've been working to turn this large, empty space into a ballroom. The fireplace is lit and there are tiny clear LED lights strung everywhere. I've setup a table for two near the fireplace. Nicole slowly spins in the center of the room taking it all in. "Dinner is heating in the oven. Would you like a tour while we wait?" She nods. I give her the tour of the house, never staying in one place for too long because if we do, we will end up skipping dinner. It's a two-story, four-bedroom, four and a half bath house. My watch beeps, alerting me that dinner should be ready. I lead her back downstairs and to the table. I serve her dinner.

"Once again, this looks amazing Liam." Tasting her food, "Your nannies and chef were great teachers."

"I'm glad you like it."

"Liam, this house is beautiful. Why do you have so many houses out here?"

"Well, I was thinking this could become a community. I still would like to convince a surgeon and dentist to move here. I stopped looking for a while, but I'm going to ask the guys if they know anyone. I think it's a good idea to have a medical team up here since it isn't just me anymore."

"I know you must know someone."

"Those that I asked said they would take their chances out in society. The ones who said they would think about it, I've lost contact with. But I don't want to talk about that right now." Changing the subject to something I know she'll want to talk about, "I was surprised you agreed to let Renee virtually babysit. He really is safe over there."

"Lee, there's something about me I haven't told you." Moving her food around on her plate with her fork, "You know how you've been able to get glimpses of the future?" I sigh, thinking she's mocking me. "Liam, I'm not mocking you. I...," she pauses. "I can see the present."

Chuckling, "Yes, we all can see the present."

"Now you're mocking me." She smiles, "Stop laughing and listen. I see, sense, and sometimes feel pain and fear of people closest to me, when I'm not with them. So, I agreed to it because I know that if Zion is scared or hurt, I'll feel it. Do you think I'm crazy?"

"No, but can you give me an example?"

"The very first time was when I was seven and Renee was fifteen. She got beat up walking home from school because this stupid girl's boyfriend said she was pretty. I saw it happen as if I was Renee. I felt every kick and punch. Ten years later, my dad was killed in the line of duty. He was a DEA agent, and it was a drug deal gone wrong."

"Wait, your dad was DEA?" She nods. "And he never taught you how to use a gun?"

"Mom made him promise to keep guns away from us. Anyway..." She smirks.

"Sorry. Please, continue." I give her a little smile.

"I really needed therapy after that one. But my mom knew I wouldn't be able to live a normal life once people found out about me. Then, three years ago, I saw my mother's last moments, but it was comforting. There was no pain or fear, just peace." A solemn expression comes over her face. I reach across the table and take her hand in mine, bringing her back to the present. She looks up at me and takes a breath before continuing. "The first time with Zion was when he was a year and a half. I was in the middle of a lecture, and this overwhelming fear came over me. I felt my throat began to close. My students thought I was having some kind of seizure. I saw my mother through his eyes. She was panicked but was able to get the grape out of his throat. When it was over, I apologized to my class and stepped out before I started bawling."

"Oh, my God. That must have been terrifying." I bring her hand to my lips and kiss it, hoping that it will help comfort her. "So, it's only people you know?"

"I don't think so. Sometimes I have nightmares that don't feel like mine, but not often. The most vivid ones are always someone close to me. With Zion, I feel everything, every bump, bruise, sore throat... Thankfully, he doesn't get sick often."

Silently taking in this new information about her, I realize she's even more special than I knew. I try to lighten the mood. "Too bad you can't sense good intentions. I almost got my ass handed to me this morning."

Nicole releases my hand and holds her hands up. "Hahaha. Okay, I guess now is a good time. I was planning to apologize to you for my attitude this morning."

"No need to apologize. I understand. Honestly, I should have just said something. I could tell how disappointed you were when the six weeks were up, and I didn't make love to you. You must know that I wanted to. I've wanted you since the first day we met. I just wanted to make it special."

"Thank you, but it will always be special with you, simply because you're you."

"Mmm." I smirk and wipe my mouth with my napkin. Standing up from the table, I go over to the wall comm unit. I put on some soft jazz before walking back across the room to ask, "Dance with me?" She takes my hand as I help her up. I lead her to the center of the room and pull her into my arms. She gently places her right hand into my left hand and rests her left hand on my bicep and her head on my chest. We slowly move to the rhythm of the music. I relish her—the way she feels in my arms, the soft, sweet scent of her skin, the gentle sway of her hips, the rise and fall of her breasts. "You honor me with your company. I love breathing the same air as you. There isn't anything I wouldn't do for you. If I could give you the world, I would. I love you that much, Nicole, and so much more."

She looks up at me and tears fill her big brown eyes. "Liam, I know. And you have given me the world. You've risked your life for me and Zion. 'I love you,' doesn't begin to do justice to what I feel for you."

That does it. I wipe her tears as they roll down her cheeks. "I am so grateful that I found you." I kiss her gently on her forehead, then each eye, her cheeks, and then my lips find hers. I kiss her softly at first, planting slow kisses on her lips. I suck her bottom lip, release it, and then slide my tongue into her mouth. I feel her breasts rise and fall against my chest. She takes her right hand from my hand and runs it up my chest, to my shoulder, my neck, until she runs her fingers through my hair. She pulls me down closer to her, allowing our tongues deeper access to each other's mouths. I wrap both my arms around her tightly, pressing our bodies together. The pressure from her body rubbing against my erection fuels my hunger for her. Our breathing turns to panting. Without breaking our kiss, I lift her up in my arms and carry her across the room to the stairs. As I climb the stairs with her in my arms, she kisses my neck. I feel the heat between us rise with every kiss.

Carrying her into the master suite and putting her down, I let her slide down my body. She gazes up at me, and my jaw clenches. She kicks off her heels and I kick off my shoes. Reaching up, she pushes my jacket off my shoulders, letting it slide to the floor. I loosen and take off my tie as she unbuttons my vest and shirt. I reach to my wrist to undo one cufflink; she helps with the other. Our eyes remain locked on each other. She rubs her soft hands up and down my chest, then across my shoulders as she pushes my vest and shirt off.

Breathlessly, she whispers to me, "I love your body."

I sigh with a low growl and unhook the clasp of her dress at the back of her neck, freeing her breasts. The dress slides down her body to the floor, leaving her wearing nothing but a black lace thong. I reach out and cup her breasts, rubbing my thumbs over her nipples. They harden under my touch. She bites her lower lip and grabs my belt. With her eyes still locked on mine, she unbuckles my belt, unbuttons, and unzips my pants. She grabs my pants and boxer briefs at the same time, pulling them down to my quads. I help them the rest of the way until they're off. I pick her up again and carry her to the bed.

As she lies back on the bed, I remind myself to be as gentle as I can with her for the first time. I remember how tight she was when I fingered her in the woods. I need to make sure she's ready for me. Bathing her stomach with kisses as I pull her thong off, I make my way to the top of her slit. I use my fingers to spread her folds. I drag my index finger from her clit to her wet hole, spreading her wetness back and forth until I insert one finger into her pussy. Her body tenses slightly. "Relax pretty lady, I'll go slow," I reassure her, but I know she's nervous about being able to accommodate me. I begin slowly licking her clit as I slide my one finger in and out. She relaxes as I speed up my tongue. I add a second finger. Nicole moans with pleasure as she strokes my hair with one hand and grips my shoulder with the other. My fingers slide in and out of her pussy as I continue my efforts to ready her for my cock. I pump my fingers in and out as deep as they will go. She raises her pelvis to me, and I hear her softly panting my name. Faster, I stroke inside of her, needing it to be my cock instead. I feel her pussy spasm around my fingers as she has her first orgasm of the night. "Yeah, there it is. Come for me, baby." She trembles in sheer pleasure until her orgasm slowly dissipates. I pull out my fingers and move up her body until we're eye to eye.

Hoping she'll say no, I whisper to her, "Do you want me to put on a condom?"

She shakes her head no, "I only want to feel you."

I'd hoped she would say no because I don't want anything separating us tonight. Even though we've only been together a short time, I know I want Nicole to have my baby. Whether or not she gets pregnant, I'm going to have the time of my life trying. I simply respond to her with, "Mmm, good."

She spreads her legs farther apart to accommodate me. I rub my mushroom tip along her slit, mixing my pre-cum with her wetness. I guide myself to her opening and gently push myself inside her. She winces and shuts her eyes. I stop. I haven't gotten all of my head in. Using my forearm for support, I whisper in her ear, "I know you want me inside of you as much as I want to be inside of you, so trust me not to hurt you. Open your eyes and look at me." She opens her eyes and locks them on mine. Her body relaxes as I push my head inside of her. She releases the sheet and grabs my hand. Our fingers interlock. I push in a bit more. She sucks in a breath through her teeth in anticipation of receiving more of me. I keep my eyes locked on hers and softly kiss her lips. With my cock only halfway in, I pull out and thrust back in with a little more force gaining a couple more inches. I feel her stretch around me, and I stop to allow her to feel me. "Are you ok? Can you take more of me?"

She shifts her body under me and grabs my ass, pulling me closer down to her. Nodding her head for me to continue, she leaves no doubt. "I need to feel all of you. Never hold back with me."

"Mmm, yes, baby." I thrust hard and deep inside her. Her eyes widen and she lets out a loud groan, squeezing my hand and tensing. Only an inch of me isn't in her, but I know with time, she'll be able to take all of me. I pause and look down into her eyes. I reach down between us and massage her clit until her body relaxes. Now she's relaxed; I find my rhythm and begin slowly pumping in and out of her. She feels so good, I'm breathless. "Oh, Nicole, you feel so good, too damn good. I'm not going to last long."

After a few thrusts, she relaxes even more and moves beneath me, matching my rhythm. I pump slowly in her, stroking her clit with every motion. Now fully enjoying the moment, she wraps her legs around my waist. I slide my hands under her perfect ass, tilting her hips slightly upward. This motion gives my cock that extra inch of access and I'm able to be in her balls deep.

"Oh, God, Liam! Please don't stop."

"Never, pretty lady. I'll never stop pleasuring you. Mmm, Nicole, come for me." I bury my face in her neck trying to concentrate on not coming before her. I lick and suck her neck as I move deep inside of her hot sex. She trembles and moans loudly with pleasure like I've pushed her into a new gear. I work her neck with my tongue.

"Oh, Liam! Yeah, baby. Just like that. Mmm, Liam, please don't stop. I'm coming." Her pussy clutches my cock tightly as she climaxes, sending electric waves throughout her body. Feeling her body vibrating, trembling hard against mine, triggers my climax. I grunt as I shoot hot cum inside of her. Still spasming, her pussy milks me for every last drop of my seed. I stay inside her, enjoying the feeling of her throbbing walls as her body recovers.

The sensations I'm feeling are new to me. Sex must have always felt like this, must have, but if it did, I certainly do not remember. Maybe it's because it has been so long. No, it's her. I know it with every part of myself. Lifting my head to look at her, her eyes tell me that she is as lost in me as I am in her. For whatever reason, I choose to lighten the moment instead of allowing us to live in this vulnerable moment. Slowly, I pull out of her. "That was so amazing." I look at her and smile devilishly, "Your neck is very sensitive."

Blushing, she laughs, "Yes, I know."

"Why didn't you tell me?"

"Because it's more fun to let you discover some things on your own. And damn baby, I won't be able to walk in the morning. I should have stretched."

"Hmm, I am nowhere close to being done with you tonight. Don't move, I'll be right back." I jump out of bed and run to the bathroom for a warm towel. She tilts her head and gives me a little smile. "I've made a mess and I need to clean it up." I nudge her from her side to her back. I see my white cum spill out of her. I reach between her legs and gently clean her.

"I love the way you take care of me. You are a very attentive lover. Have you always been like this?"

"No. Not that I haven't been respectful or caring in the past. You, you are the treasure I've waited my whole life to find. So yes, I'm going to cherish you and take care of you for as long as you'll have me."

"I have no intentions of ever giving you up, Liam."

I smile and take the towel back to the bathroom. Lying down next to her, she walks her fingers up and down my chest. I take her hand in mine and bring it to my lips.

"Is this what you meant when we were in the forest, and you talked about wanting to learn how my body responds to your touch?"

"Absolutely, and for the record, that was me making love to you. But I am going to fuck you so hard when we get back home, you'll be speaking another language." I kiss her hard and deep. "Come on, let's get dressed. As much as I'd love to just lie here and hold you, we need to get back to Zion so Renee can go to bed."

# CHAPTER 18
# INSIDE
### (Nicole)

We make it back home in hardly any time. When we enter the room, Renee looks up from a book and smiles. "He's been out for about forty-five minutes." She smirks and says, "Well, aren't you two just glowing?" Liam picks Zion up off the floor and puts him to bed.

Smiling at Renee, I shrug. "Thanks again for doing this, sis."

Liam joins me in front of the screen wrapping his arms around my waist. He gives Renee a wicked grin. "Yes, thank you Renee, from the bottom of my heart." He leans down and kisses me on the neck in his newly discovered favorite spot on my body. "Goodnight, Renee." Renee giggles as he cuts the comm line.

"Our room. Now. I need to be back inside of you," he whispers in my ear.

We rush into our room and shed our clothes. Before I can get to the bed, he grabs me from behind and begins to kiss, lick, and suck my neck. I moan and clutch the arm that he has wrapped around my waist. "Baby, you're going to make me come before you're inside of me."

"I plan to make you come at least three more times tonight." He continues to assault my neck. He grabs my breast and squeezes my nipple with one hand and slides his other hand down to my pussy and begins to work my clit. In no time, I feel my body tremble with pleasure. "Yes, come for me, pretty lady," he commands. And I do. In a low, deep voice, he says, "One."

He moves us over to the bed with his arm around my waist. I feel his huge cock pressing into my back as he lifts me onto the bed. "Spread these beautiful legs for me," he orders me. I do. He guides my shoulder down so that I'm on all fours. "I'm going to fuck you from behind now so I can watch my cock slide in and out of your perfect pussy." Without hesitation, he slams his huge cock inside of me. I can't believe I'm taking all of him. I've always had a thing for tall men, but I've been afraid that they may have big cocks. It feels amazing, though. So amazing, I decide I want to fuck him back. I take control of the rhythm and rock back on him. He stills himself and lets me have control. "Oh shit," he growls. "Yes, Nicole. That's it, fuck your man, baby." I look back over my shoulder and see him mouth, "Damn." As he watches my ass ripple while I work my pussy along his long, super thick shaft. He grunts loudly and takes control back. Gripping my hips tightly with his large hands, he slows our pace, "Your ass is perfect, and your anus looks tight and inviting." My body tenses at the thought of his cock in my ass. He bends over and kisses my neck. I relax. He slowly moves inside me. He places his middle finger in my opened mouth and commands, "Suck." I suck his finger as he sucks and nibbles my neck while still slowly pumping in and out of me. Both of our breathing gets heavy as the pleasure continues to build. He pulls his finger out of my mouth and lifts back up to his knees. He begins to thrust faster and deeper and without warning, he puts his large, wet finger on my anus and slowly but forcefully pushes it in. I gasp in surprise at this new sensation. I've never felt anything like it. It doesn't hurt, but it is just his finger. I moan in pleasure. He pumps his finger in and out of my ass as he continues to fill my pussy with his cock. "Mmm, enjoy me filling all of you. Do you like it?"

"Yes."

"Say it."

Breathlessly moaning, I tell him, "I like you filling all of me."

He drives into me deep, hard, and fast. I feel his sweat drip on my back and ass. He pulls his finger out, grabs both of my hips and continues to drive into me. He grips my hips so hard. I'm sure I'll have his hands imprinted on me in the morning. Grunting and growling with every thrust, coherent speech has left him. Knowing that I've turned my big, strong, mountain man into goo sends a wave of pleasure through me that I can't contain. My insides explode as I come hard on his cock. He responds with own climax filling me with his seed again. He holds me tight and close in a plow position. There is no space between us. I can feel his balls deflate as they empty into me with my labia gently grazing them. He continues to hold me in place until he's emptied every drop into me. "Mmm, fuck! Two," he grunts out. As he withdraws from me, I realize he had been holding me up. We both fall onto the bed panting and laughing.

"Are you okay," he asks.

"Yes. The bigger question is, are you okay?"

"Yes, I'm great. And I'm sorry you were on the receiving end of that."

"I'm not. That was intense."

"It's been so long and every inch of you is pure perfection. I'm going to have a hard time controlling myself around you. I thought it would take a few times for you to accommodate all of me, but it's like your body was made for me. Like you were made for me. I can't get enough of you, Nicole. Are you tired?"

"Seriously?"

"I don't need to come again, but you're only at two. I owe you another orgasm. Come ride me for a minute."

"A minute? You are definitely not a minute man, but I can't deny you." I sit up and climb on top of him. We spend the rest of the night consuming each other. He gets me to orgasm two more times before we fall asleep with him still inside of me.

I wake up first, hoping to get up early and make a nice breakfast for my men, but the big man in bed with me is gripping me so tightly, I'm surprised I can still breathe. With my right leg pent under his huge right leg and my left leg draped over his right hip, I try to shimmy up and off of him. I feel him waking up inside of me. I whisper, "Don't even think about it, Dr. Sinclair." He grunts with his eyes still closed, but a wicked smile slowly spreads across his face. "Come on, baby, I'm sore as hell, but I still want to make you breakfast."

Opening his eyes, "I'm a little sore too from being gripped all night by this tight pussy." Just barely moving, he gently pumps inside of me, and I feel him expand inside me until he is fully erect. "I want to wake up like this every morning for the rest of our lives." I feel myself getting wet for him. "I'm sorry you're sore. Does this hurt? Do you want me to stop?" I look into his deep blue eyes and shake my head. He keeps his pace steady and slow until we both gently climax. "Mmm, good morning, pretty lady." He kisses me on my nose and slowly pulls out of me. We untangle our bodies, and he gets out of bed.

Trying to get up myself, I ask him, "Where are you going?" I realize my leg is numb from being under him all night.

"To run a bath for us. Just relax, I'll bring you in when it's ready."

I check the time. Hopefully, we're up a couple of hours before Zion. I haven't had a man in my life since becoming a mother. I need to figure out how to juggle my sex life with my mommy duties. I decide to test my legs and get out of bed. I don't make it one step before feeling how truly sore I am. *This man has murdered my vagina.* My legs feel like rubber. I look up to see Liam standing in the bathroom doorway with a guilty look of satisfaction.

"I'm sorry you're sore, but last night was the best sexual experience of my entire life. Let me help you." Walking over to pick me up, I stop him, but hold on to his hand for support. He guides me down into the huge sunken tub. As with all things with Liam, so far, it's perfect. My body feels better right away. We take turns washing each other before I settle down in front of him, laying my head back on his chest.

*"Good morning, Dr. Sinclair. I apologize for the intrusion."*

I damn near jump out of my skin, "What the hell! You said…"

He interrupts me, "What's wrong, Gisele?"

*"Mr. Christopher Ito has sent an urgent message after not being able to reach you."*

"Gisele, please play the message."

Chris' voice comes over the intercom, **"Lee, man, my little sister is sick. I need your help. Please call me."**

Rushing to get out of the tub he says, "Baby, I…"

"Go, I'm fine. I'll be right behind you in a few minutes."

# CHAPTER 19
# AIRBORNE
## (Liam)

D read fills my heart that a new virus may have been released. But anger also fills my heart at the thought that Chris' little sister, Tiffany, could be affected. She is so kind, and full of hope and love. She has traveled all over the world in the name of peace and social justice. We can't lose her.

Waiting in the lab, I ask, "Gisele, what's taking so long to connect?"

*"It is unclear. Do you want me to continue?"*

"Yes."

Nicole finds me in the lab. "Sweetheart, what's going on?"

"Still trying to reach him."

"What can I do?"

"Nicole, I'm worried about her. I'm worried for the public that this could be a new virus. It's serious enough that Chris needs my help." She sits me down on a lab stool and pulls over another. She rubs my face with one hand and holds my hand with the other. Suddenly, we have a connection and Chris appears on the screen. "Chris, what's happening?"

Chris' location is clear right away. "I had to get her to the lab you built for me."

"Good. What are her symptoms?"

"Vomiting, diarrhea, fever, lesions, and possibly nosebleeds."

"Possibly? Chris, what do you mean, possibly?"

"She called me to come pick her up from Houston. She was down there with a team of humanitarians rendering aid to both sides on what was supposed to be neutral ground. Eight of the thirteen have symptoms and three of those are experiencing nosebleeds." Chris stares at me with frustration.

"Gisele, please connect to lab 841 and begin a constant bio scan on the active table." I try to speak as calmly as I can.

*"Connecting. Connecting. Connection complete."*

"Chris, I'm going to need a blood sample. Go to the supply cabinet and enter 8-4-1 and scan your hand. There are fifty green bags."

He opens the cabinet. There are rows upon rows of medical supplies. "These?"

"Yes, I need you to get one. Open it and place it around the bend of her arm."

He walks over to an unconscious Tiffany and takes her arm in his hands. Chris wraps the cuff around her arm, and it snaps into place. "Got it."

"Good. Attach the enclosed tube to the cuff but leave the caps on until I figure out what this is and what we need to give her." I remotely access the cuff. The cuff, of my own design, allows me to view the veins to set up a PICC line for IVs and to draw blood. I get a blood sample. "Chris, it's time. Do I have permission to activate your chip?"

"Fuck. You know I wasn't happy when we put it in but go ahead."

"I promise this is self-contained and I will turn it off when this is over, but I need to be able to monitor you in case your vitals suddenly change."

"Is it going to hurt?"

"Dude, you've been shot a dozen times!"

"It's only been twice! That other time was just a graze! Man, just do it!"

"It's already done. And I'm getting some helpful readings already." Tiffany shifts on the table behind Chris. "Hi, Tiffany. How are you feeling?"

With a very weak voice, she tries to respond, "Lee?"

"Yes, Tiffany, it's Lee. How long have you been sick?"

"Lee, I don't feel well."

"I know, and I want to help you feel better. Do you remember when you first started feeling bad?" She doesn't respond. "Tiffany? Tiff? Chris, did she tell you anything?"

Rubbing her back, Chris looks very concerned. "No, she's been in and out since I picked her up. It took six hours roundtrip to get her here."

"She's stable right now if you want to relax. Gisele is processing the blood sample for me. It may take a few minutes."

ALORA CRAIGHTON

"Nicole, go call Renee and tell her to put their masks on the docking stations, and tell her to tell Sergio to do the same. I need to send an update so the masks can detect this new threat. Do you mind calling Thaddeus too?" Nodding her head, Nicole brushes my hair out of my face with her hand and kisses me on the forehead before leaving the room.

Chris watches us and nods. "She's good for you, man. Beautiful too. Seems like things are working out for you two."

"Yeah, she's an amazing woman." I smile but bring us back to the current issue. "I wish I could get more information about how Tiffany may have come in contact with whatever this is."

"The virus has been isolated, sir. We have a match in the system and a simulated cure. Sending it to your screen now."

"Now we're getting somewhere." The virus code I intercepted and the virus inside Tiffany appear side by side on the screen. They are identical. The most unsettling thing about this is that I found it only four months ago. This means that someone weaponized it very quickly. "Okay Chris, she's right. I have a cure, but the tricky part is going to be figuring out the dosage and best delivery method."

"Delivery method?"

"Yes, pill, IV, or gas. I'm going to take a blood sample from you too. I'm going to check your blood every hour over the next 48 hours, or until the appearance of the virus."

"So, you're sure I've been exposed?"

"Exposed? Yes. Infected? That's what I'm trying to find out. Did you drink anything other than your own bottled water?"

"Of course not."

"Did you come in contact with anyone's bodily fluids?"

"No, not even Tiff's."

"Ok, so if you are infected, it's airborne. Were you wearing your mask the whole time?"

"I kept it on until I got Tiff on the plane. Shit, I wasn't thinking. I should have kept it on the whole time."

"I would like to know if they were working inside or outside. Is there any way you can get me in contact with Tiffany's team?"

"I'll go through her social media accounts and her phone. I'll have them contact me since I'm still on the grid."

"This shit is really out of control. Have you talked to any of your friends in D.C.? How close are they to getting a handle on these conflicts?" Chris has a lot of military and political connections.

"I talked to Republican Congressman Moon three days ago. He said the House was working on some legislation. He also said that he spoke with Democratic Senator Greenhart and she wants to drop all political affiliations, at least for now, so that they can present a united front. Personally, I think we're well beyond that. I never thought I'd say this because you know I've been down for the revolution since forever, but we need to start eliminating extreme radicals on both sides. It may be safer for me than you on our side of the country. But believe me, there are still some strongholds where people who look like you would still lynch me just for breathing. No, it's long past the time for rhetoric, it's time for action. Just so you know, if we lose Tiff, I'm going back there to blow some shit up."

"Okay, man, calm down. We're not losing her. Stay focused. Why don't you check your phone for messages, I saw it light up."

*"Dr. Sinclair, there is…"*

"Thank you, Gisele, I see it." I cut her off and manually enter a command to turn off verbal updates on Chris' vitals. His temperature is going up, but I need him alert and calm for as long as possible. "Any responses?"

"Yes, two. I will send them your way."

"Chris, did you put your masks on the docking station?"

"Yes."

"Maybe you should plug your phone in there as well."

"Lee, we've been friends a long time and I know you. I'm going to assume that you're getting some concerning information on my vitals. Can I eat something? I'm hungry."

"Your temperature is rising. If you can eat, you should. Make sure you drink as much water as you can. I also want you to grab a cuff and put it on." My stomach is in knots. I should eat too, but I don't know if I can. Almost as if she heard me, Nicole comes back with eggs, toast, and chamomile tea. I give her a hesitant smile.

She whispers in response, "Keep working. You need your strength to work through this. I'm going to sit here and feed you while you work. Zion is up and eating next door in the comm room. Where is Chris going?"

"To go get food. His temperature is going up. I need to figure something out. We're getting responses from people who were with Tiffany. I need to review that, too."

"Babe, let me help you with that. Qualitative and mixed methods are my specialties. I'll read the messages, pull out data on person-to-person contact, location, time, symptoms, onset of symptoms, food and beverage intake… I got this," she says while feeding me eggs.

"Clearly. That will be a huge help. I'm running simulations on dosage and delivery methods based on Tiffany's and Chris' weight and other factors." She gives me a bite of toast. "You give me strength in so many ways. Thank you. It will be nice to have someone to work with. You can use that station over there." She feeds me more.

"I think I'm going to transfer everything next door so I can at least be in the same room as Zion. You stay in here and I'll check on you and bring you food. We can't leave him on his own like this. I will send you data as it becomes available or changes." She feeds me the last of the food on the plate, hands me the tea, and tells me to drink up. I take a sip. I'm not really a fan of the taste, but I know it will help calm my nerves. She wipes my lips with her thumb and tenderly kisses me.

Chris clears his throat. "Um, I've been back, but didn't want to interrupt you two. But I figure I should stop you now. I don't need to see y'all getting freaky."

Nicole laughs. "There will be none of that. He has to get you and your little sister healthy again. Hang in there, Chris. Babe, let me know if you need me," she says as she leaves.

A few hours go by. Tiffany's condition is unchanged, but Chris' symptoms are worsening. The preliminary results coming in from Nicole shows that the virus is airborne and transmitted through close contact. I start with a fluid to administer by IV since Chris has started vomiting. It's also easier because both of their cuffs are now attached to their beds which are attached to the pharmacy I installed in the walls of the lab. I'll work on the pill form to ship out from here, but it will take a couple of days at least to produce it and ship it to them by drone. But I fear Tiffany may not have two days if we don't turn this around. She's already on fluids, but I need to start the medication drip. Nicole informed me that our sample is up to fifty-two. Tiffany's contacts, who knew of others who were also sick, had them contact us and they are also sending useful information.

Finally, I'm ready to administer the first dose. I give the smallest dose I think will be effective and will repeat every four hours. I also administer a sedative to both of my patients. I keep working on the pill form so I can send it to a contact I have in Houston as soon as possible, but I can't start the production process until these first four hours pass.

Four hours later, I check back on my patients. It's working, but at this rate it may take five to seven days for the medication to be effective. I doubled it for the next dose, but both had increased heart rates and tremors. I scaled the dose back, but now I have to try different doses. Chris would come back and kill my ass if I killed them, not because I killed him, but because I killed his baby sister. Another eight hours later, I'm seeing positive results with temperatures stabilizing, and the virus slowly dying. As I predicted, it is going to take at least three days before the virus is out of their systems.

Nicole has compiled data and contacts for ninety-three people in the last fourteen hours. She's been a huge help, collecting and analyzing data, making breakfast, lunch, and dinner, and taking care of Zion and me. I couldn't have gotten through all of this today without her. She told me she was going to work from a different room so Zion wouldn't be alone all day, but she knew I needed my process and space. Ms. Cassie always told me that the right woman would give me the space to be myself. I needed that kind of support today.

## CHAPTER 20
# FOR ETERNITY
### (Nicole)

I haven't done this much data analysis in four years. It feels good knowing I can make a difference in this way. Today, I counted my blessings one by one. I'm blessed to be alive and healthy. My son is healthy. I finally found the love of a good man. We have food to eat, and a safe place to call home. And I can finally use my education to help someone in need. I am grateful.

I follow Zion to bed and continue working, sending updates to Liam as they come in. It's late and Liam hasn't responded to my last three updates. I need to go check on him. I kiss my perfect big boy and tuck him in.

As soon as I get to the door of the lab, I see Liam face down on the desk. There is a large timer running on the top of the huge, floor-to-ceiling monitor displaying the lab where

Chris and Tiffany are. Walking over to him, I see his dinner. I guess if I don't feed him, he won't eat. I touch his face and he doesn't move. He is out like a light. How do I move this massive man to the bed without disturbing Chris and Tiffany? I'm going to have to wake him up. "Liam," I whisper. "Liam, baby, come on let me help you to bed." He groans. "You have two hours before you need to be up. Please come rest your body for a while." Still, I get nothing but groans. Finally, I resort to kissing him. He moans softly and kisses me back. I quickly shush him as he slowly opens his eyes.

"Mmm, hi my love. I missed you."

"I've been with you all day, sort of. But let's talk about this in the bedroom."

"Babe, I can't leave."

"Sweetie, the bedroom in the lab." I point to the open door. "I wouldn't dream of asking you to leave this lab."

"Oh yeah. I'm sorry. I'm so tired."

"I know. Come on." I take him by the hand and lead him to the bedroom in the lab just a few feet away from his desk. "Go ahead and lie down. I'll see you in the morning."

"Wait, stay with me. It's only two hours and then I have to be back up."

"Yes, two hours that you should be sleeping."

He closes the door and smiles, "Don't you want to put me to sleep, pretty lady?"

"I didn't think you would want to tonight, or that you'd be too tired."

"If today has taught me anything, it's how quickly we can lose that which is dearest to us. I want every possible moment I can have with you. Besides, a good release may help clear my head." He gives me a seductive smile.

Of course, I want him, I'll always want him. "Okay but, we need to be quiet."

"Oh, but I like the way you moan for me." Sitting on the bed with me standing between his legs, he takes me in his arms. Kissing me softly, he pulls down my pajamas and slides off his sweats. He grabs me behind the knees and pulls me to him, forcing me to straddle him. He lifts me up and down onto his long, thick shaft. I've missed the way he fills me. We grip each other tightly as I move up and down on him. The silence is only broken by the sounds of our breathing. He puts his hand under my shirt and cups my breast. Not being able to have full access, he lifts my shirt up and off and sucks my breast hard while flicking the nipple with his tongue. I whisper in his ear, "You make me feel so good." He switches to my other breast, giving it the same attention. Holding me tightly, he turns, laying me down on the bed. He quickly sheds his t-shirt and puts his body on top of mine. He stills himself inside of me.

"Nicole, I love you."

"I love you too, Liam."

"I need you, Nicole. Promise me you'll always be mine."

"Forever." Placing my hand on his chest at his heart, I ask, "And are you mine?"

"Heart, body, and soul for as long as my soul lives on. I promise to love you for all eternity."

He kisses me, stopping any comment I may make. Beginning to move slowly inside of me again, I feel a shift in him, and he shows me a vulnerability that I haven't seen in him before. He strokes me like he's trying to merge our bodies into one. I can feel his heart pounding and I swear my heartbeat is syncing with his. I feel him pouring the essence of himself into me and, without warning, tears begin to roll down the side of my face. I grip his shoulders tightly, trying to let him know that in this moment there is nothing else in the world that matters, just our love. I whisper, "I love you so much. I want to be with you forever." He breathes heavily as he grinds down on me. "I'll always be with you. I'll take care of you." I clutch him tighter as I ride out an orgasm. Breathless, I end with, "I'm yours." He climaxes as he exhales one long, passionate sigh. Releasing me, he looks at me and sees my tears. He moves his hands to wipe them from my face. I reach up and wipe away his tears. I whisper to him, "Talk to me."

"I thought I was going to be alone out here for the rest of my life. When I buried my mom, it hurt so badly. I truly felt alone. I wished I had someone to hold me. My brothers are great men, all of them, but they couldn't fill that void. In everything you do and say, you fill it with love. You support me, encourage me, and strengthen me. As a man, you become accustomed to standing on your own, only projecting strength."

He pauses for a moment. "My father beat me one time. It was when my mother first left. I was only five and was crying because I missed her. He slapped me hard across my face, then he took off his belt and whipped me, hitting me wherever he could. I had welts everywhere, some of them bled. Even though she wasn't there, I've always believed that was the last time he beat my mother. After he was done, he told me that crying was for babies, bitches, and sissies. I never cried in front of him again, not even when I was in pain. It became easy to be the alpha male the world expected Liam Sinclair the Third to be. But on the inside, I hurt and cry for the people I've lost, and the pain humanity is suffering. I hate bullies and I hate to see people in pain, so I try to fight back. I will always fight for what is just. I was shot for trying to do the right thing. Then, you came along. You see me, all of me. In my strength and weakness, you accept me for all that I am. So yes, I will love you for all eternity."

"And I love you too. You have been fighting a long time, whether it was your father, big pharma companies, or against social injustice. I know you're tired. I saw it when we first met, and I saw it today. I also saw fear and worry in your eyes. You are a wonderful man, and I am blessed to have you in my life, but I need you to keep fighting. We all need you to keep fighting. It is extremely unfair that you have to bear this weight under these conditions, but you are not the first person to be called to sacrifice for the greater good of mankind. Like those before you, you can't give up. I will do whatever I can to lift you up so that you can continue fighting. Do whatever you need to do to survive, but you are safe with me." A smile spreads across his face. Before he can speak, I put my finger to his lips, "On that cheerful note, close your eyes and go to sleep."

"Stay with me for a while?"

"I'll stay until it's time for you to get up. Now, shhh. Go to sleep." Tonight, it's my turn to hold him. He fell asleep quickly in my arms, but now I'm wide awake. Listening to him breathe, I wonder how he has made it this long on his own. I know that he's strong and I'm not questioning his strength, but I don't think that I would have been able to go through what he's been through alone. My heart aches for him. I feel safe with him and being here on this mountain, but I'm beginning to get concerned that the people who shot him will start to look for him again. Until now, all I could see was the good he tries to do. Now I fully understand why he's hiding up here. He is an asset to the cause for world peace. There's wealth in wars and in keeping people sick. My Liam is a threat to them, and that makes him a target for violence.

# Chapter 21

# RECONNECTING

## (Liam)

My alarm wakes me up. Time to get back to work. I realize that I'm not in Nicole's arms. Once I sit up, I see her sitting at the desk in the back of the room watching me. "Nicole, is something wrong?"

"No. Go check on Tiffany and Chris. I'm going to go downstairs and try to sleep for a couple of hours. When I get up, I'll start scanning news outlets to see how widespread the outbreak is. Is that ok?"

"Yes, that's perfect. Thank you. But why did you get out of bed? What's wrong?"

"I was just thinking about everything. I don't want you to concern yourself with what's in my head right now. We can talk about it later. I need you to focus on the task at hand. Just know that nothing has changed. I love you and I will support you in whatever comes our way." She stands up, walks over to me, and kisses me. "Get back to work and I will see you when I get up." She leaves the lab.

As much as I hate leaving whatever this is unresolved, she's right, I need to focus. I get dressed and head in. I see green on all of my screens. This is very good news. It means that all of their vitals are stable and returning to normal. Though they were in different stages of the virus, the medication attacked the symptoms at the same rate. However, the virus is still alive, and they will need to quarantine at least 48 hours after it dies.

Now I'm rethinking the pill. This virus just might need immediate in-patient care. I really need to talk to Dr. Varma, but it isn't even 6 a.m. and she may not be awake. Now is not the time for courtesy. She will understand if I wake her up. I rush next door to the comm room, so I don't disturb the patients.

"Gisele, I need a level five secure line to Dr. Prisha Varma."

"*Yes, Dr. Sinclair. The line is connecting.*"

Dr. Varma answers. "This is Dr. Varma."

"Hello, Dr. Varma. It's nice to hear your voice."

There is a pause, but I hear her breathing. She responds in a hushed tone, "Dr. Sinclair? Liam Sinclair?"

"Yes. Hi, Prisha."

"It is very nice to hear your voice! I thought you may have died."

"No, I just needed to disappear for a while. Did I wake you?"

"After the news broke about your shooting and that you were in critical condition, the story just faded away. There were never any updates, and no one saw you again. And no, you did not wake me. I have been at the hospital going on twenty-four hours seeing patients that all seem to be infected with some stomach virus that causes nosebleeds."

"Have you had any luck fighting it?"

"No, as a matter of fact it's getting worse. One of my nurses who treated the first patient is experiencing symptoms. I have two patients whose symptoms worsened and are now in critical condition. Is that why you called me?"

"Yes. I can help. Do you have a way to produce a fluid if I send you the formula?"

"Yes. I am good friends with the head of the lab here."

"Good. Tell me how I can send it securely to you. You'll need to make it known that you did not come up with the cure, but that it was anonymously emailed to you. Can you do that?"

"Yes, but how did you come by it?"

"I was contacted by two people who had been exposed to the virus. I began administering the medication by IV. A little over twenty-four hours later, both are stabilized, and the symptoms are basically gone. The virus is still active but has been dying at a steady rate. I expect it to be fully eradicated from the host in approximately forty-six hours. I am administering eight cc every four hours."

"Dr. Sinclair, that is great news, but you know I cannot administer a non-FDA approved medication to patients. I will lose my license."

"Then, people will die. And from what you told me, the first two deaths will happen soon." She goes silent. I continue, "What happened to the Dr. Varma who was going to save the world one person at a time? Now is your chance."

"Okay, send it. I have seen what you can do, and that is the only reason I am trusting you. If this kills them, I will have to give your name up. I really do not want to do that."

"You won't have to. I will send it over. Keep me posted."

"One more thing Dr. Sinclair…"

"Yes?"

"If it works, FDA is going to want a principal investigator on this."

"I'll figure out the P.I. You'll have the formula within the hour." I end the call.

She's right. I need to make this look legit. I haven't spoken to the Bennett twins in two years, but I need their help on this. "Gisele, please video call James Bennett."

He picks up right away. "Lee? Lee!"

"Hi, Jimmy."

"EDDIE, GET IN HERE!"

Eddie runs in from another room. "Liam! Oh, my God! Well, this makes coming into the office today worth my time."

"I wasn't sure if either of you would take my call."

"Why would you think that?" Jimmy asks.

"You weren't happy with me the last time we spoke."

"Aww, come on man! You know Jimmy gets emotional when he thinks someone he cares about is in danger."

"You weren't exactly happy with my decision either, Eddie."

"True, but you're my brother from another mother. I think that's how Thaddeus says it."

"Yeah, Lee. You should be here in London living it up with Eddie and me, not hiding out in some godforsaken cave."

"Look guys, I don't have time to debate this right now. I need your help. There has been a biological attack here in the states. Chris and Tiffany were infected. I have a cure and I'm caring for them, but I need to get it out to the public."

"Shit, what can we do?" Jimmy asks.

"I need help to set up a company. But I need a paper trail that isn't going to lead back to me here."

Confused by my request, Eddie responds, "You can set up a shell corporation in your sleep. What do you need us for?"

"Well, I don't want it to trace back to me here, but there may come a time that I need to claim intellectual ownership of it. I would like to have a physical place to have it trace back to in London. Can you help?"

"Of course, and I know just the place. We recently purchased a building and there are a ton of offices. I'll set up a server and have it ping off of some random satellite. Jimmy can handle the financial side."

"Yeah, I have a few favors I can call in at banks across Europe."

"Great guys. How long is this going to take? I need an email address so I can send the formula out."

"I can have you setup within the hour." Eddie says and Jimmy nods in agreement.

"Great. Please set it up as S&S Biological Enterprise, Incorporated."

"S&S? Did you have a kid? Did we miss something?"

"Look Eddie, I don't have time to go into detail right now, but yes, I met someone. Her name is Nicole Simmons. She has a son who I have chosen to help her raise as my own."

"Ah," Jimmy says. "Now you're making sense. You want us to help with an exit plan."

"No, it's a safety net. If anything happens to me, I want you guys to help her get out of the country and make sure they are taken care of."

"Blimey, Lee! That's a lot! On that note, I'm going to go get the ball rolling. Will message you when the server is up. Tell Chris and Tiff I said hello when they get better."

"I will. Thanks for your help, Eddie." He leaves the office.

"Listen, Liam, now that Eddie is gone. I'm sorry if I made you question our loyalty. You are family. Always remember, brothers are allowed to fight, but they are not allowed to give up on each other. When all of this is over, I want to hear all about the woman who has won your heart."

"I promise. Hey, Jimmy? If I'm your brother, does that make us triplets?" We both laugh.

"Still a smartass. Go take care of Chris and Tiffany."

"Alright. Talk to you soon."

I head back into the lab and am shocked by what I see on the screen. "What the…"

Tiffany is awake and sitting up. "Lee?"

"Tiffany, you're awake? Don't try to stand."

"Lee, where am I? What's wrong with Chris and how long have I been out?

"You're in your brother's—well one of my labs. Your brother contracted the virus you were carrying. You were unconscious for almost two days. The virus is still in your system, but the medication will kill it completely in about thirty-six hours."

"I know you said not to get up, but I have to pee." Tiffany was always self-reliant. Being ten years younger than Chris with parents who were always busy, she had to be.

"Tiffany, you have an IV. You need to be disconnected."

"Well, tell me how to disconnect it."

"Don't make *me* put you back to sleep. Hold on." I turn the drip off. "Ok, there's a…"

"Too slow! I did it already. I swear you guys are getting old. Do you have cameras in the bathroom?"

"Yup!" She flips me off as she stumbles off to find the bathroom. The lab door opens. It's Nicole with breakfast.

"Good morning, my love. Sorry breakfast is so late. I slept longer than I should have. Wait, where's Tiffany?"

"Feeling better and mouthing off." I shake my head and smile knowing that she's feeling better.

"I heard that! And who are you talking to?" Tiffany calls out from the bathroom.

"Shhh! You're going to wake up your brother. Get back in here and plug back in."

Tiffany comes out of the bathroom, "I asked you… Hi."

"Hi, Tiffany. I'm Nicole. I've heard a lot about you. Glad to see you're feeling better."

"Um, Lee? You want to tell me what's going on?"

"Nicole is…" I hadn't really thought of a label for what we are. "Mine." Nicole smiles.

"Your what? I'm sorry, Nicole. This is more about Lee and less about you. Are you saying you guys are together? Because there is no way you're pulling a beautiful woman like this."

Rolling my eyes, "Whatever, Tiffany. You're just jealous. Sit your ass down and plug back in."

Laughing, Nicole flirtatiously responds, "Well, thank you, Tiff. May I call you Tiff?"

"You, beautiful, may call me anything you like." She flashes my woman that damn Ito smile. Tiffany has dimples like her brother.

Watching Nicole blush at the compliment, I jokingly jab at my overly flirtatious patient. "Okay, now that's enough of this shit! Good night, Tiffany."

Tiffany glares and points at me. "Liam, you better not put me to sleep!"

"Well, stop flirting with my woman."

A low, deep voice sounds off in the lab. Chris is coming around. "Ew, I hate hearing my little sister flirt."

Tiffany giggles. "Why? You taught me everything I know."

"Welcome back, Chris! How are you feeling buddy?" I take his vitals, and everything looks great so far.

"I don't know yet. I'm just glad my baby sister is feeling better."

"Yeah, I feel much better. Now tell me, have you seen Nicole? Aren't you impressed that Lee was able to pull a beauty like her?"

"Stop frontin' Tiffany. You used to have a crush on Liam."

"Ok, Lee, now you can put his groggy ass out."

Nicole jumps in, "No, no, no. I need to hear about you crushing on my man." Nicole leans over on the desk I'm working on. I rub her bottom and pull her on to my lap. This is a good time for all of us to exhale a bit.

"All the guys would come over from time to time. Liam was my favorite. Yeah, he's fine, but I was attracted to his heart. I'm ten years younger than the guys so I was just everyone's little sister. Imagine explaining that you're pansexual to your six, straight, big brothers."

Nicole nods at Tiffany. "I think it is amazing how close you all are. I'm glad Liam has all of you."

That reminds me that I need to tell Chris about my conversation with the twins. "Speaking of our family. Chris, guess who I talked to."

"Hmm?" He groans.

"Jimmy and Eddie." I let the news just sink in,

"What!" Chris slowly sits up to see me better. "How did that happen?"

"Well, I had to get this cure distributed." I wrap my arm a little tighter around Nicole's waist. "I needed to set up a contingency plan to make sure it doesn't come back to me. But if it does, I need to make provisions for Nicole and Zion." I feel Nicole's body tense up, but she gently rubs my arm with her hand. "They said to tell you both hello."

"I'm sorry this is pushing you out of your comfort zone, but I'm glad you reconnected with the twins. They really missed you." Chris knows how badly things were left between the twins and me.

"I'm sorry to break up this tender moment," Tiffany interrupts. "But who is Zion?"

"Zion is my, our son." I respond and realize how natural it feels to call Zion mine. "You'll meet him soon."

Complete shock covers Tiffany's face. "Wait, you had a kid? You said I was only out for two days."

"No, Tiff. Zion is my son, but Liam has stepped into the role of daddy. I know you're wondering about how long we've been together."

"Nope, not I. I have fallen in love at first sight twice. You will get no judgment from me. You both look incredibly happy so, that's good enough for me. I'm happy for you guys."

"Thanks, Tiffany. I'm going to go downstairs and check on Zion." Nicole kisses me on the cheek and leaves the lab.

"Liam, that woman is worried about you. Tiffany and I are on the mend. You should go talk to her."

"Yeah, I know she's worried. It started last night. She told me we will talk about it after you two are well and I have helped with the cure as much as possible."

Tiffany winks at me. "Lee, you deserve to be happy. Hold on to it."

Chris nods in agreement. "I agree with this one. Go talk to her. At least try. We're not going anywhere. Though Tiffany could make herself useful and go make me a sandwich."

"Damn it, you two! Look, I'll make a deal with you. I will go talk to Nicole if you promise to stay in bed."

In unison, "We promise!"

# Chapter 22

# Time to Adjust

## (Nicole)

---

This is the second time I've shown too much concern around Liam. I love his life's mission and I completely support him. I have to get my nerves under control. I hear Liam coming down the stairs, but before either of us can say anything... "Daddy!" Zion runs and leaps into Liam's arms. "I missed you. I didn't get to see you at all yesterday. Mommy said you needed to focus on Uncle Chris. Is he all better now?

"Almost. I'm sorry we didn't get to spend any time together yesterday. Do you forgive me?"

"Of course, daddy. It is important to make people feel better."

"Hey buddy, is it okay if I talk to Mommy for a bit?"

"Sure. I'll just read my book. Mommy said I have to read for an hour in the morning and an hour after dinner."

"Good job." Liam pats Zion on the back before turning his attention to me. "Nicole, can we talk?" He gestures for me to follow him down the hall. He leads us into the theater. I raise an eyebrow at him. "There are seats and it's soundproof. Have a seat, pretty lady." We sit. "What's on your mind?"

I try to not sound overly sarcastic. "I thought you wanted to talk to me. What's on your mind?"

"Tell me what's bothering you, Nicole. Don't hold back. I can't bear to think that anything I'm doing is hurting you. Please, Nicole, talk to me."

Taking his face in my hands, I look into the oceanic depths of his deep blue eyes. "Sweetheart, you are not hurting me. I am so proud of you. I am in awe of who you are."

Smiling, he looks down and takes my hands away from his face. Holding both of my hands in his, his expression changes back to one of concern. "Thank you, but I need us to talk about what was concerning you this morning when you left the bed, and again a little while ago when you left the lab. Talk to me. You can tell me anything."

I take a moment to gather my thoughts. "I'm afraid that I'm going to lose you, that they will find you and kill you. I'm also afraid that Zion can get hurt."

"Nicole…"

"Please, hear me out." He nods his head. "I understand you may die for this cause, and I get that. It is a just and noble cause, but I'm not prepared to lose you. I just found you."

"Oh, Nicole, I'm so sorry. You know, if this happened before I met you, I would have simply patched Chris and

Tiff up and went back to living this life of exile, but you give me courage."

"Great, so my showing up in your life is what's going to get you killed."

"That is not what I meant, and you know it. Let's just say that now, I have two new reasons to fight to help make things better. What can I do to put you at ease?"

"I don't know if you can. What if they find us out here?"

"I doubt that will happen, but I'm prepared for it if it does."

"I'm not. You said you were bringing us somewhere safe. Now we might be out here dodging bullets and fighting assassins."

"What if I teach you how to protect yourself? I'll teach you how to shoot and some self-defense moves that could even take me down. Would that help?"

"It wouldn't hurt. The only thing that will help is keeping my family safe and you staying alive." I grab his hand. "Stay alive and stay with us... with me."

"I don't want to die, and to prove it, I've been hiding up here on this mountain like a coward. I couldn't do that this time. Hundreds, thousands of people may be saved because of this formula. Please don't ask me to stand by and just watch."

"Okay, Liam. At some point, one or both of us stopped listening. Let me try this again. I want you to help however you can. You have a moral obligation to help. If you didn't help, I would lose respect for you. Last night, as I held you in my arms, I realized how important you are to this fight. I also realized how dangerous you are to the powerful people who want to cause harm. That's what scared me."

"Does it scare you so much that you don't want to be with me, or for me to be involved in Zion's life?"

"Of course not. It makes me value each moment we have together even more. If you die tomorrow, I will be grateful for the time that we had together. Baby, this is about me taking the time to adjust to the danger involved. That's all."

"Come here." He pulls me into his lap and wraps his arms around me. "You have all of me, but if my body dies, my love will stay with you. I'll watch over you and Zion always. I am only one man. If I have to die so that hundreds may live, I'll accept my fate." My eyes drop at the thought of losing him, but he softly caresses my cheek and lifts my chin so that I will look at him. "No, it isn't fair to you, and we would still be in bliss if Tiffany and Chris didn't get sick. When I took you into the lab the first time, that's when I should have told you. I should have tried to make you understand what could happen. We hadn't made love yet, so you could have decided without emotions clouding your judgment."

"It wouldn't have mattered at that point. I had already fallen for you. You've had years to adjust to the fact that you are on someone's kill list. I just found out. I need a little time to catch up."

He nods his head. "Just don't give up on me."

"Never." We kiss and he squeezes me tight.

"I wish I could take you out on my yacht and spend a couple of weeks out on the water."

I jerk away from our embrace with excitement. "A yacht. You have a yacht?"

"Sure do. She's beautiful. It's one of the few toys I kept."

"Don't tell me any details about her. I want it to be totally new when I see her for the first time. I have always had a thing for yachts."

"Really? How many yachts have you been on?"

"Just one. It was for a work function. Having a yacht didn't make you more popular with the ladies?"

"No. In fact, you are only the second person, outside of the crew, who knows about it. I never even told my brothers. I disappeared a couple of times when I needed to clear my head. My mother knew where I was, but like you, she gave me the space I needed. When things settle, I promise to take you on an extended vacation on the water. Would you like that?"

Almost giddy, I screech, "Yes!"

The theater door opens. "Mommy? Daddy? May I come in?"

"Yes, come on in buddy." Liam tells Zion. He comes in and sits in the leather recliner at the end of the six-seat row Liam and I are cuddling in. "I was just telling Mommy that when all the crazy stuff stops, we're going to take a vacation on our yacht. What's something you want to do when we don't have to hide anymore?"

"I want to go to Disneyland! We used to go all the time. It was a lot of fun. Do you like Disneyland?" My child beams as he remembers the times we shared.

Liam's smile is gentle and full of love. "I sure do. I miss it too. I really miss the turkey legs and Dole whips."

"I miss the churros. Mommy, what do you miss?"

"Mmm, the popcorn and corn dogs. Disneyland has the best corn dogs." I wink at Zion.

Liam squeezes me and kisses me on the cheek, "One day we'll get to do normal things, like a normal family." He sits us up and reaches out for Zion's hand. Holding both of our hands, he says, "No matter what the future holds, we are a family. I will not abandon you two, in this life or the next. Do you believe me?" Zion and I both nod. "Good. I think we should watch a movie. Zion, you choose."

"What movies do you have, daddy?"

"There's a 99 percent chance that I have any movie you can name. What's your favorite movie?"

"It used to be the first *Toy Story*. Now, I like anything in the Marvel Universe. Do you have *The Avengers*, the first one?"

"Sure do. I'll put it on, and you guys get started. I'm going to make popcorn and check on Chris and Tiffany. Let them know we sorted everything out." He winks at me and kisses my forehead before heading out.

"Mommy, I'm going to sit in the front row!"

"Go ahead."

I watch Liam as he leaves the room, feeling only slightly comforted by his words. I will let him train me. Knowing how to handle a weapon is a good skill to have. If my seven-year-old can shoot a gun, I'm sure I can too. God, I can't believe my baby has shot a gun. I hate guns and I always hoped to keep violence out of our lives. Now our lives are becoming dependent on weapons. At least Liam is making sure we are properly trained.

# CHAPTER 23
# HITTING THE MARK
### (Liam)

---

After my Tiffany and Chris quarantine watch was over, I moved out of the lab and tried to get on with life. Nicole says she's fine and puts on a happy face whenever she knows Zion and I are watching. But I see her zoning out, getting lost in her thoughts when she thinks we aren't watching. Though she tries not to be, she's guarded with me.

I walk over to her and kiss her softly on the lips. "Good morning, pretty lady. Penny for your thoughts." She shrugs but smiles. "Feel like doing some shooting today?"

"Sure. You know I'm nervous about it."

"Don't be. I will be right there walking you through every step. Besides, you were ready to shoot that kid on our hike here."

"That was different. I was defending my child."

"And that's what you need to think about as we train. Everything you are learning is for you to defend yourself and those you love. I'm not teaching you to shoot for sport. This is not about having fun. I am training you to be an efficient shooter."

"Meaning?"

"Meaning if anyone shows up here unannounced, I want you to be able to incapacitate them with one shot. You won't learn it overnight. It's going to take a lot of practice. We'll start downstairs in the indoor range. When you get good enough, I'll take you outside. I think we should bring Zion with us. I've taught him general safety rules around guns, but he should hear it again."

"He told me you were teaching him how to shoot."

"Yes, but that was a BB gun. I figured I'd start him off small. I'm going to start you out on the little Glock you pulled on that kid."

Laughing, "You know that's not funny. And besides, you drew on that kid first. I was just following your lead." We both laugh, harder than the situation calls for. "I really needed this laugh. Thank you." She hugs me tightly in an unguarded moment. It didn't last long, but it was a moment worth freezing in time.

"Zion, want to go to the shooting range with Mommy and me?"

"Sweet!" He squeals with excitement.

Once downstairs, I sit my two favorite people down and go over the rules. "First and foremost, always, always point the gun down unless you are aiming at a specific target or tracking." They nod. "I will show you guys how to load and clean each weapon as we go. Zion, for now, you'll be mostly watching."

"Why?" He asks with a slight attitude.

"Because if anything bad happens, Mommy and I would rather fight than have you get hurt. I promise once she learns, you'll have two teachers. Deal?"

"Yes. Is it okay if I go sit down over there?" He gestures to the chair in the corner.

"If you like, but you won't be able to see from over there."

"I'm fine, Daddy. I'm just disappointed. I thought I would get to shoot today."

"How about this? I'll help mom until she can practice on her own and then I will work with you. I'm not blowing you off."

"Okay, you two, my turn." Nicole jumps in to calm the room, like she frequently does. "We've been through a lot over the last couple of months. We've grown as a family, and we do not compete for attention. Lee, babe, is there an intercom in here, or monitor down here?"

"Yes. Why?"

"I don't think we need to hold Zion captive today. What do you say, kiddo? What would you like to do for the next couple of hours? I don't think you should spend the day just sitting here."

Zion looks down at his hands and whispers, "I'm tired of being inside."

Zion's words cut deep. I know I've been busy saving the world, but I didn't realize I was being neglectful. "Why didn't you say anything? Zion, when did you stop talking to me?"

"You've been busy taking care of people, and Mommy said we needed to leave you alone."

I wish Nicole hadn't told him to leave me alone. "I'm sorry I haven't been there for you buddy."

Nicole grabs us and pulls us closer together. "Okay, guys, stop it. No one needs to be sorry. This is our new life. Daddy has a job, and I will help him whenever I can. We will both take care of you the best way we know how, but you have to help us take care of you too. You have to tell us when you're lonely, when you need our attention, when you need to talk, and most of all, when you just need us all to stop. But Zion, we are the grown-ups, and we have to try harder to anticipate your needs. When one of us is busy for a very long time, the other has to be available for you. Does that work for both of you?" We both nod in agreement. "Good. So, Zion, what would you like to do inside for the next couple of hours?" Nicole just rattled off what sounded like a list of demands to our seven-year-old.

"May I have some snacks in the living room? I'll read for a little while and watch TV."

"Yes, you may. Liam, will you please take him upstairs? I will stay here and wait for you."

I take Zion upstairs and get him settled before coming back to find Nicole in the range facing the wall, leaning her head on it.

"Okay, what's wrong, Nicole?"

She snaps back to reality. "Oh, hey."

I walk toward her to close the distance between us. "Are you going to make me ask you again?"

"I don't want us to fight, but I don't want Zion shooting guns. I know you've already started teaching him, but I'm not ready to watch my baby learn to kill another living being. I, on the other hand, am ready to drop a motherfucker if they come anywhere near my family."

I chuckle until I get a smile out of her. "Now that's my badass woman." I take her by the hand and lead her to the center lane. Wrapping my arm around her waist, I feel her trembling. "I'm right here, pretty lady. We're doing this so that you get comfortable knowing that you are in control." I point to the gun, "That is just a thing. It can't do anything unless you command it to. Okay?" She nods. I reach out in front of her, pick up the gun, and place it in her hands. "This is loaded so do not put your finger on the trigger just yet. Just breathe. Everything is fine. Now, square up." I release her waist allowing her to place her right foot behind her. "Don't lock your knees. Now raise the gun, extend your right arm, and use your left hand as support for your right." I step into her to adjust her body slightly. "Damn, you look sexy."

"Dr. Sinclair, I'm going to shoot this gun for a bit and then maybe, you'll get to shoot yours." She flashes me a devious smirk.

"Sounds good to me." I place my ear protection on, raise hers to her ears, and whisper before covering them, "Aim at the target and shoot when you're ready."

"Aren't you going to instruct me on how to aim?"

"Let's see what you got first."

She squeezes the trigger and fires. "Oh my God! That's intense!"

"That hit the paper, but not the target. This time, try to hit the target." She turns her head over her left shoulder to look at me. "Because the first kill shot you get, I'm going to rip off your clothes and fuck you right here. So please, give me a kill shot."

Blushing, she says, "No, man. I'm going to practice shooting until I get tired." She fires. This time hitting the shoulder of the silhouette. "Because every kill shot I hit will make me feel better about being able to protect what's mine." She fires again, hitting the target right of center mass. She puts the gun down.

"Baby, what's wrong?"

"Nothing. Now that I'm over the initial shock of shooting, I need to reset." She stretches her arms over her head and then bends over, grabbing her ankles to stretch her lower body.

"Aw, geez! Come on! That shit is not fair! I have never needed to stretch like that."

"Well, you're not me and I was tense before."

"Well, now I'm hard."

"Back up, Dr. Sinclair. I'm ready to work." Without hesitation this time, she picks up the gun, aims, and fires, hitting the target dead center. She immediately fires two more shots, hitting in the same spot.

"YEAH!!!" Something told me she would catch on quickly.

Feeling emboldened, she empties the rest of the clip in the target's head. She puts the gun down, takes off her earmuffs, turns to me and says, "Reload."

Both turned on and impressed, I ask her, "Um, should I be afraid?"

"Not you, but any jackass who comes after my man should be."

I show her how to reload the gun and switch out the target. While I send out the new target down the lane, I decide to clarify an issue. "Nicole, you're the second wave. You know that, right? I don't want you to have to pick up a gun until I draw my last breath. You are not my body-guard." As much as I love her desire to shelter me from the world, she's mine and I can't have her risking her life for me. Though she probably thinks this is just a case of me preserving my masculinity, it isn't. I just couldn't live with myself if something happened to her.

She rolls her eyes, puts her earmuffs back on, picks up the reloaded gun and empties it with all kill shots. She puts the gun down and turns back to me with a defiant look. "I'm sorry, but how do you plan on stopping me?"

I'm not getting ready to argue with her. I take off both of our earmuffs and pick her up. Before she can speak, I tell her, "No more talking." My mouth takes hers hard. She wraps her legs around my waist as I put her body against the wall. Our tongues twist and twirl in each other's mouths. I love the way she tastes, and I need to taste more of her. I lift her shirt and pull her bra down, exposing her breasts as I begin to feast. She pulls back and pushes me away. She's never done that before. "I'm sorry, Nicole. Do you want me to stop?"

Our eyes lock. There's a look in her eyes that I haven't seen before. I'm not sure what it is. It almost looks panicked.

Before I can question her, she recaptures my desire. "I want you inside of me now."

Still holding her against the wall, I take her shoes off and pull her leggings off with her panties. Then, I lower her to the floor. With her standing in front of me naked from the waist down, I ask her, "Do you remember that sexy stretch you did earlier?" She nods. I grab her around her waist, turning us around so that my back is to the wall and her back is to me. With a low growl I tell her, "Spread your legs, bend over, and grab your ankles."

"Really?" she asks.

Unbuckling my belt and dropping my jeans, I can barely maintain control. "Yes. Please." I say, practically begging her to let me have my way with her body. She sees the burning in my gaze and complies to my commands. I have the most beautiful view of her perfect ass and wet pussy. I can see her glistening wetness as I slowly slide into her. "Mmm, you're so wet." I grab her hips and thrust into her hard and fast. I watch as I slide in and out of her. The sight of my cock getting more covered with her feminine fluid with each thrust is going to make me come faster than I intended. "Mmm, fuck. You feel too good." I shake my head to maintain my composure, but it doesn't help. "Oh shit, baby! I'm sorry, I'm already about to come." My head drops forward. "You're just so damn perfect." I grip her hips tightly as my cum floods into her. "Goddamit!" I growl. "Sorry." My cum continues to fill her. "Oh shit. I'm sorry." Totally breathless, I manage to apologize one more time as my last bit of cum flows out of me. "Sorry, baby."

She grabs my hands as I slowly withdraw, and she stands up. "Why are you apologizing?"

"I came before you. I'll make it up to you."

Nicole turns around to face me and kisses me softly. "Is my man satisfied?"

"Yes, very."

"Then that's all I can ask for."

"What?" She shrugs at me as I look at her with complete confusion. "Did you not want to have sex?"

Looking at me as if I had just made a stupid joke, she presses her lips together and shakes her head. "Um, you just said how wet I was. Do you think I would be wet if I didn't want you? I will always want you," she reassures me. "Everything about you is sexy. I love your eyes, your smile, your hair, your nose, your voice, your thick neck, your broad shoulders, your back, your chest, your arms… God, your arms. I love being in your arms." She continues her surveyance of my body as she caresses each part. "Your hands, I love how you use these hands to help me, protect me, guide me, comfort me, cure me, provide for me, and pleasure me. I love wrapping my arms and legs around this waist." Her hands move gently around my waist to my lower back and down. "This perfect ass was chiseled by the gods. Even Atlas himself would have to bow before it."

I blush, having never had my body appraised by a woman. Her hands move forward again, and I know where they're going. "This cock," deliciously biting her bottom lip, "This cock is what women across the world imagine when they touch themselves, and it's all mine." My head drops back, and I suck in air through my gritted teeth as she strokes me. Her touch triggers an erection. I grab her and begin kissing her. My hands find their way to her breasts and start to grab and squeeze them. She stops me, "Mmm, baby. As much as I would love a round two, we need to get upstairs."

"Really?" She nods and leaves my embrace to put on her pants. "Well, can I make it up to you tonight?"

"I already told you; I love you and there's nothing to make up. Now, put on some pants please." She giggles knowing how badly I want to be in her again.

"Fine. Come on, let's go find Zion."

She grabs my hand before I make it to the door. "Liam, why don't you take Zion camping tonight? It would be nice for you two to have some one-on-one time."

I was hoping that I would be spending the night in bed with her and now she's sending me off camping. Maybe she needs some space. "I suppose we could go camping. The weather is great, and Zion would love being outside. Will you be okay by yourself tonight?"

"Yes," she says a little too quickly.

"What's going on, Nicole? Are you trying to get rid of me?"

Sighing loudly, "No, Liam. Everything is fine. Where are you going to set up camp?"

"I actually have a campsite within the compound. We'll be close by. I do enjoy sleeping under the stars, especially in the summer. I even put in a fire pit. I'll make sure Zion has a great time. Maybe I can get him up high enough to see fireworks in the distance."

"I forgot about holidays. I didn't even realize today is the fourth. Zion loves fireworks."

"Then it's settled. Are you sure you don't want to come, pretty lady?"

"I'm sure."

# CHAPTER 24
# DOES MY EXISTENCE MAKE YOU NERVOUS?

(Nicole)

---

"Thank you for letting us go camping, Mommy! I wish you were coming with us."

"This is a boys only camping trip. No girls allowed. Besides, you haven't had a lot of time with Daddy lately." I help him put on his backpack. "Do you have everything? Did you grab some snacks from downstairs?" Zion nods with a big smile. Turning my attention to Liam, "And you've packed everything you need to keep my baby safe?"

"Mom, I'm a man! We're men!"

"You will always be my baby." I grab him and kiss him on the forehead, messing up his hair, which I know he hates. "Geez, Mom!"

"Yes, I have everything we need including this phone that's connected to the house's comm system. You need me for anything, you call it. We'll be about a ten-minute walk away."

"Okay, okay, okay. Just go." I turn him around and walk them to the door. "Zi, kisses." He hugs and kisses me. Standing up and turning to Liam, I tug his lightweight jacket and smooth it out. "I love you."

"I love you too. I'm going to miss you tonight. Keep the bed warm for me." Getting up on my toes as he comes down to me, we kiss passionately.

Zion shrieks, "EW! Daddy, did you just put your tongue on mommy's tongue? I think I'm going to be sick!" He covers his mouth and turns his back to us.

Liam and I laugh, and I push them both out of the door. "Have fun!" I watch them until they are far off in the distance. I love them so much, but I need some time in the lab without them interrupting or hovering. Earlier today when I was with Liam, he hurt me a little, but I didn't want to freak him out. Plus, I've been more emotional than usual. I thought maybe my period was coming, but it hasn't. The only other time my breasts have been this sore was when I was pregnant with Zion.

I scan into the lab. "Gisele?"

*"Good evening, Professor Simmons. How may I assist you?"*

"How are you this evening, Gisele?"

*"Because I am an artificial intelligence database, I do not have feelings."*

I can't believe I'm trying to butter up a freaking computer. "Gisele, how often is the lab entry file accessed?"

*"The lab access log has been active since my system came online. It has never been accessed. What date would you like me to access for you?"*

"No, Gisele, I do not wish to access the log. Are you required to report every entry and bio scan to Dr. Sinclair?"

*"Please rephrase your question."*

"Does Liam, Dr. Sinclair, know that I am in the lab."

*"No. Do you want me to notify Dr. Sinclair?"*

"No, thank you. I would like for you to run a bio scan on me, but I would like to keep it private for now. Can you do that?"

*"Yes, Professor Simmons. You have administrative access."*

"What does that mean, Gisele?"

*"You may access, update, or change my programming."*

"Okay. I do not wish to change your programming. I'm going to lie on the examining table, and I would like for you to run a bio scan."

*"What tests would you like for me to run?"*

"I need to know if I'm pregnant."

*"I will perform the bio scan if you like. However, I can perform a urinalysis."*

With the bio scan all I need to do is lie on the table, but I don't know how to give Gisele a urine sample. "What supplies do I need?"

*"You may use one of the plastic tubes by the console with the receptacle that is labeled 'Insert here'."*

Great, this looks like something to collect blood in. Whatever. I'm not going to argue with the scary AI lady. I collect my sample and carry it over to the console. "Gisele, do I put it into the console where it says insert?"

*"Yes, Professor Simmons. Professor Simmons, are you nervous for your result? Or does my existence make you nervous?"*

"Both."

*"My existence should not alarm you. I was created to help. Prior to your arrival I also served as a companion. Friend is what Dr. Sinclair named the programming. It allows for friendly conversations. For example, speaking to you in a friendly tone will help to calm your nervousness."*

Not likely. "How long before I receive the results?"

*"Two minutes and twenty-eight seconds. Would you like for me to play music for you?"*

"No, thank you. Gisele, do you have any pictures of Liam when he was a baby?"

*"Yes, Dr. Sinclair has a family album downloaded."*

"Do you think he will mind if I see them?" Images begin appearing on the screen in front of me. "I guess not."

*"No, he loves you. Since your arrival I have logged many anomalies in Dr. Sinclair's breathing and heartbeat. I researched his symptoms and sexual arousal, which can lead to love, or vice versa is the only logical explanation."*

Laughing, "Wow. Really? Um, okay."

*"The result of your pregnancy test is complete."*

"AND?"

*"It is positive for pregnancy."*

I stare, in silence, at the baby pictures scrolling on the screen in front of me. I'm pregnant. It's real. I'm really pregnant, but this time it's for someone that I know and love. Now, how, and when will I tell him? Will he be happy?

"*Professor Simmons, are you okay?*"

"Yes, thank you."

"*Please be advised that I sent a message to Dr. Sinclair regarding a new virus that was picked up during a sweep of labs we investigate.*"

"Is he coming back home?"

"*His heart rate is slightly elevated, but he isn't moving. I'm receiving a command from him to begin a global sweep to confirm that the virus is still theoretical. It is highly probable that Dr. Sinclair's decision to return home will be based on the results of my analysis.*"

"Is there anything I need to do to clean up? You know put the lab back the way I found it?"

"*No. Dr. Sinclair will not have any inclination that you used the lab. Is your pregnancy the result of sexual intercourse with Dr. Sinclair?*"

Why am I having a conversation with her? "Gisele, I do not believe that question is relevant to my medical care."

"*Apologies for speaking in a familiar tone. However, I know that Dr. Sinclair is in love with you, but because you do not have a bio chip, I cannot detect your heartbeat. I detected your nervousness based on your breathing pattern. Do you love Dr. Sinclair?*"

"I do, very much."

"*I recommend you inform him as soon as possible. He enjoys positive news.*"

"Well, thank you for the conversation. I think I'll go downstairs. Gisele, you won't tell him, right?"

*"Your pregnancy is marked as a confidential medical issue in your file. It can only be activated with your voice."*

"Thank you."

Do I love Liam? She's lucky she's a computer. I don't know when I'm going to tell him. He has another virus to study. And I cannot cause him to be distracted. If he's distracted, people can die. I don't want that. I'm going to step up my training in the shooting range. I need him to show me how to handle the rifle. Now I have three people to look out for. *What am I going to do about prenatal care and vitamins?* Gisele is right. I have to tell him sooner rather than later.

CHAPTER 25

# THEY WILL DIE IF YOU STAY

(Liam)

Tonight was a good night before I received the message from Gisele. The night sky is amazing out here. Nicole would have benefitted from some time outside too. There weren't many fireworks as I don't think a lot of us feel like celebrating. I pointed out all the stars and constellations to Zion that I could remember. We roasted hot dogs and made smores. We told spooky stories and laughed as we told silly knock-knock jokes. I tried to get him to go to sleep, but he was too excited. I sang Jason Mraz's "Have It All," Rascal Flatts' "My Wish," and I finally got him to sleep with John Lennon's "Beautiful Boy." He loves being out here and I love having someone to teach and take care of. I love being a dad. I want to be everything to Zion that my father wasn't to me. Most of all, I want to teach him that there is strength in love. It is not a weakness. I watch the flames in the fire pit as they lull me off to sleep.

*Things are light and happy with Nicole and Zion. I don't know how I've lived without them. Their presence brings peace. Nicole's smile casts a golden glow as she stands over the stove making breakfast for Zi and me. Watching her take in our happy home forces me off of the sofa where I have been watching football with Zion. As I walk to her, her beauty overwhelms me. "You are the most beautiful woman I have ever seen."*

*"Please, you have to say that because you love me. It's okay. I know I'm big as a house." She giggles and shrugs.*

*"No, Nicole, you are even more beautiful today than the day I met you. Pregnancy agrees with you. Besides, how can I not see beauty in the process of what I helped to create." I wrap my arms around her big, pregnant belly. "I'm still not sure we should name him after me, since that is also naming him after my father."*

*"Liam, we've been over this. Naming our son after you is reclaiming your name. We're naming him Liam. Now grab some plates, please. The food is ready."*

*"Yes, ma'am." I kiss her on the cheek and turn my back to take the plates out of the cabinet.*

*"MOMMY!"*

*I turn around just in time to catch her before she hits the floor. The dishes fall in slow-motion and shatter as they hit the floor. "Nicole? Nicole, baby, what's wrong?*

*Nicole!" I shake her, but she won't open her eyes. "GISELE, WHAT'S HAPPENING?" I get no response. I pick Nicole up and run with her up the stairs. I never stop calling out to her. Zion follows closely behind me crying. I try to be strong for him, but I can't as my tears flow. "Nicole, please don't leave us baby. We need you. I need you. I love you so much. Nicole, please baby. Please don't go." I get her to the lab. "GISELE, WHY AREN'T YOU ANSWERING ME?"*

*"I will not be enough to help you save her. She and your son will die if you do not get them a surgeon. You cannot stay here. If you stay, they will die."*

*"FUCK YOU, GISELE! DON'T SAY THAT! FUCK YOU! I HATE YOU!" I squeeze Nicole in my arms as I continue to cry out her name and shake her. "NICOLE! NICOLE! NICOLE!"*

I hear Zion screaming, "DADDY, DADDY, WAKE UP!"

I open my eyes and realize it was just a bad dream. My face is soaked with tears and Zion is crying. I can't catch my breath to console him yet. This can't be happening again. This can't happen. I grab Zion and hug him tightly, still barely able to speak. "Zi, it's okay. Everything is okay, son. I had a nightmare." Shit, this can't become our reality. My breathing stabilizes.

"Daddy, can we please go home?"

"Yes. Let's pack up and head home." The morning sunlight casts a beautiful glow over the entire compound. Instead of giving me hope for a new day, it feels like the calm before the storm. Everything in me feels on edge. Either Nicole is pregnant, or she is going to become pregnant very soon. I will have Gisele run a pregnancy test today. If it is negative, we will start using condoms, maybe even get her on the pill. I simply cannot lose her. But, if it is positive, I need to work fast to try to get to us to London, or at least get someone here to perform a c-section and provide care for a premature baby. We're going to have another son. This is stupid. I can't keep her here. The risk is too great.

We make it back home and are both eager to see Nicole. Our bedroom door is open. Zion and I go in and find her sleeping peacefully. I rub the back of my hand on her cheek. She opens her eyes and sees us. Zion leaps on the bed and goes straight for her arms hugging her tightly. "Zi, buddy, let's be careful with Mommy."

"Why, Daddy?"

"Yes, why does he need to be careful with me?"

Before I can answer, Zion begins to tell her about our morning. "Mommy, Daddy had a really bad nightmare about you. He was screaming your name and crying. It scared me. Are you okay?"

"Yes, sweetheart, I'm fine." She smiles and kisses Zion but doesn't look at me.

I lie down with them and wrap my arms around both of them. We quietly embrace each other with all the affection we can give. This is my family. "I love you all. I'll do anything to keep you safe. I need to go check things out in the lab. Nicole, will you please come find me later?" I kiss her tenderly on the lips and get out of bed.

Once in the lab, I pull up the information on the virus being studied in a bio-tech lab in Florida. I hate the ones that come up in the states. It means they're too accessible. "Good morning, Gisele."

*"Good morning, Dr. Sinclair. Do you require assistance with running scenarios for the new virus?"*

"Not right now. Gisele, I'm going to need two new bio chips. I am going to have you complete a bio scan for Zion and probably a pregnancy test for Professor Simmons today. I will need to speak with her first, but I want us to be ready in case she agrees to everything. Will you help me with that?"

*"Yes, Dr. Sinclair."*

I analyze the virus and realize that something isn't right. It's a designer virus, but it's harmless. I worry that it was planted in hopes of being able to track me, or worse keep me working on an inconsequential virus while they pass through something that could cause another pandemic. "Gisele, please take the virus scanner offline. I need to work on the programming." The lab door opens behind me.

Nicole comes over and kisses me. "You wanted to talk to me?"

"Yes. You and Zion have been here three months. I think it's time for bio chips, but I know you may need to think about it. Chris was hesitant but agreed as long as I kept it turned off. We turned it on for the first time when he was sick. Thaddeus said, 'Hell no.' It's really just a way for me to check vitals, but it also has tracking. Gisele, please pull up the data from my bio chip and run a demo for Nicole."

"You're right, I don't like the idea, especially for Zion, but I understand why it is necessary. Just make sure no one else will have access to our chips."

Trying to reassure her with my smile, "I promise."

One of the things I love most about Nicole is she knows me almost better than I know myself. "So, are you going to tell me about your nightmare? Was it one of your special dreams?"

Tears begin to fill my eyes again as I somberly nod. She takes my hand and leads me to the bedroom. We sit on the bed. Holding her hand, I begin. "We were standing in the kitchen getting ready for breakfast. You were pregnant. I hugged you from behind and rubbed your very pregnant belly. I turned away for one second to grab some dishes out of the cabinet. Zion screamed as you collapsed. I grabbed you before you hit the floor, but you wouldn't wake up." Tears flow from my eyes. The pain of losing her feels so real. "I called out to Gisele, and she wouldn't answer me. I ran to get you to the lab, and I yelled at her asking why she wouldn't answer me. Then, she said, 'I will not be enough to help you save her. She and your son will die if you do not get them a surgeon. You cannot stay here. If you stay, they will die.' I have to find a way to stop this. I have to." I look at Nicole. She's crying too. "Nicole, I want you to take a pregnancy test today. If you are, we'll figure it out. If you're not, we'll start using condoms and get you on the pill."

She takes a deep breath. "I am."

"You are what?" She looks at me through tear-filled eyes. "Pregnant?"

She nods, "Yes." Then she smiles through her tears. "We're having a boy?"

I smile back because this should be a time for happiness. "Wait, how do you know?"

"Yesterday when we were in the shooting range, you touched me, and my breasts were very sore. I sent you camping so I could use the lab."

"Gisele ran the test?" She confirms with a nod. "And she didn't tell me."

"I asked her not to. But we're having a boy!"

"It looks that way. I hate that I'm too afraid to celebrate this moment. Nicole, you're having my baby!"

"I'm having your baby!" She kisses me. "Let's just focus on that. You said in your dream that I was big, right?"

"Yes."

"Okay, then we have time." Nicole squeezes my hand to reassure me that we are in this together.

"I need to call Chris and see if he can drone drop some prenatal vitamins."

"We have to tell Zion first and I need to tell Renee. Can whatever you're working on, wait a few minutes?" She asks me to refocus my attention.

"Yes, it was odd anyway. We'll go tell Zion. And then, we'll all come back up together, and I'll put the chips in. Deal?"

"Yeah, about that, I'm going to leave it to you to talk Zion into letting you cut his arm open." She pats me on the chest. "Good luck with that." We leave the lab, walk downstairs, and find Zion in the living room.

"Zi buddy, Mommy and I need to talk to you." He stops working on his Lego set and joins us on the sofa. "First, I want to apologize for scaring you this morning."

"It's okay, Daddy. I've had scary dreams before."

"Zion," I reach over to Nicole and place my hand on her tummy, "You're going to be a big brother."

He squeals and jumps up and down. "Finally! Is it a brother or a sister?"

"We don't know yet, but Daddy has something else to talk to you about. I'm going to go get a snack."

"That's cold! You'll pay for that later, pretty lady." Zion looks up at me waiting to hear what I have to say. "So, buddy, now that you and Mommy are a part of my life, I need to make sure that you are healthy and safe at all times. To do that, I need to put a chip in your arm."

"Cool! I'll be part machine, like a cyborg!"

"See, Nicole, he's fine with it!"

"Yeah, okay. Tell him how you put the chip in."

"What does she mean, Daddy? How do you put the chip in?"

I look over my shoulder at Nicole, smirking behind me waiting for me to traumatize our son. "I will put a small incision in your arm and put the chip under your skin."

"Incision? What is an incision? And under my skin? Wait, is incision cutting? You have to cut me open? Mommy, is he going to cut me open?"

"Zi, I will numb it. You won't feel it."

"Mommy, you said he can cut me open?" I reach out to touch him and he jerks away. "No, Liam!"

"Excuse me, young man? Liam? That's Daddy to you and I would never do anything to hurt you. You know how much I love you."

"But you want to cut my arm open. What if I bleed to death?" He runs to his mother.

I look over at Nicole, the smirk is gone. Concern fills her face. She instinctively bends down to pick up Zion, but I jump up quickly and remind her that she's pregnant. I pick up Zion and carry him back to the sofa. Nicole sits with us.

"Zion, sweetheart, your daddy loves you so very much. He chose you to be his son. That means that he will put your safety and health before his own the same way I do. He already has a chip. And we can use Gisele to find out wherever he is on the planet if someone tried to take him from us. He wants the same thing for us. I am getting my chip today too. Do you think you can be brave for all of us?"

"I'm scared."

I put my arm around his little shoulders. "Do you know what scares Mommy and me most?" He shakes his head no. "For something to happen to you. We always want to be able to find you. We'll both be with you the whole time."

"Okay." He hangs his head and looks up at me with just his eyes. "Daddy, I'm sorry for calling you Liam."

"That really hurt my feelings, but I forgive you, son. I will never stop being your daddy, not even when you get upset with me."

I take them to the lab and successfully install their chips. Zion doesn't cry. The incision is so small that they will barely notice it tomorrow. Unlike with Chris, I activate both chips right away and show them on the monitors all three of our vitals and locations. I suddenly remember the reason it was so important to do this today—my nightmare. My heart rate speeds up and my breathing changes. They notice it on the screen and turn to me as I stare at nothing in particular. Nicole takes my hand and holds it against her womb. "Today is today, and today is perfect." She smiles at me tenderly, trying to take away my fears. "If we're done here, I want to go tell my sister our good news. Are we good here?" I nod and let her leave.

CHAPTER 26

# JUSTICE'S LAW

(Nicole)

"Hi, little sis!" Renee greets me with a smile.

I shriek at the unexcepted appearance of my sister when I pick up my tablet because I did not hear it ring. "Oh my God!"

"What!"

"I was getting ready to call you, but when I picked it up, you were staring at me." I laugh at myself.

Renee laughs at me too. "Yeah, you have always been skittish. I was calling to check on you."

"What, you had a feeling, Ree-ree?"

"Yes, but I'm not the one with a gift. Anyway, how are you? Why were you calling me?"

"So, before I tell you why I'm calling, I have to tell you again that you do have a gift. Even before you became a nurse, you were a healer. Every kid in the neighborhood would come to you to get bandaged up after a fight they didn't want their parents to know about. Hell, even the injured neighborhood stray animals would end up on our doorstep. Then all the girls started coming to you for advice after a breakup. You always attracted broken men who needed their hearts put back together. You, my dear big sister, are a healer."

"Yeah, well, it isn't helpful if I never get to be made whole myself."

"But you are whole, Renee. You are amazing. And you're going to make an amazing aunt."

"Please, I'm already an amazing aunt."

I smile at her and put my hands on my tummy. "You are and you will be again." She jumps up and screams. My nephews and niece run into Renee's room. Zion and Liam burst into our bedroom. Zion and Liam understand the madness, but Justice, Journey, and Joy stare at us with confusion. "Hi, my babies! Your mom is just excited because she's going to be an auntie again." Journey and Joy join their mother in celebrating. Justice, on the other hand, does not seem amused.

"Excuse me, Liam, may I have a word?" Liam, taken by surprise, nods. "Mom, may I borrow this? I'll bring it right back." Renee hands the tablet to Justice.

I hand my tablet to Liam and shrug, "Uh-oh."

He takes the tablet into the bathroom but leaves the door open. "What can I do for you, Justice?"

"My aunt is like a second mother to me. I love her very much and her happiness is important to me. So, are you going to marry her?" *Aw, my nephew wants to know Liam's intentions.*

"I would like very much to marry your aunt and formally adopt Zion. I have actually asked one of my friends to contact a lawyer so that we can start the adoption process. I have not formally proposed to your aunt because I am hoping to do it under better circumstances. I understand you're a military guy."

"Yes, I was in the Corp. I got injured while I was deployed. When I got stateside, they issued me an honorable discharge because of my injury and PTSD. Why?"

"I'm sorry. I didn't know about the PTSD."

"It's fine. I'm better. I even tried to re-enlist, but all of this bullshit went down, and I couldn't leave my mom."

"Well, I have a friend who owns a security company. They are great at what they do. If you ever need work, let me know. Truthfully, I could use a weapons guy out here."

"For what? I thought you guys were high up in the mountains and safe. Are my aunt and little cousin in trouble?"

"Justice, let me explain. I don't mean to upset you. I possess the knowledge and ability to create cures for various diseases. This knowledge has gotten me shot. That is why I am out here, but something came up recently and I was able to help. The people who shot me thought I was dead and had stopped looking for me. They may start again now that I've poked my head up, so to speak. I couldn't just stand by and let thousands of people die when I could help."

"Okay, well I guess there's really only one thing that matters. Do you love my aunt?"

"Very much."

"Do you promise to protect her?"

"I will protect her, Zion, and the baby with my life."

"That's really all I need to know. If the shit gets real, let me know how I can get there to help. And Uncle Liam, welcome to the family." He smiles and takes the tablet back to his mom.

Liam comes out and hands me the tablet. Not wanting to let on that I eavesdropped on the conversation, I rush back to bed and ask, "Everything alright?"

"Yes, your nephew just needed to know if he was going to have to shoot me or not." Justice laughs at the comment.

"Listen kids, I need to talk to Renee and Lee for a bit. Zion, why don't you go to your room and call Joy. Joy, is that alright?" She nods and Zion runs to his room. Liam closes the door behind him. "Babe, I need you to tell Renee about your gift."

He looks at me with confusion. "What gift?"

"You know, your premonitions."

"Is that why you were talking about gifts earlier? Even he has one! I guess the ancestors really didn't think I was worthy."

"Come on, Renee, this is serious. Go ahead, baby, tell her."

He drops his head and sighs. "I have had one dream that predicted the future. Which is what led me to coming out here. I recently had another dream, a nightmare." He takes me by the hand and squeezes tightly. His eyes fill with tears again. "I held a very pregnant Nicole in my arms as she died."

"WHAT?" Renee reacts, but then calms as another explanation occurs to her. "Maybe this was just anxiety about becoming a new dad. Maybe it's nothing."

Though Liam doesn't want it to be true, the gravity of the premonition weighs heavily on him. "Renee, this was before I found out she was pregnant. And this was no ordinary dream. It was definitely a warning. I need to get her off this mountain or get a surgeon out here." He weeps. Renee sees his anguish and begins crying too.

At this point, I'm just tired of the tears. It feels like Lee is just accepting that I'm already dead. "Okay, that's enough, you two. I love you both, but I need you to stop. I wanted you to know because I need us to be on the same page with my care and coming up with a plan."

"Liam, you have to understand, she's my baby sister, my only sister. Promise me you'll take care of her."

"I understand, Renee. And as long as there is breath in my body, I will do everything in my power to keep her alive. After we're done here, I'm going to go put some things in motion. I can't lose her." He turns to me, "I can't lose you, baby. You and Zion are my life now."

I place my hand on his cheek and kiss him gently. "You can go, babe. Renee and I need some sister time. I love you." He kisses me on the forehead and leaves.

"Nicole, I know you believe in the mystical, but are you afraid?"

"Yes. I am terrified. Liam is so strong and to watch him right now, like this, it's breaking my heart."

"He loves you. I wish I could be there with you both. I think we'd be really close friends. Plus, Zion needs someone stable right now. I can tell, you are the air in Liam's lungs. If you die, he's going to fall to pieces."

"Come on, Renee, don't say that. Not that I am resigned to dying, but he would totally step up. He wouldn't leave Zion hanging. He's proven that's he's in this."

"Oh, there is no doubt in my mind about that. I'm just saying that losing you will break him. Just in your quiet time, remind him that Zion needs him and that he can't ever checkout. He's made that commitment, not just to you, but to Zion as well."

"I hear you, big sis."

"Good. Now, hear this. I'm pulling your grown card."

"Great. You haven't done that in years. What do I have to do?"

"From here out, you must check in with me every day. Nicole, e-ve-ry day! You got it?"

"Yes, I got it. I love you."

"Love you too."

# CHAPTER 27

# THE INNER CIRCLE

(Liam)

---

"Gisele, please get Chris on the line." Chris appears on the screen. "Hey. Thanks for always being available to take my calls."

"Hey, Lee. I'm supervising a mission right now, not waiting around for your ass to call." He laughs. "Besides, all the business you send my way and the huge retainer, I should pick up."

"Plus, I saved your life."

"Saved yours first!" We both laugh. "What's up, since you rarely call just to catch up anymore." He sighs, "I didn't mean that how it sounded."

"No worries, man. Nicole is pregnant."

"What? Congratulations, man! I mean, that's a good thing, right? Aren't you happy? I mean y'all are two highly educated individuals. And I pranked you with enough condoms to last a lifetime. You intentionally didn't use them. So, what's the problem?"

"Yes, you're right in that I wanted this, but I had a dream that the pregnancy will kill her. I'm afraid for her, man. The fear is debilitating."

"Dude, I know you sometimes get premonitions, but that isn't what every dream is. Sometimes, it's just a dream, or in this case, a nightmare. I think we should just be happy and celebrate the moment."

"Yeah, that's what Nicole said too. Uh, is there a way to get some prenatal vitamins to us?"

"I guess you really didn't consider using the condoms." He laughs, "As an additional joke, I buried six bottles of prenatal vitamins underneath the condoms." He winks at me. "See, I can take care of you too, brother."

Shaking my head, "You, my man, are a lifesaver. But seriously, I need your help whether or not you want to believe me. If I stay up here with Nicole, which has been safe so far, I must get a surgeon here, but that's just the tip of the iceberg. What if we get the baby out and he needs neonatal care? The bio scans will show most things, but I never tested it on a fetus in utero. And if we leave, how do we get out of here? I don't want to give the location of this place up in case we need or want to come back. Where do we go? London?"

"You've got a lot of questions, and this is big news. Who else have you told? Does Thad know?"

"No, you're the first. I needed prenatal vitamins. And I was hoping you knew some people who might know a surgeon who would be willing to come out here. Money is no object."

"Lee, breathe. Hold on and breathe. Give me a couple of minutes and we'll brainstorm."

I place my head in my hands and try to imagine the future...a future where Nicole delivers a healthy baby. I imagine holding her and baby Liam in my arms as Zion kneels on the bed in front of us, meeting his little brother for the first time. I imagine us all together, happy, and most of all, healthy. My thoughts are interrupted by my name being called. I look up from my hands and see all my brothers looking at me, all of them. Chris even got Thaddeus to take his call. We haven't all been face-to-face at the same time in six years, since I announced I was leaving civilization.

Thad speaks first. "Lee, what's wrong? Chris said you need us."

"You all are here."

Sergio smiles, "Of course we are. And if any of us needed you, you'd be there for us. So, we're here now. Whatever you need, your brothers have your back. What's going on?"

"Nicole is pregnant, and she won't survive the pregnancy if we stay out here alone."

Chris interjects, "Lee has had a nightmare that he believes is another premonition. He needs us to help him come up with a plan. We either need to get a surgeon to them or we need to get them off the mountain."

"How far along is she," Eddie asks.

"Just a few weeks, we just found out."

Eddie continues, "Have you thought about not having it?"

Before any of us can respond, Jimmy throws a book at Eddie. "Shut up, you wanker!"

"No, we haven't thought about not having it. We would be celebrating if it wasn't for the nightmare. I would like to find a safe way to get Nicole through this pregnancy and for my son to be healthy. Does anyone know a surgeon who would be willing to come here? I could come pick them up from the resort."

"No!" Thaddeus says adamantly. "You can't come here, Lee. Do you hear me? You—can–not come here."

I don't like the tone in his voice. "Why, Thad? What happened?"

"A few weeks ago, Devon and his men raided the resort and the camps just behind the resort. They killed a lot of white guys. He has the kids working for him and the women he has cooking, cleaning, and of course some are being used for sex. He has them in his camp and promises those who are willing to service them, will be taken care of. I have been forbidden to board or assist any whites in any way. He threatened Alicia; she's pregnant too. I couldn't call you, Lee, because he's monitoring everything."

Chris groans loudly. "I know we don't talk like we used to, but you are still my brother, Thad. If you couldn't call Lee, you should have called me or Serg. I can get you out of there in the morning. And congratulations to you and Alicia too."

"No, Chris. Thank you, but I need to stay here so that I know what's going on. I'm Lee's first line of defense. I can't go."

"Thad, I appreciate that, but you have to put Alicia and the kids first. If you need to go, go. All of you guys are putting yourselves out on a limb for me."

"No, Lee, we're all protecting you so that you can protect the rest of us," Chris responds to my plea for them to stand down.

"This is total bollocks! All of you need to pack your things and come here. We have our own castle in the country. You all could live like royalty here," Jimmy tries to reason with us.

Chris isn't going to pass up the opportunity to remind the Bennetts that it isn't all roses over there either. "You all may not be experiencing the civil unrest that we are, but we saw how your country treated your Black royalty. I think I'll just stay here and keep putting foot to ass."

"Yeah, that made us look bad," Eddie admits.

I need this not to turn into another US versus the UK debate between Chris and the twins. "Guys, let's get back on topic. Nicole and baby Liam, how do I save them?"

Thad says, "Like I said, you can't come here."

"I can send out an inquiry."

"Serg, Lee knows doctors he can ask, but it will mean nothing if he won't let me land an aircraft to drop them off. Which means we're looking for surgeons who are willing to parachute in since Thad is saying they can't meet up at the resort."

Jimmy sighs, "Lee, what if you let Chris land a helicopter and air lift the three of you out of there."

"Guys, my lab is here. All of my data is here. To give up this position is to surrender any chance of survival we have."

"Do you love her, Lee?"

"From the moment I met her, you know that, Thad. She is everything to me, my light, my air. You guys know how angry I've always been and how lonely I've been. Well, she's cured me of my anger and loneliness. When everything stills around us, our souls speak to one another. Nicole is my soulmate."

"Damn, Lee. You're a poet too now?" For once, Eddie allows the weight of my words to sink in.

Chris brings us back to the sobering reality of the situation. "Then one day soon, you're going to have to choose between saving her, and saving the world. All of us already know the choice you'll make, and it's the right choice. Just don't take too long to make the call."

I feel a hand on my shoulder and all the guys shift their attention. "I didn't hear you come in." I kiss her hand. "For all of you who haven't met the love of my life, this is Nicole." They all greet her with hellos, congratulations, and how great she looks.

"Hi, guys. Thanks. Listen, I'm not freaking out just yet. Like I told Lee, right now, I feel great, amazing in fact. Liam has a job to do, and this situation is making him irrational."

Chris cuts her off. "Nicole, I think I've gotten to know you best out of all the brothers, so I'm going to talk to you like you're my sister. Fuck his job! Just because Liam wants to be a martyr doesn't mean you need to be. You worked side-by-side with him, helping him save Tiff and me. For that, I will always be grateful. Nicole, you need to put yourself first. Think of Zion too. If you want off that mountain, you call me, and I will come."

A bit annoyed, I need to see Nicole's reaction. I look up to find tears welling up in her eyes. "Thanks for that, Chris, but I think I can take care of my family. I get it and I know you're being supportive, but we'll let you know what and when we decide." I pull Nicole around to me and sit her in my lap. "Guys, thanks for the support. I love all of you. Let's talk later. I need to tend to this beautiful woman right now." They all say goodbye and wish us well. I end the connection and direct my attention to Nicole.

"You know I'll die before I let anything happen to you, right?"

"I know, Liam."

"I don't want you to spend this pregnancy waiting to die. If Zion wasn't with me when I had the nightmare, I never would have told you."

"Don't do that. We tell each other everything. No secrets."

I nod my head. "Okay, then tell me what you want to do. If I didn't have the means to fight this biological war, what would you want?"

"That's not fair. That kind of defines you. We wouldn't be out here, and we never would have met if you didn't have this purpose."

"That doesn't define me, not anymore. I want to be the best husband and dad that I can be. That's how I choose to be defined now. So, what do you want me to do? Tell me and I'll do it. I will give all of this up for you."

"Great. Once again, I'm the one that gets to decide if hundreds of thousands, or millions of people die. I won't have that on my conscious or yours. Let's give it three months and keep Chris on standby."

"What if I can get a surgeon to come here? Would that help?"

"Can you talk to your doctor friend and ask for an OB/GYN? Maybe we can send my vitals and ultrasounds? Maybe we can see if there is something wrong with Little Liam."

For the first time since my nightmare, I breathe a sigh of relief. "You are a genius, Dr. Nicole Simmons! Why didn't I think of that? Yes, I'll send my contact a message right now! Then, we will get an ultrasound so that we're ready to send it off when we get a doctor. I love you so much!"

She smiles, "I love you too. And don't think I missed that 'husband' comment."

"Glad, you caught it." I wrap my arms around her waist. "What do you think about that?"

"Why? Are you asking?"

"Not officially. I want to wait until I can do it right, but it is what I want."

She smirks in that cute way that I love, "Well, when you are ready to ask me officially, I will be ready to say yes officially."

# CHAPTER 28

# FLASHING LIGHTS

(Nicole)

---

Over the last few months, I've helped Liam with his work and homeschooled Zion. I've done as Renee asked and checked in with her every day.

"Hi, Renee! Whatcha doing?"

"Hey. Reading a romance novel. We can't all find our perfect man out of the blue. What's up?"

"Well, now I don't want to tell you."

"Why not?"

"You seem to be in a mood."

"I'm not. You know I love these books. I want my tall, beautiful chocolate man to find me already. Does Liam have any single friends?"

"Yes. There's one that comes to mind but he's a tad lighter than us, not exactly chocolate, but still gorgeous. He's Black and Japanese. Um, but that's not why I called you."

"True. What's up?"

"Nothing much. I just can't wait to make things official with Liam."

"Yeah, I know. I see the way you guys are together. He adores you. I'm glad you two found each other."

"Thank you. Don't tell Lee that I'm getting impatient."

"Uh, do you think Liam and I are shooting the breeze when you're not around? Besides, the only topics we ever discuss are you and Zion."

"What about Nicole and Zion?" Liam comes in. "How are you tonight, Renee?"

"Hey Lee. I was just asking Nicole if she and Zion were excited about baby Liam. She says they are. What about you? Still nervous?"

"I will be nervous until he is safely here in his mother's arms and she's resting comfortably in mine."

Renee fake gags. "You guys are disgustingly adorable."

Suddenly, an alarm sounds with flashing red lights. "Lee, what's that?"

"Shit! No, no, no! Stay here!" Liam runs out of the room. Zion is standing in the hallway, visibly shaken. "Zion, get in the room with Mom, and stay there!"

"Nicole, what's going on?"

"I have no idea, Renee, but I'm sure as hell not staying here. I'll call you back."

"Do not hang up!"

"I love you, big sister, but don't call back. I promise that I or Zion will call you back as soon as we can." She nods and I disconnect. "Zion, sweetheart, do you remember our epic hide and seek battles?" He nods. "Do you remember the hiding places where Mommy and Daddy couldn't find you?"

"Yes, and Daddy showed me a secret passage that leads to the house next door."

"Okay good. I want you to go hide. Try to stay on this side, but if someone gets in the house, go next door, and hide. I will find you with your chip." I hug him tightly and kiss him. "I love you so much." I punch my code into the safe and pull out my Glock.

"I love you too, Mommy. Please don't get hurt."

"Okay, I'm going to open the door. Use the stairs if you need to go up or down. Love you. Let's go." I slowly open the door and peek into the hallway. It's clear. Zion follows closely behind me. I don't know where his hiding spot is, but we stay quiet. We get to the stairs; he squeezes my hand. I head upstairs and he heads downstairs. *God, please watch over my baby.* I quickly make it to the comm room. I spot Liam talking to Chris. The alarm stops as I enter the room. He turns around quickly and glares at me. I guess that means he's not happy with me. "What's happening?"

"We have a security breach in Sector Two."

"What does that mean, Lee?"

"A dozen armed men parachuted down into Sector Two. Chris and I broke up the sectors by distance. We are in Sector One. They are a day away from the Sector One border. Once they hit Sector One, they will be three hours away."

"That's too damn close, Liam!"

"Hey, Nicole. I've deployed a team. My guys are elite, all ex-special forces. Whoever these guys are, they're going to regret taking this mission. I heard you're pretty deadly with that gun." Chris makes small talk to get me to calm down.

I take a deep breath and allow myself to breathe. "Yeah, no one is messing with my family."

But Liam is still agitated. "Nicole, go get my son and bring him up here."

"He's hiding. I don't know where he is."

He grits his teeth and pulls up Zion's location on the monitor. "There he is. Now, go get him."

I huff and roll my eyes, "I guess someone is pissed."

# CHAPTER 29

# THE TARGET

## (Liam)

---

"Liam, dude, what the fuck man? Why'd you talk to Nicole like that? What's going on? You two *not* okay?"

"Come on, Chris, just watch the monitors."

"Man, this is what I do. I don't tell you how to run your lab. I got this. My men are a few minutes from the drop. Now talk. What's up?"

"I told her to stay in the room with Zion! You saw her come in here with a loaded gun, without him. She put herself and my sons in danger!"

"Man, don't do that. She's fine. Calm down and talk to her about it later."

"Whatever. Let's just get these bastards out of my backyard."

Nicole and Zion come into the lab. "It took me a while to find him. He's great at hiding. He did great. You did great, Zi."

"Zion, I'm sorry this is scary. One day it won't be like this. I promise. Babe, can you take him and find him something to do?" She nods and I grab her by the hand before she walks away. I take her hand and kiss the inside of her wrist. "I love you. We'll talk later." She nods.

"Lee, I'm going to share one of my screens with you. My guys came down in front of them and are headed straight for them. They should intercept soon. Sit tight, I'm going to give out some last-minute orders.

Alright team, listen up. This is the mission that we've been preparing for when we're in between missions. There can be no mistakes. I want clean single kill strikes except for two. We keep two alive until we get answers. Alpha leader, on your mark, bring me some goddamn answers."

The screen Chris shares with me displays POV images of what each member of the team is seeing. The visors on their helmets are equipped with night vision and heat sensors. In less than two minutes, the intruders come into view. They are not prepared. Our team leader takes out the first target before they realize they are in the crosshairs. One by one they go down. One tries to run, but he gets tagged as one we'll extract information from. The last guy drops his rifle and falls to his knees. He surrenders but doesn't appear to be afraid. "Chris, watch that guy, something's not right."

"Lee, chill. My guys are the best."

The team binds the big, cocky guy and drags back the runner. The runner is ready to talk right away. "Hey Boss, he'll talk. Can we get rid of this one?" The big guy lifts his head, exposing a large tattoo on his neck of an American bald eagle with its wings back and talons extended to catch prey. He looks up at his captures for the first time. "Oh, shit! Boss, are you seeing this?"

The big guy smiles and says, "What the fuck?"

I don't understand what's going on. "Chris, talk to me. Do you guys know this man?"

"Hell, yeah! We know him, he was a SEAL with a couple us." Chris talks to one of his guys. "Breeze, let me talk to Raptor."

"Go ahead, Boss."

"Raptor, what the fuck are you doing out in these woods with these idiots?"

"Boss, I was running low on funds, man. I needed work."

"So what? You just thought you'd sign up with these assholes, and what? Why didn't you come to me? I would have taken care of you."

"After what happened with Tiffany, I thought you hated me."

"Tiffany is a grown ass woman and has made plenty of bad decisions since you. Right now, there's only one question I need answered. Whose side are you on today?"

He flashes our SEAL team tat, "For life!"

"Raptor, does any of the equipment have tracking?"

"Affirmative, Boss." He points to the lead so Breeze can disable the device.

"Breeze, cut Raptor loose and have someone take care of the runner. Hurry and get back to base so we can debrief Raptor." One shot rang out.

"Lee, you still with me?"

"Yes. I'm really not comfortable with this guy, but I trust you, Chris, with my life. What's going to happen when whoever is behind this contract comes looking for their team?"

"You are my biggest client, Lee. Cleanup is in your contract. No one will ever find them. It will look like they simply vanished. It will be about a couple of hours before we can question Raptor."

"Hours? I need answers now."

"It may not be as safe as bringing them in, Lee."

"You're not going to tell him my name or location so it's safe enough. Besides, our signal is bouncing all over the planet. Now, please, Chris."

"Breeze, we're going to do a field debriefing."

"What? Now, Boss?"

"Yes. Sorry, I know it isn't how we do things, but our contractor says it's extremely time sensitive."

Breeze conveys the order to the team. "Alright fellas, we have to do a field debrief. Form a perimeter. Boss, are you recording?"

"Yes. And I'll take point. Raptor can you hear me?"

"Yes, Boss."

"Who sent the team?"

"I was hired by a security team that I sought out. It's headed up by a Russian woman who goes by the name Nastia. It's clear she has had some training. My guess is she was a hired gun at some point. Anyway, I don't know a lot about who she is working for, but I overheard her talking to someone she called Dr. Volkov. They seemed to know each other intimately. I know some guys on the team jokingly called him Dr. Poison."

"Okay, what was the mission?"

"None of these idiots were killers. They thought they were, but I doubt any of them had seen any real action. This was supposed to be recon with the possibility of a snatch and grab."

"Recon? Explain."

"A signal was picked up somewhere out here. We were only a mile and a half out from the final place the signal was detected. I don't think they know exactly who they're looking for."

"So, there was no photo of the target?"

"No. You know me; I always keep an ear out. I overheard Nastia asking Dr. Volkov if he really thought it was 'him.' She said someone named Trigger was her best guy and that he put two bullets in the dude's chest. That's all I know."

"Okay, Raptor. We have to get you off the grid for a while. Come back to base with my guys and we'll figure out something. Breeze, clear out and get everyone back to base. I'm going to get everything squared away with our contractor. I'll cut the audio but keep visual. See you when you get back."

"Lee, fuck man. Did you get all that?" I can't speak. "Liam? Nicole, are you still in here?"

"Shit, Chris! Don't call her in here!"

"I didn't know if you were in shock or what. What the fuck, man! How did they track you? Was it from when you helped Tiff and me? I'm so sorry."

"Chris, it wasn't that. It was me, man. I fucked up. I got a weird hit on a virus a few weeks after I treated you. It was the same day I found out Nicole was pregnant. It wasn't a real threat. It was like someone planted it. I immediately changed my algorithm, but they must have already intercepted the signal."

"What are you going to do Lee? You have to tell Nicole."

"Man, she's really beginning to show, the temperature has plummeted on the mountain it's raining off and on. It'll be snowing soon. We can't safely come down the mountain. I am definitely not telling her."

Chris suddenly looks like a deer in headlights. "Um, yeah, okay, good luck with that. Good night, Nicole." He rushes off the call.

I turn to look over my shoulder at Nicole. She glares at me and simply says, "Don't."

"Nicole, I just don't want you to worry."

"I specifically asked you not to keep anything from me, Liam. You can't do that!"

"I'm sorry, but if it's something I can handle on my own without stressing you out, I will."

"No, either we are in this together, or you can stay on this mountain by yourself."

"Okay. You have my word, but we need to get your rifle training in. It's time. I don't like it one bit, but I'm certain the same people who tried to have me assassinated are going to send another team after losing today's encounter. Or we can leave right now."

"I'm just about five months along, and I'm getting big. We can't go to the resort, but I just don't think we should give up this position yet."

# CHAPTER 30
# ZION FEST
(Nicole)

This is Liam's first year taking part in our family tradition. Zion's birthday is two weeks before Christmas, so to make it feel special, we have Zion Fest. Because his birthday is right before Christmas, he only gets one gift from me for his birthday, but we do everything he wants to do. Watch what he wants to watch. Play the games he wants to play and eat what he wants to eat. It is all things Zion.

Liam got me up early for some outdoor shooting exercises. I was able to pick up the rifle right away in the indoor range, but Liam says it's different while standing still. I need to be able to move around and pick off targets if necessary. There are targets hidden throughout the compound. He has given me an hour to clear them. Each cabin has the usual front and back doors, but each cabin also has a unique dedicated entrance to the tunnels that run underneath the compound. It makes getting in and out easy without being detected. I quickly find the targets inside and outside. With the butt secured by my right shoulder, right hand on the grip, and left hand on the hand guard, I take the target from behind the built-in cabinets. I slip back into the tunnels and come back up through the floorboard in a different cabin. This target is right above the hatch that I come up through. I quickly release my rifle and pull my Glock and fire one shot—target down. I go back down into the tunnels. The last cabin has an entry that is proving more difficult for me to access. I guess my belly is getting big enough for me to notice the extra weight. I try climbing up what I can only describe as an attic ladder, but the task proves to be too much. I backtrack and go back up through the cabin I just cleared. I take the back door, stay as low as I can and come around the corner. I spot the target on the stairs leading to the front door of the cabin I couldn't access. I take it out with one shot from my rifle. As I scan the area for more targets, I come to the corner edge of the cabin and a hand quickly grabs the barrel of my gun. I release my rifle and draw my Glock, pointing it at Liam's head.

"Damn, you're quick!"

Breathing hard, I see my breath in the cold, crisp air. "Just like you taught me."

Liam gives me a quick peck on the lips. "I was worried that you wouldn't be able to access the last cabin through the tunnel. How do you feel? Are you ok?"

"You're right. I couldn't clear it. What do we do if I need to get in there? It's the farthest from our bunker, but the closest to the entrance of the compound. It's pretty important to have a plan for it, don't you think?"

He lifts my chin up so that our eyes are locked. "Yes. But how are you?"

I see the concern all over his face. I place my hand on the side of his face. "I'm tired, but I'm okay."

"You did great. Let's get you home. Are you cold?"

"Yes. It's freezing. I'm not used to these temperatures."

"I'm hoping we'll have a white Christmas."

"That will be a first for Zion and me."

"I can't wait to watch the two of you experience snow for the first time."

Just as if he had willed it into existence, something cold and wet hits my face. I look up and gasp. Holding out my hand, I watch as tiny snowflakes land in my palm. "Liam." I look up at him, but he's already looking down watching me.

"The only thing that would make this moment more perfect is having Zion here, but first…" He lowers our rifles to the ground, pulls me into his arms. "I want to seal this moment in time with a kiss." He passionately kisses me as the snow falls around us.

"Wow, I almost forgot what that felt like."

He gives me a small smile, picks up the rifles, and takes my hand. "Come on. Let's go get Zion."

"You know you're being ridiculous, right?"

"Nicole, you know I want you all the time. I'm just not taking any chances, so why work myself up by kissing you like that? Hell, woman, I'll be stroking off to that kiss tonight."

"But it's okay for me to be out here running around?"

"No, it's not, but I need you to be ready. If I had it my way, you would be on bedrest, but I know you. I would have to strap you down."

"Why, Dr. Sinclair, I didn't know you were into bondage."

Rolling his eyes and laughing, "You know I'm not. If I tie you up, I can't feel your hands on me, and I love your touch. Shit, Nicole, knock it off!"

"Damn it, Lee, you haven't made love to me since you found out about the pregnancy. You know all about the human body. And, you know what, never mind. You're just as stubborn as I am. Little Liam is going to be one headstrong kid."

We reach the front door of our luxury bunker. Liam opens the front door and calls out to Zion to get dressed and come outside. Once outside, Zion's face lights up like a lightbulb. It reminds me of the first time he saw Mickey Mouse at Disneyland, sheer amazement.

"Daddy, can we have a snowball fight?"

"There isn't enough snow for a snowball fight yet, but I promise you we will have many snowball fights this winter."

I watch my guys watching the quiet snow fall for a few minutes. "Hey guys, I'm going inside to finish the food for Zion Fest. I'll see you in a bit?"

"Yes, go ahead. We can use some daddy-son time," Liam beams with parental pride as he shares this new experience with Zion.

I go inside to prepare pizza, fried fish, french fries, corn on the cob, and of course birthday cake. I'll also make a batch of sweet tea. We haven't had any for about a year, but my baby loves my sweet tea. It's a total carb fest. Zion is totally my kid. As I prepare the food, I reminisce about when Zion was born, something I always do on his birthday. He was an absolutely perfect baby. I didn't get to have him lay on my chest immediately since I had a c-section, but I remember the first time I heard him cry. It was the most precious moment of my life.

The food is ready, and I've not seen my men for quite some time. They are probably somewhere playing video games. I set the table and pick up the pizza to carry it over to the table. I feel a burning sensation along my right arm. I don't recall burning myself, but I take a look at it anyway. There's nothing there—not sure what that's about. I continue bringing the food to the table. While carrying the fish and fries I feel another burning sensation, but this time it's on my right knee and shin. *That's clearly pain.* I wonder what the hell Liam has Zion doing, or is it Liam that's banging himself up? I finish with the table since I'm only feeling pain, but no fear. I take the elevator down to the rec level. As soon as I get off, I hear a sound that I've not heard down here before. *He wouldn't.* I push the door open to Liam's skate park. *He did.* There they are laughing and having fun. Zion goes down a small ramp and wipes out. I feel the fall.

"Are you alright?" Liam calls out to Zion.

"Yes." Zion pops up. "I'm going to go again."

"How about you don't?" I shout to Zion.

"Mommy, look what Daddy got me! It's so much fun! Daddy says I can pick any decals I want to decorate it."

I look over at Liam and he's grinning from ear to ear. "Daddy should have talked to Mommy first before getting you a skateboard."

"May I keep it, Mommy?"

"We'll see. Now let's go upstairs please."

"But, Mommy, it's Zion Fest. Don't I get to choose?"

"Not right now."

Liam looks at me with annoyance. "What's the problem, Nicole? I love skateboarding. I just wanted to share this with my son." They both head towards me and the door. When Liam gets close, I kick him in the shin; hard enough to cause a bruise, but not enough to really hurt him. "Shit, woman! What was that for?" I give him a death stare as Zion turns around in shock at the language. "I'm sorry, kiddo. It's just that Mommy has lost her mind. Go on upstairs and wash up. We'll be up in a few minutes."

Zion looks at us both and smirks, "Good luck, Daddy."

I glare at him, "Go, Zion." I close the door behind him.

"Ok, Nicole. What? He was having fun."

"Yeah, fun that I felt upstairs."

"He wasn't scared."

"He fell twice before I came down here." Liam's face tells me that he is catching on to the conversation we're having. "I specifically told you I have felt every scraped knee that kid has ever had."

"I am so sorry. How bad was it?"

"Just bad enough to get my attention. Now I need you to talk him out of skateboarding."

"Aw, come on, pretty lady, please don't make me do that."

"Lee, you should have talked to me first. Not to ask for permission, but just to have a discussion. What did you get him for Christmas?"

He hangs his head, "A BMX."

"Yeah, well, you know that's a no. What else?"

"Some video games, but come on, Nicole, he should still get to have fun."

"And what's going to happen to him, or you when one of you breaks a bone out here? Huh?"

"Well, I know how to handle broken bones." I give him a dirty look. "Okay, okay, I get it. I'm sorry. Now let's go try to enjoy the rest of Zion's birthday. I mean you only turn eight once, right?"

# CHAPTER 31
# TAG!
(Liam)

---

Even though nothing really happened, I feel bad about causing Nicole pain with my gift choices. As I sit across the table watching my two favorite people in the world giggle about everything and nothing at all, I appreciate how truly blessed I am. I have an amazing family. "So, guys, what are we doing next?"

"I want to go back downstairs to the skate park." Zion grins from ear to ear.

I can feel Nicole's annoyance without seeing her face. "Zion, how about we do something that Mom can do with us."

"Laser tag! All four levels are in-bounds."

I love his enthusiasm. Smiling, I say, "How about three levels? Comm room and lab off limits. What do you say?"

"Works for me. Mommy, do you want to play?"

"Play? I am getting ready to take you both down! I call blue!" Nicole loves to compete. I love that about her.

"You always call blue. It's my birthday."

"You're right, son. Do you want blue today?"

"No, I'll take green. Daddy, red for you?"

"Red is fine with me. It doesn't matter because I'm going to kick both of your butts."

"You old people sure like to talk a lot." Zion giggles at calling us old.

"Daaang, baby, he called you old!" Nicole laughs as she tries to remove herself from Zion's crosshairs.

"Sorry, pretty lady, but he said 'people.' That includes you too." We all jump up and grab our laser tag gear. I go over to the comm box and grant Gisele access to the other three levels and the laser tag gear. "Gisele, please start free-play laser tag, first player to fifteen points wins."

*"Affirmative. Would you like for me to call out each point?"*

"Yes. Also, please dim lights to 15 percent and start a thirty-second countdown." The countdown begins and the three of us take different routes, but all end up on the recreation level. Gisele finishes her countdown, and the guns and targets signal the start of the match with a flash and buzz. I hear a buzzer go off in the skate park; it has to be Zion. I run down the hall and into the park. It's dark. My target lights up and so does the green target.

*"Blue, two points."*

Dammit, Nicole is in here. I aim at the green target as my target lights up again.

*"Green, one point. Red, one point."*

Both of our targets light up again. *"Blue, three, four points."*

"Dammit, Nicole! Where are you?"

"It's my birthday, Mommy!" Zion yells out in frustration at his mom's competitive nature.

*"Incoming transmission from Blue reads: I always play to win, boys."*

"Zion, are you thinking what I'm thinking?"

"Yes, Daddy, we need to take Mommy down!"

*"Incoming transmission from Blue reads: Bring it."*

I signal to Zion to go left as I go right. We clear the area, but neither of us see Nicole. We meet back up at the door, but I haven't heard her leave. Just then both of our targets light up again.

*"Blue, six points. Incoming transmission from Blue reads: This is too easy. I'm leaving. Bye, boys."*

I look at Zion, "What the... Never mind." We leave the skate park and stand outside the door waiting for her to come out, or any sign of movement, but nothing happens. I look at Zion, "Is your mom a ninja? Are you holding out on me?"

Zion giggles, "This is your fault, Daddy. She wasn't always this good."

"Okay, we need to split up. She can't be in more than one place at a time. You take the basketball court, I'll take the pool, and then let's meet up at the bowling alley." Just then the lights are restored to full power and Nicole is standing barefoot in the hallway with her gun pointed at us. We both jump with surprise.

"Aww, man, Gisele! You're supposed to have my back!" Nicole calls out to Gisele.

*"Sorry for the interruption. Dr. Sinclair, I'm receiving an urgent message from Dr. Varma."*

"Please play the message, Gisele."

"Hi, Dr. Sinclair. This is Dr. Varma. We have a problem. One of my colleagues in Boston just contacted me saying that they are getting a lot of visits to the ER with a virus that is rapidly attacking the liver. People are coming in with signs of liver failure after only displaying symptoms for one to two days. Liam, he has a six-year-old on dialysis. Call me, please help."

Nicole looks at me with concern. "Liam, please help that baby."

I take off my laser tag gear and hand it to her. I kiss her on the forehead and kneel down to Zion. "Buddy, I'm sorry, but I have to work now. I promise you I'll make it up to you as soon as I can."

"It's okay Daddy. I used to get upset, but now I know my Daddy is a superhero. Go ahead, Daddy. Go save the world. I'll take care of Mommy and baby Liam."

I smile, trying not to cry. I kiss him on the forehead, "I love you, son." I stand up and head off to the lab.

# CHAPTER 32

# EXQUISITE

## (Nicole)

Tonight, has not been a normal family night. After that last outbreak, things have been tense between Liam and me. It proved to be more challenging to get the virus under control this time; took Liam almost a month. At seven months pregnant, I'm really starting to freak out about Lee's premonition. I couldn't bring myself to eat dinner with Liam and Zion. Really, I only ate to make sure I fed baby Liam.

For Christmas, Liam got me a shipment of candles and body care. Tonight, I need some aromatherapy. I light six candles and run a bubble bath. I step down into the sunken tub. The warm water feels amazing. I think little Liam likes it too. He's been doing somersaults since this morning. He's settling down, or maybe he's tired himself out. I settle into the tub and recline with my hands on my belly. I think about everything that has transpired over the last few months, but my focus isn't on the danger. Instead, I remember all the special moments that have happened. I focus on the love and the unbreakable bonds we have created. I'm afraid I'm going to miss Zion grow up. Tears roll down my face as I continue to rub my pregnant belly. I close my eyes and talk to my baby.

"My sweet, sweet, baby boy. Mommy loves you so much. Daddy does too. We're both just scared because we want to keep our family safe. Your daddy is a great man. He's kind, gentle, loving, brave, and strong all at once. Sometimes, Mommy still thinks he's just a dream. Then, I feel you moving so strongly inside my tummy, and you show me that I didn't just dream him up. I pray that you and I get to have many happy years together. But if I'm not here, I want you to fight to be here so that you can take care of him and your big brother for me." The thought of Zion being a big brother warms my heart and brings a smile to my face. I sniffle, "Zion is going to make the best big brother. He'll love you and protect you fiercely. Always listen to him." I hear sniffling in the room, other than mine. I open my eyes and find Liam in his boxer briefs, kneeling at the edge of the tub.

"Nicole, I hope that you're not preparing our baby for a life without you because a life without you is not a life I want to live. I didn't want to come in while your eyes were closed, but may I join you?" I nod my head at him in approval. He takes off his boxer briefs and steps into the tub. Settling on his knees in front of me, "Hi, my pretty lady." I can't help but smile in response. "Nicole, my love, I don't want to fight with you. I won't fight with you. I'm sorry I upset you earlier, with all of my new restrictions for you. I'm just getting more anxious by the day. I want to cherish every moment I have with you." He leans in and gently kisses me. "You are so beautiful, Nicole, inside and out. I don't know what I did to deserve you, but I am so thankful for your love." He moves behind me and pulls me back into his arms. As he rubs my belly, Liam kicks softly. "Hi, son. I need you to help me take care of Mommy. I'll take care of her out here, but I need you to take care of her in there."

I look up at him over my shoulder. Tilting my head up with his hand under my chin, he kisses me softly. I feel his hand move under my baby bump and he begins to massage my clitoris. He whispers, "Is this okay?" I nod yes, and he continues to kiss me. I interlace my fingers with his hand that is resting on my belly. I reach my free hand up to the back of his head and pull him closer to me, kissing him deeper. I pant against his mouth as he continues to pleasure me with his fingers. "I love you so much, Nicole." I grip his hand tightly and call out his name as he brings me to orgasm. He gently kisses my lips for the next few minutes.

"Nicole Dawn Simmons, you are the sun that warms my life, the gentle breeze that soothes my soul, the water that washes away all my pain, and the rock that anchors me when chaos tries to swallow me. You are the very air I breathe. You are my cure; you make everything right in my life. I need you. I love you. And even though this is not my idea of the perfect proposal, I need to hear you say it at least once, so… Will you marry me?"

"Oh my God, Liam. Nothing could be more perfect. Yes, Liam Owen Robert Sinclair the Third, I will marry you. I long for the day that I officially become Mrs. Nicole Dawn Simmons-Sinclair."

He chuckles, "Simmons-Sinclair, huh?" He tickles me.

"Hey, all of my degrees say Simmons."

"Well, maybe we'll all just have to be Simmons-Sinclairs."

"You'd change your name for me?"

"Pretty lady, for you, there's nothing I won't do. Now let's get out of this tub. We're turning into raisins. Plus, I really want to make love to my fiancée for the rest of the night. Is that okay?" I blush and nod excitedly in agreement. It's been far too long since Liam has been inside of me, and I've missed him.

He stands, takes my hands, and leads me out of the tub. Drying me off ever so gently, Liam leads me to our bed and lays me on my side. With his hand on my hip, he slides in behind me. I close my eyes and relish in every touch and kiss as he tenderly caresses me. He kisses my neck and runs his hand down the length of my body. I lift my leg. He grabs my thigh and holds it in place as he pushes inside of me from behind. I softly moan with pleasure. "Is this okay, baby? I'm not hurting you, am I?"

"No. It feels amazing. You feel amazing."

"Mmm, so do you. I'm sorry it's been so long. I was afraid of hurting you. Mmm, I wish I could make up for lost time."

"Liam?"

Breathing heavily, "Yes, baby."

"Shut. Up."

"Just one more thing." I glare at him over my shoulder. "I love you so much." He slowly pulls out a bit.

"My fiancé always knows what to say."

He slowly slides back in. "Say it again."

Moaning with pleasure, "My man."

"Keep going," he growls.

"My fiancé."

Panting, "Mmm, come on wife."

I clutch his arm, "My husband."

Liam takes his time with me tonight, making me feel like time is standing still, loving me, and worshipping my body in the most exquisite ways. "I need to see you," he says. He climbs over me and pulls my hips towards him. My belly is quite big these days. It's like having a basketball between us, but my man has skills. It doesn't even phase him as he slides back inside of me as I face him lying on my side. My body quakes with pleasure and from exhaustion from the countless orgasms I've had in the last hour. Just before I fall asleep wrapped in my husband-to-be's arms, I hear him whisper, "Always remember that I will love you for all eternity."

## CHAPTER 33
# REPARATION AND RETRIBUTION
(Liam)

I wait long enough for the love of my life to fall into a deep sleep. Then I slowly and quietly get out of bed. Though I don't want to, I go into one of the empty rooms and shower before I dress. I hate washing her scent away. I pray that I am back in her arms sometime tomorrow. My nightmares have gotten worse and are happening more frequently. With Nicole right around seven months, she's really looking like the size she is in my nightmares. I have to get Dr. Morris up here sooner rather than later.

I stop to check in on Zion. He's sound asleep. I go in, kiss him on the forehead, and tell him how much I love him. I can't spend too much time, but I've left private messages for each of them in case something goes wrong. I leave out of his room and take the stairs to the lower level. The ATV is ready to go, full tank and fully charged. I've got food and water, and guns with ammo. Fear sets in. I'm afraid that I won't see Nicole and Zion again. I'm afraid that I'll go and come back only to find Nicole and Liam dead. "Oh, God, please let everything work out. I will gladly sacrifice my life in exchange for you keeping them safe. Please, God." I take a deep breath and scan my hand to start the ATV. Once safely out of the compound, I check the time. It's almost 1 a.m. If I haul ass on the flat terrain and slow up on the rough, figure in a five-mile hike on foot, I should get to the resort right around 6 a.m. I need to find a way to shave off an hour. I can't risk being seen once the sun comes up.

As I drive down the mountain, I reminisce about falling in love with Nicole on our hike up here. I thought I was rescuing a damsel in distress, but really, she has been my salvation. She gave me her heart and has allowed me to be Zion's dad. Many women in her position would pull rank or constantly remind me that I'm not really Zion's father, but she has never done that. She respects me and allows me to lead our family. "Oh, God, please help her to forgive me and know that I am just doing what I believe is best for our family." I've never prayed this much in my entire life.

Maybe I should have told Chris I was going to the resort. No, I'm sure he would have told Nicole. It's both good and bad how much my brothers have taken to Nicole. It's great that they all love her, but it's bad that they think I can't take care of her. What they don't understand is that we're a team. She supports me in a way that only my mother and Ms. Cassie have. She never discounts nor discredits me. Mom and Cassie would have absolutely loved her. They'd have love Zion too.

Zion, my precious boy, how could I be so cruel? He's been longing for a daddy for all of his short life. I barged into his life, and he welcomed me with open arms. He is going to feel so betrayed when he finds out I'm gone. I've tried to share as much of my knowledge and time with him as I could, in anticipation of this moment.

Okay, that's enough. I am taking a huge risk, but I have to be positive. I'm going to sneak into the resort. Once I'm in my tunnel, I'll let Thad know I'm there. If it isn't safe to come up, I'll stay there, and he can bring Dr. Morris and her family to me. This whole mission is to grab the doctor and get her back safely to my wife-to-be, and that's what I intend to do.

I've made great time and reach the spot I plan to leave the ATV just before 4:30 a.m. It's cold out, but very little snow is on the ground down here. I load my guns, one in my chest holster, one at my thigh, and one at my ankle under my pant leg. I throw on my jacket, backpack, and lean my rifle against a nearby tree while I camouflage the ATV. Once I finish, I grab my mask out of my bag and put on my shooting gloves. I sling my rifle around me and start on my five-mile run. I packed lighter than how I trained so I'm able to get within a mile of the resort quickly. I slow up so I can get a lay of the land and catch my breath. Using my night vision goggles, everything appears to be clear. I get back on track and move briskly, but cautiously.

Only a half mile to the resort and I hear movement. I freeze, but before I can reach for my gun, I hear an order. "Don't even think about it. Show me your hands." This is definitely not a kid. I slowly raise my hands. I see men surrounding me with weapons drawn. I start to reach for my mask. "Slowly!" He yells. I slowly remove my mask.

"Please, I don't want any trouble. I will pay for safe passage."

A voice sounds off from the crowd. "Hey, this is the guy I was telling you guys about."

"So, the white ghost is no longer an urban legend. On your knees whitey." I drop to my knees and the head guard emerges from the group. "You called too much attention to yourself on your last visit. Gave the white people around here a false sense of courage." I look up at him. "Don't worry, we took care of it." He winks at me. "So, you said you're willing to pay for safe passage. How much?"

"I have fifty thousand dollars on me. I can get more. Just, please let me pass."

"Well, sucks to be you because today is not your lucky day. I'm going to help lighten your load by taking that fifty grand off you, and then I'm going to take you to Devon." Before I can speak, I see the butt of his automatic rifle coming at me. I feel the pain and warm blood trickling down my head. Then blackness.

I don't know how long I have been out, but I am awakened by a splash of cold water to my face. My shirt has been ripped opened. I open my eyes to see that I'm in a room with a concrete floor. My hands are bound tightly behind my back, and I'm pulled up from the ground so that I once again rest on my knees. A man enters the room flanked by six armed guards. He's about five-ten, athletic build, but not buff. His perfectly groomed locks fall just below his shoulders. His wrist and neck are laced with gold and diamonds. He's a good-looking man. "So, you're the white ghost?"

"That's what I've been told. You must be Devon."

"You've heard of me." He walks over and sits on a table near the fireplace.

"Only from your guard who robbed me and knocked me out."

He shrugs, "The way I see it, that was reparation and retribution. We're big on those two principles around here."

"Is that what you call it? I, personally, have not, to my knowledge, wronged any person of color. My grandmother was Black."

"Oh, so which one of your parents is Black?"

"Neither. My mother was white, and my grandmother adopted us."

"Oh, so I was right. You're just another white boy reaping the bounty of my people. Did your Black granny nurse your white mother? I bet she raised her and then your family treated her like shit. I fucking hate your kind. I'm going to make an example of you. All your people you gave hope to… I'm going to do everything to you that your people did to mine in front of them." He smirks evilly, "Someone bring shit-scrapper to me. I want him to see this."

"Man, you have me all wrong. I loved my grandma. I took great care of her and made sure she never wanted for anything. I'm not like those idiots who believe white skin makes us better. I believe we're all just people trying to find our way." The door opens. They bring in a dirty young white boy. I recognize him right away.

"Hey shit-scrapper, is this your hero you're always talking about?"

The kid shakes his head no when he's zapped with an electric cattle prod. I yell out, "Yes, I recognize him. Please don't hurt him."

Devon tilts his head curiously. "I wouldn't worry about him as much as myself if I were you. Hey shit-scrapper, come closer so you can get a good view." Devon nods at the guards behind me. They come and grab my shoulders, holding me in place. Devon grabs something from the fireplace. "You know, when the slave master bought a new slave, he marked that slave to show ownership." He walks toward me. He's holding a long rod. At the end of it is a "W" in a circle with a line going through the W. *This crazy son of bitch is going to brand me.* I tense up, take a few quick deep breaths, and brace myself. He presses the hot metal against my flesh on my upper chest on the left side. I grunt but breathe through the pain. Then, I swear, I see, feel, and hear Nicole. Oh my God, she felt that. Tears begin to fill my eyes, but I fight it because I refuse to let Devon see that any of this is affecting me.

"Take him to the kennel and put him in one of the cages."

## CHAPTER 34

# MY FEAR WILL MAKE
# HIM WEAK

(Nicole)

---

Tossing and turning, I sit up out of my sleep and grab my head. *What was that?* "Liam? Baby? Are you in here?" It's really early and I want to go back to sleep. I turn over and my senses are overwhelmed with anger and pain. I sit back up, "Oh my God. Liam, baby, what are you doing?" I scoot to the side of the bed, dangle my legs off and push my upper body up with my hands. Once sitting up, I stand, but I'm a bit dizzy. I manage to get to the door and open it. I use the hallway walls to support myself. Zion's door is closed — it's usually opened. "Zion, sweetie? Will you please come here?" I push the door open. He's usually a heavy sleeper, but he's sitting up sleepily looking at me.

"Mommy, are you okay?"

"No. My head is hurting really badly and I'm afraid."

"Where's Daddy?"

"I don't know. Will you help me get to the comm room?"

He gets up and helps me to the elevator as I balance myself using the walls. Once we get to the comm room, Zion helps me to Liam's seat in front of the large screens. "Gisele?"

*"Good morning, Professor Simmons."*

"Gisele, where is Liam?"

*"Dr. Sinclair is at an unspecified location near Mr. Masters' resort."*

"Mommy, Daddy left us?"

"Sweetie, he thought he was helping me. Gisele, please get Chris Ito on the line."

*"Right away."*

I turn from the screen to face my son, "Zion, I think Daddy is in trouble. I'm going to need you to be strong and brave. Do you remember when you were younger, I would get sick when you got sick?"

"Yes, and you always knew when I was hurt or scared. Do you think Daddy is hurt and scared?"

"I think so, baby. Listen, there's a part of me that I kept from you because I didn't want to scare you, but now you have to know." I take his hands, "I can actually feel the pain of people I love. That's why…"

"That's why you never wanted me to get hurt or play sports. That's why you won't let Daddy teach me how to skateboard."

"I'm sorry, son."

I hear Chris' voice, "Nicole? Are you okay? Where's Lee? Do you need me to come get you?"

"Hi, Chris." I put my hand to head. The pain is pretty bad. "I'm pretty sure Lee is in trouble. He went to the resort, but I'm certain he didn't make it. Will you please get Thad on?"

Within moments, all the guys are on the screens in front of me. "Chris, I said Thad."

"Sorry, Nicole. This is an all-hands-on-deck situation. I need Jimmy and Eddie to access the high security functions of our satellite. I need Sergio to work our connections while I work command. And I need Thad for recon. Everything that we tried not to do to protect your location is about to get initiated."

"Nicole, are you sure Lee is here? I specifically told his ass not to come!"

"Yes, I tracked his chip. He is close to the resort, Thad."

Sergio has been quietly observing. "Nicole, I'm sorry to pull the focus off of Lee for the moment, but I have two questions for you. Why is Zion in here for this, and why are you clutching your head?"

"Guys, Zion is here because Liam has been teaching him everything about the lab and the comm room. I think he can help with some things that I might not be able to, and I'm clutching my head because it hurts. Chris, I asked for Thad only because I didn't want to freak everyone out." I pause before continuing, "I can feel Liam's pain."

They all stare at me in confusion. Eddie speaks up, "So, Lee is having a headache. Got it. Is there anything else we need to know, Nicole?"

I sigh and roll my eyes at him. "Sometimes I think you're funny, Eddie, but right now, you're being an ass. It's more than a headache. I think Liam was hit in the head with something."

"Sorry, Nicole," Eddie says.

"Thad, if Lee was captured, where would they take him?" Chris asks.

"Only one place. To Devon."

"The psycho you guys mentioned before?" Jimmy yells out. "Didn't you say that guy is into killing white men?"

"Yeah, he's bad news." Sergio chimes in.

"What I didn't tell you all, especially Lee, is that Devon has been looking for this 'white ghost.' There have been stories about a white man who came into town and disappeared. They say he gave the white people around here hope. He was said to have money and weapons, but the most damaging thing is that three youngsters told the guards that they saw him traveling with a Black woman and a child. The Black woman who defied the guards while protecting her mixed-race child. Of course, people claimed they saw them come into my resort, but never saw them leave. I denied it, but that was when I was told I could no longer assist whites."

Shaking my head in disbelief, "Let me make sure I understand you, Thad. This Devon guy is pissed off because I wouldn't let him touch my child and he thinks Liam saved us from him. Liam is his idea of the 'white savior.' He's going to kill him. He's going to kill my Liam." Tears soak my face as Zion hugs my arm.

Thad reluctantly continues. "Nicole, it's so much worse. I'm sorry, but Lee will probably be tortured before Devon kills him."

My eyes say it all to the guys. "Chris, please help him. Help me. Please."

"Nicole, we will get him back. I promise you. Okay, boys, let's get to work. Jimmy and Eddie, I'm going to need the skies cleared. No one in or out starting from the compound's position for a hundred-mile radius, don't initiate until I give the order. I need you guys to cut all signals except the one we're on now because we need an open line to Thad. I know what you guys are capable of, so fuck up everyone's shit except ours! Roll out the red carpet for us, boys. How long do you need?"

"About six to eight hours," Jimmy answers.

Chuckling deviously, Eddie admits, "Oh, I hope I get to vaporize his ass!"

Confused, I shake my head and ask for clarification. "What? Chris, what is he talking about?"

"In case you haven't caught on, Nicole, Eddie has a rather wicked sense of humor. The satellite is equipped with a high tech, very accurate laser that can literally vaporize a person. We almost didn't get the satellite launched because of it, but our contact decided that one day the US government might have use for it."

I smile for the first time today. "Eddie, I think I just found our common ground. I love sci-fi and James Bond movies too. Sorry for interrupting you, Chris."

"Serg, time to put that PR degree back to use. I've sent over a list. Everyone on that list owes me a debt. I'm calling in all my favors today. Start at the top and work your way down, get me appointments for today. The two elected officials on the bottom are friends. I'll contact them myself."

"Thad, you have the most important..."

Suddenly, I begin to hyperventilate. *Oh my God, I can see what Liam is seeing!*

"Nicole, what is it?"

"I can see Devon! No, no, no, please!" I feel an overwhelming sense of fear, but I think it's my own. I think Liam is feeling my fear. "Devon is going to brand Liam!"

"What the fuck!" Chris yells and jumps to his feet. "Thad, would he do that?"

Thaddeus squeezes his clasped hands in front of his face as he grimaces. "Absolutely, he would."

As the brand burns into Lee's skin, I feel it and the pain is unbearable. I scream at the top of my voice, my body trembles. I clutch my left upper chest, and tears flow down my face. Zion tries to catch me, but I fall out of my seat and onto the floor. He cries out for both me and Liam. The guys are all standing as if they could help me through their screens.

I hear Jimmy's voice, "Nicole? Nicole, stay with us if you can. Nicole, try not to pass out. Lee is tough. He can take whatever this monster has concocted."

I roll to my side in the fetal position and sob. "He's strong, but I'm certain he can feel me. I'm not as strong as he is, and my fear is going to make him weak. You guys must get him out of there."

"Guys," Thad speaks. "I hate to be the bearer of bad news, but Devon is capable of so much worse. And while all of you are stunned into silence, let me point out that in front of us is a very pregnant Nicole, on the floor, in pain. This can't be good for the baby. She needs medical attention."

"I'm fine for now, Thad. They're moving him. Let's stay on task please. I'll meet with Dr. Morris a little later." Zion hovers over me, filled with concern as the guys look on. I can feel the cold lab floor on my face. It's soothing. I need to focus on something soothing right now. "I just want to lie right here for a little while." Zion stands up and takes my seat in front of the screens.

"Uncle Chris, what's the next step to rescuing my daddy?"

Chris takes a deep breath and continues laying out the plan. "Thaddeus, once we're the only ones with a signal, I need you to put on that watch I got you for Christmas. You didn't throw it away when you were mad at me, did you?"

"No, I'm not stupid. I knew you wouldn't give me a hand-me-down watch. It's not your style, so I figured it must be some kind of decoy. What does it do?"

"It has a built-in camera. It has a worn look, so it doesn't attract attention. Put it on and hook your thumb into your pockets or belt loop, as long as the face of the watch is outward. I need you to pay Devon a little visit."

"Damn it! I knew you were going to ask me to do that. Honestly, if I know Devon like I think I know him, he's going to summon me soon. I'll have to act like I don't know Lee. Jimmy, Eddie, you guys need to work quickly on the signal because I can't control when I get summonsed."

"No, Thad. Hear me. You cannot wear that watch in there with any other active signals. We need to give them time to get this right. You may have to stall if he sends for you before Jimmy and Eddie are ready."

"Chris, you don't stall with Devon. Come on man, he just branded our brother! You think I can stall him? He will burn down this resort with me and my family in it and roast marshmallows while we burn to death."

"Guys, chill! We'll be ready with the signal." Eddie breaks up the back and forth. "We have our assignments. Let's do this. We need to get Nicole up off the floor. Lee isn't here to do it, so it's up to us."

I sit up and slowly find my way to standing. "At least the pain from the brand stopped the pain in my head." Tears still flowing, I bend down and kiss Zion. "Thaddeus, please have Dr. Morris get in contact with me. I'm going to the lab."

# CHAPTER 35
# THE GHOST AND THE TRAITOR
### (Liam)

---

D evon fights dogs for sport. There must be twenty to twenty-five dogs in here, but enough cages to hold thirty-two. The guards throw me into one of the empty cages next to a beautiful, gray pit bull. This poor animal has seen better days. He doesn't bark. He just stares at me with his sad, puppy dog eyes. Once the guards leave, the rest of the room gets surprisingly quiet. I wish I could hurt myself without hurting Nicole just so I can get the connection back and tell her I'm sorry. At least I know she and my brothers know where I am. They won't let me die here. The only thing I fear is that Devon will keep hurting her through me. Dumbass is just sadistic. I get that he's mad at the world. His people have been treated like crap for centuries. And yes, I am ashamed of my ancestors, my father included. But how do we break the cycle of violence? I'm just pissed that

Nicole and my sons will have to see this scar as a reminder that I messed up.

I close my eyes and try to go to my happy place, Nicole's arms. It's as if I'm transported to her. She softly kisses, barely touching my chest. "We'll get through this." I swear I can smell her sweet scent. I close my eyes even tighter, I whisper, "Nicole, are you here with me?" She smiles through her tears and simply says, "Always." I feel her hands caressing my face. "Fight for us, baby. Stay alive. We're coming."

I'm brought out of my head by the sound of barking dogs. I open my eyes and see the kid come in. He walks over to my cage. "Hey mister, do you need to use the bathroom? I brought in an extra bucket. There's no one outside. I won't look."

"Thanks kid. I'm good for now. My name is Liam. What's yours?"

"Shit-scrapper." He drops his head.

"That's not your name and I'm not calling you that. What's your name?"

"Jesse." He goes to start his task of cleaning the cages.

"Nice to meet you, officially, Jesse."

"Why did you come back, Liam?"

"Don't take this the wrong way, Jesse, but I'm not really in a trusting mood."

"No, I get it. Clearly, Devon holds all the power in my world. I could be on a fact-finding mission for him. I'm not, but I get it."

"So, he brands all of us?"

"No, just the ones he plans to make submit to him. It's a power play. I had a crew, so I have a brand and I'm cleaning up dog shit. At least I'm not dead," he shrugs.

"I'm sorry, Jesse. Where is your crew?"

"They have better jobs than me. Devon humiliates me around them all the time. I'm pretty sure you got branded because of me. I'm sorry. I put a target on your back."

"No, kid, it isn't your fault. You just confirmed that the woman he wanted to defile was with me. That was my choice, and I'd make the same choice if I had to do it again. Besides, I grew up being humiliated all the time, I'm well-versed in that tactic."

We're interrupted by the door opening, the dogs bark. I sit up as much as I can in my cage, trying to look as unbothered as possible. Devon enters after his guards, but he isn't alone. I try not to react.

"White ghost, I'd like you to meet Thaddeus the traitor. Oh, but you guys have already met."

Before Thad can speak, I say, "Sorry to burst your bubble, Devon, but I've never seen this man before."

"Are you sure about that? I'm sure you and your little white man's whore stayed at the resort next door."

I glare at him for calling my fiancée a whore.

Thad speaks up, "Devon, man, I have repeatedly told you that I do not see every guest that comes through my resort."

"We spent one night and moved on," I tell him.

"So, Devon, you caught your white ghost. What are you going to do with him?"

"Why do you care, Thaddeus, the traitor?"

"Your reputation is spreading, and with it, my profits are plummeting. I want to get my business back on track."

Devon looks down at me with a sick sense of satisfaction. "I plan to do to him everything his people did to us." Shaking his head, "We could have avoided all of this if I would have thrown that little bastard off the dock and fucked that bitch right on the dock in front of the whole port. Made her submit and remember what good Black dick feels like."

Unable to control my reaction at this point I yell out, "Fuck you, you piece of shit! You'll never lay your filthy hands on them!" He smiles and I immediately regret not keeping my damn mouth shut.

"I think it's been a while since I've shown everyone around here why I'm the boss. Take the white ghost outside. I think I'd like to break in my new whipping post and whip."

Thad's eyes grow big. "Devon, is this necessary? Maybe he cares for the woman. Even you would be upset to hear another man talk about fucking your woman in front of everyone. I just think you're going too far."

"I don't give a shit about what you think you Uncle Tom, traitor, motherfucker." He turns to the remaining guards, "While you're at it, escort this traitor out and make sure he's close enough to me to hear my whip crack the air."

The guards drag me out of my cage and walk me outside. They finish ripping my shirt and attach my wrists over my head to the post. A crowd gathers. I've been whipped before with a belt so I'm not afraid, but I'm terrified for Nicole to be whipped. She doesn't deserve this. I need to find a way to submit sooner rather than later. If it was just me, I'd let him swing until his fucking arms fell off, but Nicole wouldn't be able to bear it. I recognized Thad's watch. I helped Chris pick it out. I'm sure Chris is watching, and I can only assume Nicole is too. God, I hope they don't let Zion watch this. I see Devon enter the area, whip in hand.

"Some of you need a reminder about who is in charge and why. You've gotten comfortable with my hospitality and generosity. I've brought you all out here to meet the white ghost whose praise you sing for defying my guards, for having money, for bearing arms, and for saving two people I marked for disgrace. Well, I have your white ghost and now he's going to bow to me and my whip!"

Devon takes his first swing, and his whip connects to my back. I suck in air at the sting on my back, but I don't scream. Nonetheless, I hear Nicole scream; I feel her presence. "I'm so sorry baby. I love you, Nicole." He swings again and Nicole screams in pain, I can see her. "Baby, hold on to me." Tears fall down my face. I hang my head, so people won't see my tears. Devon swings again, Nicole is crying hard. "Hold on baby, don't let me go." Though the pain is real, I don't want to give Devon the satisfaction of hearing my pain, but I know it is the only way to make him stop hurting Nicole. The fourth lash comes, and I try to muster up a scream, but it comes out half-hearted. I hope Devon didn't notice. He swings again and I feel the warmth of my blood spilling down my back. I let my knees buckle a bit.

Devon yells, "Bow, white ghost!" He swings again.

Is that all his punk-ass wants? I can do that if it will stop him from hurting Nicole. Just as I prepare to drop to my knees. I hear Devon speak to Thad, "Come over here, Thaddeus the traitor. How about you redeem my faith in you? Take a swing." Thaddeus will be messed up for the rest of his life if he has to whip me. I think quickly and make my body go limp as if I've passed out. As soon as I do, I hear a loud retching. Thad is vomiting. "The white ghost has passed out. You're vomiting like a little bitch. You both are two weak pussies! Straight rob me of the joy of this moment."

Devon prepares to walk off, but he stops to get a little more pleasure out of the moment. "Do you still want to know what I'm going to do with him?" Thad wipes his mouth and waits for an answer. "I'm going to torture him until I find his little whore. Then, I'm going to bring her right here, chain her to that post, spread her legs, and call everyone out to watch me fuck the white ghost's whore. And when I'm done ripping her insides apart, I'm going to castrate the white ghost and hang him from that tree." He points. "Just as he begins to struggle for that last breath, I'm going to set him on fire." Devon shoves Thaddeus to the ground. "Take that one back to his cage and throw this coward out of my camp. Oh, and I'm sending you the bill for my shoes, motherfucker! The rest of you idiots go find something to do. Show's over."

The guards drag me back to my cage in the kennel. Thad saved us. I'll have to thank him later. It feels like I've been here for a week, but it's just nightfall on day one. The door opens and I go limp again. I have to lie low for the next several hours until the calvary comes.

"You can relax; it's just me."

"How did you know I was faking, Jesse?"

"You're special. You're the white ghost. I saw it when we met. You faked your pain with the brand too."

"That's not entirely true. The brand and the whipping were both painful. I'm just a man. I feel pain just like you. I've just had a little more time developing the mental skills to cope with the pain. Hey, Jesse, can I bother you for a bucket?"

"Yeah, let's empty this one."

"What's all of this?"

"I empty the buckets at the edge of the camp, right next to the resort. Mr. Thaddeus hates it. So, that's where Devon demands that I dump the dog shit. Mr. Thaddeus sent you a care package."

"Are you friends with him? Yes, and so are you. If you get out of here, will you please take me with you?"

"We'll figure out something because I'm not leaving you here. Clearly, you need me." I wink at him.

"Seriously man, you don't have to shit? That's how I know you're the man. You've been branded and whipped, and you don't have to shit."

"Maybe I'm scared shitless," I shrug. "No, I haven't really eaten in two days."

"Well, Mr. Thaddeus sent you food, and ointment for your chest and back. I can help you put it on."

"No one is going to look for you?"

"No, after dark, Devon and his goons are more concerned about pussy than Shit-scrapper."

"How old are you, Jesse?"

"Seventeen."

"I'm sorry you were robbed of your childhood, but will you do me a favor?" He nods. "Stop cussing around me."

He laughs, "Okay, Mr. Liam." Jesse uses antiseptic wipes on my wounds and puts ointment on them. "I wish we could bandage them, but Devon would literally kill me."

"I know, kid. You did good. Thank you. Let's see what Thaddeus sent for us to eat."

## CHAPTER 36

# I WILL CHOOSE YOU

(Nicole)

—————————————

T had bursts through the door and onto the screen. "Zion, where's your mom?"

"Thank you for not hitting my daddy, Uncle Thad."

"I'll never do anything to hurt my family. Is your mom ok?"

Zion shakes his head. "No. First, she was in pain, then she got scared. And then, she got mad. I think she was talking to that stupid jerk's mom."

"His mom?"

Chris explains to Thad. "Yeah, Serg did some digging and found out his mom lives in Houston. Guess who got sick and almost died from the same virus Tiff and I had. Guess who benefitted from Lee's cure."

"That shit bastard!"

"Man, come on Thad! Not in front of Zion!"

"It's okay, Uncle Chris, I'm a big boy."

"You are, but we don't want you to pick up our bad habits."

"I like having a lot of uncles. Are you going to come pick us up, Uncle Chris?"

"Yes, in a few hours. We all need to sleep. I was trying to wait for your mom to come back. Plus, I'm sure she's going to want to talk to you, Thad, since you're the only one to have access to Lee."

"I'll knock on the door and see if my mom can come in here to talk to you, Uncle Chris. I'm getting sleepy too." Zion rubs his eyes.

"No need, I'm here. Thad, thank you for risking everything to check on my Liam."

"You're welcome, Nicole. I sent him some dinner and something to care for his wounds. I have a young friend on the inside. You actually met him in the woods when you left with Lee. Lee is his hero. I'm sure he's checking on him tonight."

"Thanks. What time is this operation kicking off, Chris?"

"In five hours for some of us, but I will get you and Zion in eight hours. Zion, did your dad show you how to open the roof for the helipad?"

"Yes, he made me practice the evacuation almost every day this month. I'm ready."

Chris is impressed with Zion. "You are one cool little dude. Nicole, I take it you had a productive conversation with Devon's mother?"

"It was very informative. We all need to get to bed. Thank you both for everything you did for us today. Thank you for letting me lean on you. And thank you for not mocking my gift. Today, it definitely felt like a curse."

"I'm sorry it was such a hard day for you, Nicole." Thaddeus gives me a little smile. "Zion, take care of your mom tonight."

"I will. Goodnight Uncle Chris and Uncle Thad."

"Goodnight," they say in unison.

Once the comm line is clear, I grab Zion and pull him in close. "I love you to the moon and back, my big boy. You have truly made me the proudest mother on earth. I am so grateful for you. Thank you for being the best part of me. Let's go eat so we can get to bed." We head downstairs to the kitchen. I open the refrigerator and there is enough food prepared for three days. Liam made sure we had enough food to last us until he came home. He takes such good care of us. Zion and I eat and head off to bed. I tuck him in and head off to our room.

As I lie alone in bed, I pray to God, the universe, and my ancestors. "You saw fit to give me this gift. I have never asked for anything regarding mercy, but tonight I beg you to increase my abilities. Tonight, I humbly ask that you allow me to commune with the man I love. Allow us to share one consciousness. Please." I close my eyes, exhausted from the day, but hopeful for my dreams.

*I open my eyes and I'm in my room, but I'm not in bed. I'm at the door. I'm a bit confused because I know I just* went to bed. Then, I realize I'm dreaming. I take in the room, its smell, the lighting. The floor feels like cashmere beneath my bare feet. There are sounds coming from the bed, erotic sounds. The sheets are moving. This isn't my dream. I take a deep breath. This can't be happening. The fates are cruel if they allow me into Liam's sex dream. Okay, it's just a dream. I will not hold him responsible for his dreams. As I slowly approach the bed, I hear him say, "Nicole, I love you so much." My man is dreaming about making love to me. I watch for a moment and remember how tenderly he made love to me the night before. Then, I remind myself that this is not what I'm here for. I walk over to the bed and kneel at the head of the bed.

I mock him with a whisper, "Really, Lee?"

He looks over at me, makes eye contact, and the confusion hits him. He looks down and suddenly, I'm no longer under him. He looks back at me. "Nicole? Dream Nicole or my Nicole?" He sits up on the edge of the bed and reaches his hand to my face.

"I'm here, baby."

"Nicole, how are you doing this?"

"I simply asked the givers of my gift. Let's get out of here." We stand hand in hand, facing one another. "Close your eyes. Think of nothing but me, our love." We both close our eyes. I squeeze his hands when I feel a change in our surroundings. We both open our eyes.

*Above us is the most beautiful clear sky with the night and moon on one side and the sun on the other. I can feel the warmth of the sun on my face on one side. The moon is so big and close I feel like I can touch it on the other. I look down and see that we are standing on calm, clear water. Beneath us, it is teeming with life. In the distance, under the night sky is our beloved compound. Under the day sky is calm clear waters as far as the eye can see. Here with Liam, it's peaceful and quiet. Liam is now clothed in delicate, white linen. And I am in a very pale blue chiffon, thin dress that blows gently with the calming breeze.*

*Once the first impression of our surroundings wears off, I give my man a real greeting. Taking his right hand into mine, I bring it to my heart. I greet him the best way I know how,* "Hi, my love."

"Hi, pretty lady."

*I pull him down to sit with me* "Today was a rough one, huh?"

"Yes, it was. I'm sorry for the pain I caused you. Please forgive me."

"There is nothing to forgive. You risked your life to save me and my child, again. I'm so sorry you had to endure so much pain today."

"No, I'm sorry you had to endure so much pain today. I can handle it. What I can't handle is you being in pain."

"I'm sorry for making you appear weak."

"The only people whose opinions I care about are you and my sons. I don't give a fuck about what Devon thinks."

"Yeah, I can't wait to be face-to-face with that bastard."

He looks out of the corner of his eye at me. "There's nothing I can say to keep you from coming here is there?"

Without taking my eyes off the huge moon that hangs above us, I reply with, "Nope."

"Did you hear what he said he wanted to do to you? Zi?"

"Yes, I did, but I'm not coming alone."

"Nicole, did my son see me get whipped?"

I reach down and take his hand. "Yes. I'm sorry. I needed him with me, and he didn't want to leave me, knowing that I would be in pain."

"Well, did you tell him I'm okay and not to worry about me?"

"Your brothers did, they were great. I, on the other hand, was lying on the floor in the fetal position. He's angry more than anything. I have always taught him that bullies are bad, and I think we're all in agreement that Devon is a bully."

"Devon has consumed enough of our attention. Did you ask for all of this from the higher powers so we can talk about Devon?"

"Absolutely not. I miss you and after a rough day, I just really want to be in your presence. Besides, I needed to make sure you were okay. So, um, how is it you can dream about sex after your body has been mutilated?"

"It wasn't about the sex." He drops his head, "You're my happy place, your arms, your eyes, your smiles, your scent, your spirit, you. I can face anything as long as I know you're with me."

Remembering the last words, he whispered to me before he left the compound to go to the resort, "Eternity is a really long time."

"Loving you for all eternity would be like a blink of an eye. No amount of time will ever be enough, Nicole."

I look up at him and smile, "Let's just say that our love transcends time." I lay my head in his lap.

"Nicole, will you promise me something?"

"Anything. What is it?"

"Promise me you won't die any time soon."

"Oh, Lee, I wish I could promise you that. I promise you I will fight as hard as I can to stay alive."

His head drops, "You may not want to hear this next part." I look up at him from his lap. "I promised not to keep anything from you." I nod for him to continue. "If it comes down to a choice between your life and little Liam's, I will choose you."

"I know."

"You know? You don't hate me for it?"

"Yes, I know, and I don't hate you. I won't try to talk you out of it either. I've known from the moment you thought something was wrong that you would choose me. I love little Liam; I loved him before we conceived him. But, as Renee pointed out to me, losing me will break you. I worry Zion will lose us both if I die. I know you love me, but Zion is me and you cannot check out on him if I die."

He sighs loudly, "I promise not to check out on him. I will be strong for him. Nicole, I'm not giving up on you."

"You better not. I know I said I would always support you, but this time… this time I plan to prove you wrong. I'm going to live and kick your little premonition's ass!"

We both laugh. "I have never looked forward to an ass kicking before. Come here, I want to kiss you."

We get lost in a moment that seems to last forever. An alarm sounds to end the moment. I look at my man. "It's time for me to get up. The mission to get you is already underway. Do me a favor and stay out of trouble for a few hours."

"Do me a favor and listen to Chris."

Winking in defiance, "We'll see. I love you."

"I love you too."

# Chapter 37

# RESCUE MISSION

(Nicole)

I open my eyes and find Zion standing in my room. "Mommy, it's time to go get Daddy."

"I know. I'm up. We don't know when or if we will be able to come back here. I want you to pack a few things, clothes, comm devices, whatever you think you may need."

"Okay, Mommy. Mommy, are you nervous?"

"A bit."

"Me too." He walks away to go pack.

I pack the normal stuff I may need and a few items for Liam. Then, I pack for today. My big pregnant belly won't allow me to fit comfortably into my own pants, so I throw on some of Liam's tactical pants. They are super long on me, so I cut a few inches off the legs before heading down to the armory. I grab two clips for my Glock and fill a magazine for my rifle. I put on a chest holster and a hip holster, one of his jackets, and then throw the rifle across me. Now that I'm fully loaded, I take the elevator up to the living quarters and get Zion and our bags.

"You look tough, Mommy! Let me carry your other bag."

"It isn't too heavy?"

"I will be in so much trouble if Daddy knew I let you carry your bag."

"Thank you, son. Let's head upstairs and let Chris know we are waiting for him." We both get on the elevator and head up one more floor to the comm room.

"Good morning, Gisele."

*"Good morning, Master Zion. What can I help you with?"*

"Will you please send Chris Ito a level five encrypted message that we are ready for retrieval?"

I am beyond impressed with my kid. Liam would be so proud of him.

*"Right away, Master Zion."*

"Gisele, will you please make sure everything is locked down when we leave?"

*"Yes, Professor Simmons. Good luck retrieving Dr. Sinclair. Incoming message from Chris Ito: ETA is twenty minutes. Please prepare the helipad."*

I look around not knowing if or when I'll ever see this place that I have called home for the last year. I go grab our masks out of the lab while Zion enters the commands to open the roof to expose the helipad. It isn't long before I hear the helicopter approaching. Zion and I take the elevator up to the helipad for the first time. It's cold out and there is a thin dusting of snow covering the roof. Chris and Sergio exit the helicopter to help us with our bags. Chris looks at me but doesn't say anything. Sergio greets me with a hug and a kiss on the cheek. They usher us to the helicopter. As soon as I board, I see Renee and her kids. She greets me with open arms and rubs my tummy. Zion runs over to Journey and Joy. The doors close and I hear Chris's voice.

"Nicole, no."

"Hi to you too, Chris. How are you this morning?"

"Nicole, FUCK NO!" His deep voice echoes throughout the aircraft's cabin.

Shaking my head with one eyebrow raised in defiance, "I don't know what you're talking about, Chris."

"Do you see the men on this chopper? DO YOU?"

"I'm not blind, Chris."

"Do not hold up this mission by being stubborn."

I yell at him, "WHAT DO YOU WANT FROM ME, CHRIS?"

"Give me the guns. Now!"

I reach to my hip and hand him my gun. He glares at me. I roll my eyes and hand him the gun in the chest holster.

"Can we go now?"

"No. Ankle. Liam has taught me your tricks."

"Dumbass, I'm almost eight months pregnant! I can't see my ankles, let alone reach them!"

"Rifle."

"Damn, Chris, the rifle is down. You or someone will see me if I grab it."

"The mission is to get Lee out with minimum bloodshed. We are being accompanied by six military choppers each carrying twenty men who have been trained by the U.S. government. Is there anything that you think you can do that we can't? Your job is to sit and wait for us to deliver Liam to you. Do you understand?" I nod. "I need to hear you. DO YOU UNDERSTAND?"

"YES, CHRIS! DAMN! Can we please go now?"

"Nicole, I swear to God."

"What, Chris? What are you going to do?"

"Do not make me handcuff you to your seat." He gives the signal to the pilot to leave.

I look around and see that Justice is suited up for the mission. I give him a little smile and he blows me a kiss. Renee reaches over and grabs my hand.

"You look beautiful, little sister. Well, I mean minus the G.I. Jane getup."

"Hahaha." I scoot over closer to her. "Make no mistake, big sister, Chris will not keep me out of this."

"He's gorgeous."

I turn to her. "Who? Chris?" I roll my eyes and she nods. "Yeah, he is. That's Liam's friend I was telling you about. After this is over, I'll introduce you properly. For now, I need you to do me a favor."

"Uh-oh, what?"

"Lie to him. Tell him you will make sure I stay here. He's not going to believe anything I say until Liam is back with me."

"Nicole, I'm with Chris on this. You should let them work."

"Ree-ree, a lot has changed. I'm good. Damn good."

"And damn pregnant with my nephew."

"How about this? I will stay out of it as long as I can."

"Translation, I will wait until no one is around to stop me."

"Not exactly. I give you my word that I will not do anything unless I have to. Chris is under orders to prevent bloodshed. Devon is not going down without someone bleeding. I am under no orders, and I have no hesitation about making Devon bleed. You weren't there yesterday. He hurt Liam and in turn hurt me. Devon spilled my fiancé's blood yesterday."

"They told me we were all being moved. Liam had been taken, but they didn't tell me what happened."

"Devon branded him and whipped him."

"Oh, sis, tell me you didn't feel it."

"You know I did. Then, he told Thad the plans he had for us. He wants to kill Zi, publicly rape me, castrate, hang, and burn Liam. I won't kill him because my family isn't the only one he's harmed and those families deserve a day in court, but if he doesn't go quietly, I will pick up my gun."

"I have your back little sister. Put him down."

Right at daybreak, we descend onto the grounds of Thad's resort. There are men in military tactical gear all around. Chris turns to speak to the civilians on our craft. "Listen up, Justice, Sergio, tactical team, you're with me. Everyone else sit tight." He glares at me, "Everyone, Nicole." He pulls out a pair of handcuffs.

"Chris, is it? Nicole is fine. She'll sit right here with me." Renee says sweetly as she wraps her arms around me.

"She better. Dr. Morris and her family will join you soon. We're going to make quick work of this." Chris exits and addresses the huge group of men gathered on the ground. "Good morning, gentlemen. I am retired Commander Ito, call sign Boss. Those who know me will tell those of you who don't that I have earned every bit of my call sign. You fuck up, I fuck you up, so don't fuck up! The moment we touched down, Devon and his crew started scrambling to get the upper hand. Will they get the upper hand?"

They yell in unison, "NO, SIR!"

"You're goddamn right! Now, our mission is three-fold. One, we retrieve Dr. Liam Sinclair. You've been briefed on his importance to the United States government. Second, we apprehend Devon Taylor and all of his guards. You should have all been issued a copy of his photo. Lastly, and the most difficult part of our mission, get it done without bloodshed. Those are our orders, but you know the drill. Defend yourself and your brothers. Now, let's get it done!"

"Oh, my. He's totally take-charge. I'll call him Boss. Is he nice too, or just a brute?"

"Whatever, Renee. As much as I want to smack him right now, even I have to admit that was sexy as hell." I smirk at her. "He's strong, but a sweetheart. I think you'd be good for him. Now stop trying to distract me."

"I'm not. You do you, Nicole. Just don't miss if the time comes."

"Ree-ree, I don't miss."

# CHAPTER 38
# UNVEILING THE WHITE GHOST
## (Liam)

I wake up as soon as Nicole breaks our connection. I won't be able to rest until I see her face. There's no sign of Jesse, but he left me a bucket. I hate to do this to him, but I'm worried about Nicole staying safe. I use the bucket. Hopefully, Jesse won't get in trouble for leaving it here. I'm sure Devon wants me to wallow in piss and shit. I owe that kid. The camp is still relatively quiet. I hear multiple helicopters in the distance. They must be for me. Chris is the man. There must be three or four. I wonder if Nicole is on one of them. She just woke up and I know she won't allow Chris to keep her that far away from the action. The door slowly opens. It's Jesse. He quietly closes the door behind him.

"What's going on, Jesse?"

"Do you need the bucket? I need to take it out before people get up."

"I'm done, man. Sorry."

"Are you okay?"

"I'm fine. Just do me a favor, will you?"

"Anything, Mr. Liam."

"Lie low today."

"Okay. Mr. Liam, please don't leave me."

I try to play it cool. "What are you talking about?"

"Nothing." He whispers, "Just don't leave me behind." I see the fear in his eyes. I sigh and give him the smallest smile I can. He walks over to my cage and pulls the bucket out, but he hands me something. "I have to go hide. I don't know when they will discover that it's missing." I look down at my hand, it's the key to my cage.

"I can't let you risk your life for me. You have to put it back."

"Putting it back will be more dangerous than not."

"What makes you think the rescue will be today?"

"Communications are down. Everything went down about three hours ago, but they were all too afraid to wake up Devon to tell him. It's been really quiet all night except for those helicopters I heard a while ago. No one knows what's going on. They're fighting about who is going to tell Devon and who will take the blame. They didn't notice the helicopters. Besides, our friend might have told me."

"Okay. Thanks for the heads up. Get out of here and go hide. I won't use the key until the right moment. Thank you, Jesse."

As Jesse opens the door to the outside, I see that the sun is just coming up. That's when I hear another helicopter. This one is much closer, sounds inside the resort. My Nicole is here. I hear commotion outside. There's chatter about who could be visiting the resort. These idiots are so cocky that they don't even consider that someone is here to snatch their power away. I get comfortable in my cage and bide my time. I hear one of the guards say that it's time to wake up Devon. There is an urgency in his voice. I just want confirmation that Devon is up. I'm going to knock out as many of his perfect teeth as I can. Today, he's drinking his own blood.

Not being able to sit still any longer, I get up to open my cage when a guard calls out, "Let's release the dogs!" I sit back down quickly. There are a lot of people running around. Someone yells, "BREACH! THE CAMP HAS BEEN BREACHED!" A couple of guards run in and start opening the cages, but the dogs are quiet and not moving. They give up and run out, leaving the door opened. I open my cage door. I check the dog next to me. He's alive, but fast asleep. Jesse must have put something in their food to make them go to sleep. Where would he have gotten that? I smile, "Thaddeus." People are fighting outside. I get to my feet and run out. Some of Devon's guards are fighting, but most of them are surrendering. I spot Chris. He sees me. I scan the area for Devon. I see him in the distance trying to escape. I run at him full speed and tackle him. We both get to our feet. I smile, knowing that one on one, he's no match for me. I punch him as hard as I can in the mouth. He staggers and spits out blood.

"Fuck you, white ghost! Is this all for your ass?"

"You're damn straight!" I throw a right hook to his jaw. He goes down. "That's for you thinking you could ever touch my wife!" Someone comes up and grabs me from behind allowing Devon to get to his feet. I elbow my assailant in the gut, he goes down. Another one of Devon's guys hits me in the back with something hard. I stumble into Devon who catches me and puts a blade to my neck. That's when we are surrounded by what feels like two dozen of Chris' men. Devon's men drop their weapons and fall to their knees.

Chris orders Devon, "Drop it, asshole!"

"Kill me if you want, but I'm taking this white piece of shit with me." Frustrated and angry that his reign has ended, "You know, I just don't get it, brother, you're supposed to be on my side. What is it about him?"

"I'm not your fucking brother. You have a knife to my brother's neck. I was ordered to bring you in alive, but I swear if you do anything else to him, I will kill you without a second thought."

Just then a shot rings out and Devon screams and falls onto his back as he's shot in the thigh. Everyone in the area parts as if the Red Sea has parted. It's my baby, all strapped up with her big, beautiful belly and all. I swear she is the most beautiful vision I have ever seen.

"All of these men are under orders not to kill you, but I'm not, you piece of shit! So, you want to rape me, kill my kid, torture, and murder my man? Fuck you! Boss, you got him?"

"Affirmative."

She turns to Chris, "If he blinks, drop his ass." She continues to walk toward an injured Devon. She gets to me and hands me her rifle. I take it, bend down to kiss her, and then draw on Devon. She walks over and firmly grabs him by the ear, leading him to the quad where the whipping post is. He stumbles and wails like a wounded animal the entire time. Nicole releases him and he drops to the ground like a lead balloon. Chris looks over at me as if to ask me what Nicole is up to. I shrug because I have no idea. The captured white people and Devon's guards that are in custody are all in the quad. I look up and see Thad, Sergio, and Renee. Chris, Justice, and I still have our weapons on Devon.

"Let me tell you all something about the white ghost." Nicole's voice echoes throughout the quad. "First of all, his name is Dr. Liam Sinclair." She stresses the word 'doctor.' "He rescued my son and me from this so-called pro-Black man who wanted to not just humiliate us but, as I recently learned, he also wanted to rape me and murder my innocent seven-year-old child. Dr. Sinclair found us, loved us, and cared for us." Speaking to Devon, "Something you wouldn't do for someone with the same color skin as you, so spare me your Black power rhetoric. The only person you care about is Devon Taylor."

"You're a white man's whore," Devon responds.

Nicole slaps him across the face as hard as she can. She shakes her hand from the sting, "That's from your mother."

Devon looks directly at Nicole, "My mother? You've talked to my mother?"

"Yes, interesting story you have. You graduated from college with a business degree in restaurant management, married a white woman whose daddy owns one of the biggest steakhouse companies in the country, had three adorable mixed babies and lived the good life until wifey's daddy caught you screwing the help. He kicked you out on your ass." Nicole chuckles. I'm still not sure where she's going with this. "Then, you proceeded to get two beautiful Black women pregnant and refused to work a normal job to support those cuties. Yeah, your mother was very eager to share pictures with me of her grandbabies she helps take care of. Want to know why?" Nicole pauses. "It doesn't matter because I'm going to tell everyone here anyway." She diverts her attention from Devon to the crowd. "About nine months ago, there was a virus that hit the Houston area. Guess who lives in Houston. If you guessed Devon's mommy, you're right. Guess who got gravely ill. Devon's mom? Right again." Nicole looks him in the eye. "I heard you cried like a baby when you thought she was going to die. She's a terrific lady, you should have cried. I bet you even fell to your knees to ask God for a miracle for her. Well, He sent her one in the form of Dr. Liam Sinclair." Devon glares at Nicole, not understanding what she means. I lower my rifle as she begins to deliver her final blow to Devon.

"The man you call the white ghost, the man you tortured, and planned to kill, single-handedly developed the cure that saved your mother's life. He's a hero. I say you owe him one hell of an apology." Devon spits a mouthful of blood in my direction. I take a couple of steps forward, but Nicole looks at me, signaling me that she's not done. She turns back to Devon and kicks his bullet wound. He screams in pain. "I really wanted to empathize with you. I wanted to believe that you were just trying to get justice for our ancestors. It wouldn't have made it right, but I would have understood.

Instead, you are just a miserable, lying, cheating, sadistic con artist. I hope they throw you in a cell with all of your guards who you tricked into doing your dirty work and supporting you. I hope they take turns whopping your ass. Liam Sinclair, Thaddeus Masters, that guy," she points to Chris, "are each twice the man you will ever be. And don't you ever judge me or anyone else for who we love." Finally, Nicole kicks him in the balls. He yells and topples over. "And that was for you thinking that raping me was okay." She turns to Chris and Justice, "Take him."

Nicole heads in my direction. I run to her, and we share a kiss worthy of this reunion. As the crowd disperses, and Devon is led off in shackles, people pat me on the back to thank me, forgetting that I have raw lashes across my back. It's attention that I am not used to, nor do I want. I don't do what I do for the applause, but I get why Nicole took that approach. Truthfully, I would feel safer knowing that people don't know who I am.

Renee and Dr. Morris begin walking toward us when I see Zion running our way. I think he's just happy to see me when he screams, "MOMMY!" I look at Nicole as she's collapsing next to me. I catch her. Everyone stops.

# CHAPTER 39
# DREAM WITH ME
## (Liam)

---

Oh my God, it's happening. My scream is so loud and high pitched it startles everyone around us. "NICOLE! NO, BABY! DON'T YOU DARE DIE ON ME!"

Chris yells, "MOVE! Come on, Lee!" Our entire crew boards the helicopter. Jesse runs up out of nowhere and Thad helps him onboard. "Dr. Morris, I can fly us anywhere. You just have to tell me where to go."

"I don't know, she won't make it far. The closest place that I can operate with no questions asked is about an hour and a half away. I don't think she'll make that."

With tears running down my face and my lungs burning from hyperventilating, I beg Dr. Morris for help. "What's wrong with her? Can you save her? She's my everything."

Concern fills her face as she tries to answer quickly and honestly, "I can save the baby for sure if I operate now. At this point, Nicole has about a fifty-fifty chance."

"No! She comes first."

"Liam," Renee begins.

"No, Renee! I told her, I choose her."

"Chris, try to get us to Faulkner Memorial Hospital in Seattle as quickly as you can. I will call ahead and make the arrangements. Liam, I honestly don't know if they will survive the next hour and half without surgery."

"Lee, technically the two of you are not married yet. Legally, I'm the next of kin."

I cough out all the air in my lungs and begin bawling in agony, "Renee, don't do this to me. Please."

"She's my little sister and I don't want her to die, but if she dies, I would like her sons to be a part of our lives. Don't you want that?"

"She's right, Lee." Sergio says.

I hear them, but there is no way I'm letting her go. Then, I remember last night. The helicopter is so loud, and everyone is crying. Zion and Joy are wailing. I scream as loudly as I can, "SHUT UP! Everyone, please, I need quiet. Chris, I need a headset, but disconnect it. I have an idea, but I need as close to silence as I can get." Chris hands me the headset. I look at Dr. Morris, "Do not wake me up under any circumstance until Nicole is stable. Do you understand?" She nods. I lie down in the middle of the floor with Nicole in my arms. I close my eyes and focus on the pain I'm feeling at the thought of losing her.

"Find me, Nicole." I drift off as I let go of every thought except for her.

*"You came!" I open my eyes in our dream world, but this time, it's in Nicole's peaceful place. The shining bright sun bounces off the crystal blue water. It casts a beautiful golden glow on Nicole's face.*

*"Of course, I did. Where else would I be? Are you okay?"*

*"I don't know, you tell me."*

*"What do you think is happening?"*

*"I remember being in excruciating pain; then nothing."*

*"Different location, but other than that, it happened just like in my dream."*

*"Wait, am I dead, Liam?"*

*I chuckle a little, "Do you feel dead?"*

*"I don't know. I never died before."*

*"You aren't dead, and you better not die on me. I'm here to keep your brain active and engaged."*

*"Lee, what will happen to the lab?"*

*"I don't know. I need to talk to my brothers. See where we stand with everything."*

*"I'm so glad we were able to rescue you. I'm sorry I ruined your reunion with Zion."*

*"Nicole, what do you want our life together to look like?"*

"I just want us to be happy and love each other, raise our boys to be good men like their father, uncles, and big cousins. What about you?"

"You. I will be happy with any version of the future, just as long as you are in it. You have to let me die first." I kiss her on the forehead. "I don't want to be in this world if we can't be in each other's arms. I need to feel your warmth in my bed, to hear your laugh, see the love in your eyes looking back at me, and to taste your sweet kisses."

"You always know what to say, my poet." She looks at me in the way that only she does.

There's a fire in her gaze that I pray I will always be able to keep ignited. Her love for me is unconditional and unwavering. "You know, I don't just say things that I think will impress you. I say it so that you never have to wonder how much you mean to me."

"I know how much I mean to you. Just look at us. You've followed me into an uncharted, astral plane. Something, somewhere neither of our PhDs can help us understand. That tells me you would follow me across the universe, beyond time and space. I know what I mean to you, and I accept your gift of love. I'll never take it for granted."

I smile and nod, knowing that I couldn't have articulated it any better than she did. "I guess our love reflects back on each other." Pausing briefly to take her in, "Thank you."

"For what?"

"Following me."

"Well, thank you."

"For what?"

"Kidnapping me."

I gasp and we both laugh. "Hey, you wanted to come. You saw these blue eyes and these huge guns." I flex my biceps. "There was no resisting me."

"Oh, is that what you think?" I grab her and tickle her. Her beautiful laugh almost makes me forget what's happening in the real world. "Baby, I'm really tired. Will you hold me while I sleep?"

"No, Nicole. You can't go to sleep. Think about it, how can you be tired in a dream state."

"Maybe you should pop out and see what's going on with me."

"Promise you'll stay right here and not go to sleep."

"I promise, Liam."

I open my eyes to see that we are being wheeled into the operating room. Dr. Morris sees my eyes opened. "I don't know how you're doing what you're doing, but keep doing it. She's lost a lot of blood, but for some reason, she's stable. We're here. I'm going to do my best to save them both. Keep going, Liam."

I close my eyes and try to get back to Nicole. She lets me back in. *She's sitting looking down into the ocean beneath her.*

"What is it, my love?"

"A humpback whale nursing her calf. They're beautiful." Without looking up from the whales, "What's happening out there? How am I doing?"

"You're doing great." She looks at me skeptically. "Okay, you're getting tired because you've lost a lot of blood, but we're in the operating room now. Dr. Morris is getting ready to get baby Liam out and work on you. We made it to the hospital. So yes, you're doing great. You're so strong and beautiful." The sound of a soft cry surrounds us like the sun's warm rays on a cold winter's day. I look at her and we both cry tears of joy. "He's here!"

"He's alive, Liam!"

"So are you."

"Go to him. He needs one of us."

"He's premature, they're going to take him to the NICU. I am not leaving you until I know you are going to pull through this surgery."

"What if my uterus is ruined?"

I shrug, not to make light of the situation, but to let her know that it changes nothing about my love for her. "We have two kids. Whatever happens, we'll be okay as long as we're together. I will take care of you. Will you be devastated?"

"No, I don't want to disappoint you."

"Not possible."

"Liam? Liam, if you can hear me. It's Dr. Morris. Nicole is all stitched up. She's stable. If you want to wake up now you can. You two have a son. He's beautiful. He's in the NICU when you both wake up."

*"Nicole, do you want me to go talk to Dr. Morris or stay with you?"*

*"Go. Let her tell you everything that's going on. I'm going to try to wake up as soon as possible. Will you try to wait for me to go see Liam?"*

*"I wouldn't dream of going without you. I love you."*

I open my eyes as Nicole is being wheeled out of the OR. "Dr. Morris?"

"Dr. Sinclair, welcome back. One day, you'll have to tell me what I witnessed today."

"Where are they taking her?"

"Come on, we'll go with her to recovery. Do you have questions for me?"

"Tons. How is our son?"

"Great for a four-pound, eight-ounce infant. The good news is that Nicole was actually more like thirty-two weeks instead of thirty like we thought. I won't sugar coat it, he's not totally out of the woods. If he doesn't have any setbacks, you should be able to take him home in about a month? On the other hand, he is the son of two very strong and determined individuals. He's also bigger than expected, so that's a benefit as well. Who knows, maybe a little less than a month if he hits his benchmarks."

"That's a long time. What about Nicole? When will she be able to come home?"

"In about a week. Liam, I had to make a call."

"You weren't able to save her uterus, were you?"

"No, I'm sorry. There was too much damage, and she lost a lot of blood. I'm really sorry."

"Don't be. You saved her. That's what I hired you to do. I am forever in your debt. Plus, we were prepared for that possibility."

"Not sure what you mean, but absolutely no thanks are required."

We stop at Nicole's bed in the recovery room. I kiss her on the forehead. "How long before she wakes up?"

"About an hour. Why?"

"Is there somewhere I can shower and change? I don't want to be filthy when I meet my son."

"Yes, I'm told her room is ready. Just waiting on her. I'll get the room number for you."

"Thanks. Where is my family?"

"The entire crew is waiting for you in the waiting room."

"Thank you." I ask Nicole's nurse to let me know when she wakes up and I head off to the waiting room. As soon as they see me, they all stand. Zion runs full speed to me and jumps into my arms. I weep, which causes panic in the room. "Everyone, calm down. I haven't seen my son in two days. These are tears of joy." Sergio, Thaddeus, and Chris all rush over to greet me and then give me some space with Zion.

"Daddy, I missed you. Is Mommy okay?"

"Mommy is feeling much better. Baby Liam is here, but he's tiny. He'll need to be in the NICU for a while. I haven't seen him yet. I would love to get cleaned up first."

"Mommy packed you some clean clothes."

I look over and see Chris cozying up to Renee. I walk over to them to get the bag Nicole packed for us. I say in a low voice, "I see you two have met." They both smile. "Nicole will definitely approve. Renee, can we count on you to look after Zion for a while?"

"No, I have better things to do," she says sarcastically. "I have loved Zion like he is one of mine since the day I found out my baby sister was pregnant. Nothing has changed for me. I'm here for him, whatever he needs."

"Lee, I need to talk to you. Can I walk with you?" Chris asks.

"Sure. Renee, will you please go sit with Nicole?" She nods and heads off to see her sister. "Zion, stay close to your cousins and uncles."

I grab the bag and head to the elevators with Chris. "Thank you for rescuing me and taking care of my family."

"It's not like I could just let your ass die. Nicole would kill me. You got yourself a warrior in that woman." We both laugh as we get into an empty elevator. "Some very influential people saw what went down today. Nicole's little speech about you is really making the rounds. I've gotten twenty-some requests for meetings with you. My guess is you're going to finally get that meeting with Congress that you've been wanting."

"That's great. Chris, what am I going to do about the lab?"

"So, I was thinking about that. Maybe I can bring a team and stay for a while with you at the compound. At least until you get safely to D.C."

"That isn't a bad idea, but I can't leave Nicole and Liam here."

"We need to see if Dr. Morris will be willing to move Liam Jr. You get changed and get to your woman and baby. I'll find Dr. Morris and start working on her. I should probably take Serg, he's more diplomatic."

"Yes, please." I smile. "I owe you my life, man."

"Consider us even."

# CHAPTER 40

# HE'S STRONG

(Nicole)

When I wake up Renee is looking down at me. "Hi, little sister. You gave us all quite a scare." She kisses me all over my face, the same way I do to Zion.

"Where is Lee? Where's my baby?"

"Big Liam went to freshen up and baby Liam is being cared for in the NICU."

"How is he? How much does he weigh?"

Renee looks around and grabs my medical chart from the desk once the nurse steps away. She opens it and starts reading. She tears up and closes the file. "Maybe we should just wait for Dr. Morris." She walks back over to my side and fiddles with my IVs and cords.

Taking her hand to reassure her, "It's okay. Liam and I knew that this might be my last chance to have a baby. I don't have a uterus anymore, do I?" She shakes her head. "Renee, it's okay. I'm fine. Zion is here and now, so is Little Liam. I'm happy. Ree-ree, can you sit me up? I think I'm going to be sick."

"Yeah, sweetie." She helps me sit up just as fluid begins to come up and out of me. "You always get sick after surgery, like Mom."

"I really miss her today."

"I have to say, she would be so proud of you." She wipes my mouth.

"Do you think she would like Liam?"

"Baby sister, she would have loved him. You guys take great care of each other. She would be so happy that you found someone to love you as much as Daddy loved her. I have to tell you something." I lie back down, and she holds my hand. "On the way here, I told Liam that you would want Liam Jr. to live. He told me that you knew he would choose to preserve your life over Liam's. I tried to pull rank, and I reminded him that I'm legally next of kin." I look at her with as much displeasure as I can muster, but before I can get a word out, she continues. "You should have seen him. It was absolutely heartbreaking. Do you remember when I had chicken pox and you caught them from me?"

"Of course, I remember. You gave me your cooties, got better, and then went on our annual trip to Disneyland without me. I still hate you for that." I wink at her.

"Yeah, and that was thirty years ago. Do you think Liam will hate me for that long?" She begins to tear up. "I broke his heart and I feel terrible."

Liam steps in from behind the curtain. "I forgive you. The situation was very intense."

"I'm sorry, Liam." Renee hugs him and kisses him on the cheek. "Congratulations, you two. I love you both."

My man looks even better than I remember. A smile spreads across my face. "I missed you, baby."

He bends down and kisses me. "Are you ready to see our son?" I nod. "Me too. Let me find a nurse so we can get a wheelchair."

"Uh, Liam, Nicole is still in recovery." Liam stares Renee down. "Look, I'm a nurse and I am just letting you know that there are certain things they have to check off on her chart before she leaves recovery. They're not just going to let you go wheeling her off."

Liam scoffs, "Our baby needs us."

Just as Liam is beginning to make his case to Renee, who has no power in this hospital, Dr. Morris enters the room. Before he can speak Dr. Morris interrupts him. "Dr. Sinclair you really are a control freak, aren't you? How dare you send your henchmen to bully me into releasing Nicole and Liam early!"

Liam tries to speak, "But…"

He is promptly cutoff. "No, you don't. I'm speaking and you're listening. These are my patients. I say when they will get released. I and I alone dictate their care unless I ask for a consult. And Dr. Sinclair, I will not be asking you for a consult. I know you and Nicole have this great bond, but if you try to interfere with me doing my job, I will have you banned from this hospital. Do I make myself clear?"

"May I speak now?"

"Only if the word 'yes' is coming out of your mouth."

Liam turns beet red, and I can tell he's upset. I'm not sure what this reprimand is about so I speak up. "Dr. Morris, I don't understand what's going on."

"Go ahead Dr. Sinclair. You had enough balls to send those two knuckle heads to come talk to me. Tell your fiancée what you want to do."

Not used to taking orders and being shut down, Liam takes my hand and turns his attention from Dr. Morris to me. "Nicole, I asked Chris to take Serg with him to speak to Dr. Morris. From the way the good doctor is yelling at me, my guess is that Chris barked at her and Serg didn't get to use his diplomacy skills." Focusing on my eyes, he drops all pretenses and talks to me like I'm the only one in the room. "Pretty lady, little Liam is going to need medical attention for maybe the next month. You know I would never put anything before you and our boys, but if something comes up that needs my attention in the lab, I'd like to be able to respond. You know I don't ever want to be separated from you. So, I wanted to know if we had everything Dr. Morris needs in the lab to care for you and Liam there, would she be willing to move you two."

Knowing that Liam is always trying to do the right thing, I raise my hand to brush his damp hair out of his face. He kisses the inside of my wrist the way he often does. "Baby, I trust you, and it isn't a bad idea, but I think we need to wait at least a week. Dr. Morris, is this what you understood Liam's request to be?"

A bit calmer in tone, "I was informed of the move, not asked. Besides, do you know how much something like that will cost?"

Still a bit put out after being emasculated in front of his woman, Liam responds in a low, deep voice. "Has anything you've learned about me led you to believe that I can't afford what we need?" I gently squeeze his hand and give him a look of disapproval. He doesn't apologize, but he changes his tone. "If it is possible, will you consider moving them, and what equipment will you need?"

Dr. Morris begins to list her concerns, "Liam needs around the clock care right now. I'm one person."

Liam stops her, "There is a bedroom in the lab and Renee is a nurse."

"Yes, I am. I can definitely provide assistance. I have NICU and ER experience."

Liam nods at Renee and continues, "If Liam does well this week, and you are willing to allow us to go home, I'll need a list. If I'm not around, please give it to Renee. Money is no object so make sure everything on the list is top of the line. Now, may we please have a wheelchair so that we can go meet our son?"

"No, Nicole is not able to go just yet. Besides, they are still running tests on him. I would be with him myself, if I didn't have to come back down here to talk to you." Liam flashes her a look that lets her know she should tread lightly. "Listen Dr. Sinclair, you both should get to meet your son in about three or four hours. Allow Nicole's body to come out of the anesthesia. We're taking great care of your son."

She turns to leave but stops. "Dr. Sinclair, I recognize your contribution to society is vital right now, but like you've shared with me on countless occasions, you would be an empty shell without Nicole. Hold on to that and focus on her. And yes, I will consider the transfer, *if* they are both doing well at the end of the week."

A few hours later we finally get to meet our perfect newborn. He's small, but not the smallest in the NICU. A nurse comes over and asks if I would like to hold him. Completely shocked, as I thought it would be a while before I would be allowed, I nod my head wildly while feebly trying to choke back more tears. Liam helps me from the wheelchair to one of the nursing chairs next to our baby's crib. The nurse moves the wheelchair out of the way while another nurse moves in a chair for Liam. He assists me with my gown so that little Liam can be placed on my bare chest. Our small son is hooked up to an IV and oxygen but looks to be in good condition otherwise. When they place him on my chest, his little knit cap slides off his head, exposing a full head of red hair. Liam gasps loudly and begins to sob quietly. Little Liam opens his eyes and looks at me for the first time. Like his big brother, he too has my big, brown eyes which garner another gasp from his father.

Finally gaining some composure, Liam finds his voice. "He's so perfect. When I look at him, I see my mom and you, her beautiful red hair, and your amazing brown doe eyes. After you and Zi, I didn't know it was possible for my heart to hold anymore love. But I tell you, my heart is so full of love it could burst."

Little Liam lets out a very delicate cry, and I suddenly feel the familiar awareness in my breasts. Remembering nursing Zion, I smile and ask Liam to get the nurse for me. I ask her, "May I try? Is he able?" She shrugs and tells me he was able to suck and swallow from a bottle a little bit. She gives me permission to try, but encourages me to be patient with him. Liam helps me position him. Our little guy tries and finally latches on. We both gush over the accomplishment. "Dr. Morris said he was strong." He doesn't suckle for very long, but it is a wonderful and welcomed first attempt. We spent the next several hours holding our baby and talking to him, letting him know that his mommy and daddy will always be here for him.

CHAPTER 41

# SURPRISE ON THE HILL

(Liam)

It's been three months since Red was born and things have really picked up around the compound. His Uncle Chris and Aunt Renee have given little Liam the nickname Red because of his fiery red hair. Everyone seems to think it's an adorable nickname, everyone except Nicole. She believes that it will confuse him. Dr. Morris says he's doing great. He is breathing on his own, not hooked up to any machines, and has a very healthy appetite.

The compound has been bustling with people. Renee and her family are in the cabin closest to our home. Though Chris has his own cabin, I've noticed that he spends a lot of time in Renee's. Dr. Morris, her husband, and their eight-year-old twin girls have a cabin. Six other cabins are housing twenty-four of Chris' men who are guarding the compound around the clock. Our home has become a revolving door as everyone has access to all our amenities. Just the other night I had to break up a fight between Justice, Journey, and Jesse. Justice and Journey caught Jesse trying to kiss Joy in the theater. Renee and Nicole found it cute, but Justice and Journey were not amused. Turns out, they are both seventeen, and it was the first kiss for both of them. I had to have a man-to-man talk with Jesse. It was good practice for the talks I will have to have with Zi and Red. Jesse begged me to stay with us for a while. It's the least I can do for him since he took care of me while I was Devon's prisoner. Nicole has been competing with the guys for pool time, as it's her special place. She finally had to tell everyone that the pool is off limits from ten to noon. I miss Nicole, but not all the commotion.

Today is finally the day I have waited for, for six years. Nicole sits on our bed at home holding a sleeping Red while I dress in front of the screen. Even though I traveled by private jet, Nicole and Dr. Morris decided it was best for her to stay home with the kids, since she will be leaving them again soon for our honeymoon. Having her on the screen is the next best thing. "You look amazing, Dr. Sinclair."

I wish she was here to help me get dressed. Wearing a three-piece, dark gray suit, white shirt, and electric blue tie that Nicole picked out, I ask, "You don't think it's too much?"

She gives me the biggest smile. "Absolutely not. That tie brings out your deep blue eyes, the eyes I love to get lost in. I'm going to miss your long hair, but I must admit, I love this haircut too." I roll my eyes and smile at the compliment. "Do you have your statement?" I check my left inside pocket for my cards and nod. "And you sent over your visual aides to the email address I sent you?"

"Yes, pretty lady. I'm starting to think that you're as nervous as I am." Just then, I realize that I have been pacing in front of the screen.

"I am nervous." Nicole admits. "I want you to get everything you want out of this address. Then, maybe we can have somewhat of a normal life. I love Chris, I do, but it would be nice to not have so many guns around the boys. Is Chris guarding you today?"

"Of course, you know he is not letting me out of his sight today. He also brought along twenty other men to guard me. I have more guards than the elected officials."

A loud knock sounds at the door, followed by, "Lee, are you ready to roll out?" Chris is not known for his patience.

"Okay, baby, this is it. I love you more than you will ever know. If you get nervous, look directly into the camera, and know that I'm there with you." Nicole's words are comforting. Chris knocks again. "You better go before Chris breaks the door down."

"Be out in a sec." I get as close as I can to the screen and kiss it. "I love you, Nicole Simmons-Sinclair." I smile big and cut her off before she can respond, "Okay, in two days. I just like saying it." I look down at my watch. "See you in forty-eight minutes." I wink at her and disconnect.

Crossing the large executive suite, I reach the door and open it. I'm greeted by Chris and twenty members of *Men In Black*. "Um, good morning, Chris. Is all of this really necessary?"

"Bro, you've had two attempts on your life in less than four months. You have two kids, one of which is a newborn. And you're marrying Nicole in two days. So, no, I'm not taking any chances."

I step out into the crowded hallway and let the door close behind me. Joining Chris in the middle of the hallway, there are ten armed men in front of me and ten men behind me. We take the larger cargo elevator down to the parking garage where five black large SUVs are waiting to take us to The Hill. I turn to Chris, "Let me guess, bulletproof?"

"But of course. Lee, just relax and let me do the worrying. Okay? And don't forget to breathe. You told me once that you weren't afraid to die. Remember?"

"I'm not, but I'm afraid of losing everything I've gained in the past year. Dude, I had nothing to live for. Don't get me wrong, I have had purpose. But Nicole and the boys have opened my eyes, my life, and my heart to a joy that I had never known. That is why I'm here, in this moment. Everything happens for a reason. You told me that when I showed up on your doorstep with fresh bullet wounds."

"I hear you, man. Between you and me, I'm falling pretty hard for Renee. I can't figure out for the life of me how a woman like that isn't off the market." Chris smiles at me trying to lighten my mood and change the subject. "You know I love Nicole, so I mean no offense, but that sister of hers keeps my flagpole at full mass."

"DAMN! Chris, I do not need to know how hot you are for my sister-in-law."

Chris laughs heartily. "Come on man. Tell me sex talk isn't off limits. I know Thad, Serg, and Jimmy still talk to you about their wives. We're brothers!"

"True, but none of them are screwing my sister!" I chuckle while giving him the side-eye. "You know, Nicole keeps me more than satisfied." I wink at him. "Though Red has kicked me out of one of my favorite spots."

"There he is! Hell, you never could turn down a woman with big tits."

"Like you've changed. Still following behind a big round ass."

"Shiiit, and you know this!" We both laugh long and hard. "See how nicely that cleared the air, just shooting the shit with your boy? And we're here. I've informed everyone that I could about the guards. Raptor, Breeze, and I will accompany you in, but the rest can only go as far as the front door. The MPs will take over from there. Trust me, you'll be safe. There isn't a sniper in the world who can get close enough to take a shot."

The door opens and I step out into a sea of black suits, heavily armed, though the weapons are covered by their jackets. We head inside. I'm ushered through security while my ex-SEAL guards are greeted by the MPs and have their credentials verified. Though I know I shouldn't be, I'm very uneasy and I keep my eyes on Chris. Once through security, Chris nods. Breeze gets to my right and Raptor to my left. Chris steps in front of me. "Chris, am I going crazy?" Something feels wrong.

Chris tenses and shakes his head, "No, we feel it too. There's a presence. You're being watched."

"Boss, on your two. On the stairs," Raptor says. "That's her. It's her. Shit!"

Chris, Breeze, and I look just ahead to our right. She is looking directly at me. "Raptor, who the fuck is she?" Breeze questions Raptor, "Why does she have eyes on Dr. Sinclair?"

"That's Nastia! The one who ran the mission I was on looking for Dr. Sinclair." Raptor is clearly rattled by the appearance of his former employer.

I immediately stop and then change direction. Chris reaches out and grabs my arm, "Lee, man don't. We don't have time for this. Once you enter the chamber, you'll be safe. And there's no way in hell my men are letting her out of here."

"I love you, Chris, but let go of my fucking arm." Shocked by my resolve, he releases me. I quickly close the distance between Nastia and me. I walk right up to her and look down at her. "I hear you're looking for me. Well, here I am."

Nastia glares up at me, unphased, she probably thinks she can take me. "Dr. Liam Sinclair, interesting to see you still breathing. I just had to come see for myself when I heard you were making an appearance."

"Why?"

"Simple. I was assured you were dead. I guess someone will have to die for their mistake." She scans her surroundings. "What do you think you will gain from today's little speech? You think they are going to just let you rid the world of disease? How do you think big pharmaceutical companies stay in business and operate in this country?"

"I have a PhD in biological sciences. I know everything about pharmaceutical companies. I know exactly how the man you work for stays in business. Unlike you, I was invited here. And what I plan to accomplish is none of your goddamn business. I'm finished with you. I have somewhere to be." I begin to go back down the stairs.

"I do have just one more question." I turn and look up at her over my shoulder as she stares down at me. "Will you promise that you'll die like a good little boy the next time I come to kill you?" She smiles coyly as if anything about her could have an effect on me.

I come back and stand over her again, "Come near me or my family again, bitch, and I will put you in the fucking ground myself."

Chris grabs me and tells Breeze and Raptor to continue to escort me to my hearing. He then moves in front of Nastia. She looks at him like he's a shiny new toy. "Nastia, is it? Thank you so much for coming here. I mean it takes the fun out of the hunt, but I was beginning to get bored."

Catching him off guard, "Boss, is it?" Though shocked she would know that name, Chris withholds any reaction that could prove satisfying to her. "I have diplomatic immunity. I walked in here a free woman and I'm going to walk my sexy ass right back out as a free woman." Nastia winks at him. "I hope you enjoy the view."

Chris laughs out loud and his voice echoes off the walls. It startles her as she wasn't expecting him to call attention to them. As she looks up, she sees several armed men coming her way. "I allowed you to walk your boney ass in here, but your diplomatic immunity was cancelled the second you scanned in. Though, I am amused that you actually thought you'd be legally arrested." He flashes his million-dollar signature smile, dimples and all, "When you came after Dr. Sinclair, you really didn't know who you were fucking with, did you?" His expression shifts to stone cold. "Well, now you know bitch." Nastia's eyes double in size, but before she can speak, Chris finishes her with, "Don't worry, we're professionals; they'll never find your body."

# CHAPTER 42

# JOINT MEETING

## (Liam)

O ne of the MPs met Chris and told him we were heading in the wrong direction. "My apologies, sir. There was a change overnight. Apparently, a lot of the officials demanded to be included in the hearing." As they approach me, I hear the MP say, "Dr. Sinclair will be delivering his address in the House chamber for a joint meeting." My adrenaline kicks in at this news. My heart starts pounding and my breath becomes shallow. This is much bigger than I ever imagined it could be. "I don't mean to rush you all, but we need to double time it over there. The vice president will be arriving very shortly. Secret Service will have my ass if you aren't in your designated location when he arrives."

We get to the chamber doors, I blurt out, "I need a minute."

Chris glares at me. Being the consummate military guy, he knows that this is no time for pause. "Lee, we don't have time. Pull your shit together."

"Please, just hand me a phone and give me a minute." Chris is going to kill me when this is over because I can tell I'm sending him into cardiac arrest. I quickly dial the only person who can calm me. The line connects, and she picks up right away. Completely out of breath, I can only manage two words, "Joint... meeting."

Surprised to be receiving a call from me right now, Nicole isn't sure how to respond. "Lee? Why are you calling me? Your hearing is getting ready to start."

"Yes, Nicole, and I only have a few seconds. It's a joint meeting of Congress and the vice president is coming. I'm freaking out!" Then, like always, Nicole gives me what I need.

"Dr. Liam Owen Robert Sinclair, the Third, everyone, but you, knows your value. They want you in a joint meeting because you have now stopped four biological attacks that could have quickly reached pandemic levels. And you did this while being hunted by Dr. Volkov and that Nastia woman, not to mention being captured and tortured. You are brilliant, brave, and benevolent. Now suck up this anxiety and pull your shit together!" She gentles her tone, "The entire compound is gathered to watch you. Hmph, joint meeting! Damn, right! That's my man! I love you, baby."

"I love you, too." I end the call and hand the phone back to Chris. Smiling, I nod, "I'm ready."

He shakes his head. As we enter the area and clear the path for the vice president, Chris asks, "So what did she say?"

I smile and shrug, "She told me to pull my shit together." We quietly laugh and he nods at me.

Vice President Thomas Burke enters the area with his entourage. He sees me and begins walking in my direction. I was just expecting to get in and out. Our security teams make room for the encounter. He extends his hand, "Welcome, Dr. Sinclair. What an honor to meet the man of the hour. Let me just say how impressed I am with your work. Thank you for your dedication to serving your fellow man. I am looking forward to hearing your statement."

I firmly shake his hand. "Mr. Vice President, the honor is mine."

"And Mr. Ito, thank you for your superior service to our great nation." Vice President Burke tells Chris. "We remain in your debt. Let's get this show on the road." He nods to his team, and they open the chamber doors for him.

Several minutes later, the doors open again. The sergeant at arms nods to me in confirmation that it is my time, "MADAME SPEAKER, DR. LIAM SINCLAIR THE THIRD, HUMANITARIAN!" I'm greeted with applause, and everyone is standing as I enter. I try to take in as much of this moment as I can. I'm greeted by handshakes and gentle touches on my shoulder like I'm glass. I notice people in tears and I'm not sure why. A Black woman I recognize as a senator from California, whose name eludes me, takes my hand in both of hers and she says, "I'm so sorry you had to go through that." In that moment I realize Chris has not only released the footage from the rescue but also the footage from my whipping. As I approach the podium area, I decide that I need to change my approach. I shake hands with the speaker of the Senate and the vice president. I face the applauding crowd as I wait to hear the Speaker's gavel. Though it feels like several minutes have gone by, I'm certain it's only a few seconds, but finally I hear the pounding of the gavel.

"Madame Speaker, Mr. Vice President, honorable members of the Senate and the House, distinguished guests, I thank you for the invitation to meet with you today. I am truly humbled and honored by this opportunity." I pause to take in my audience. "As I look out at your faces, I see admiration, concern, and even pity. That is not why I have come before you. It was my intent to bring you news of my ability to produce cures for bio-engineered viruses. I came prepared with charts and data to discuss the outbreaks that have occurred across America over the last year. However, it has become clear to me that you are all here to hear me discuss my encounter with Mr. Devon Taylor. I cannot in good conscious stand in this hallowed chamber and claim to be a victim. Yes, I was victimized by Devon Taylor because of his disillusioned sense of reality, but too many people who look like him have been brutalized in the same way in this country. Because of that fact, I am not comfortable in the victim role. You see, I have never wanted for anything. I am privileged. Most of life, my race and wealth opened every door I stood in front of. I was raised by a racist, homophobic, sexist, abusive father, but he was rich. At least four of you in this room knew my father, but you allowed his bad behavior to go unchecked. Just as you continue to allow men like Devon Taylor on both sides of this battle to continue to terrorize our society. This country has been struggling with racial inequality for centuries, but we have more commonalities than differences. For example, a virus created in a lab to hurt your enemy, when released into the air or water will hurt your ally as well, because we all breathe the same air, drink the same water, and eat from the same food sources. Everyone in the virus' path becomes collateral damage. Perhaps, you don't care enough to take action, but I do.

"Where my father failed, my mother instilled love, compassion, and service in me. What you did not learn about me in the video is that I have a special ability to problem-solve. I decided at an early age that I wanted to use my special talent to help those less fortunate than myself. It wasn't until my African American nanny who was like a grandmother to me, passed away from the flu that I became interested in the field of infectious disease. She was turned away three times from the ER because they didn't think she was sick enough to be admitted to the hospital. I believe that if her skin was a different color, she would have been admitted immediately. I started studying chronic conditions. I discovered a treatment that would essentially eradicate childhood asthma and an effective way to reverse diabetes. When I tried to share my discoveries, I received my first lesson in what happens when you try to take on big pharmaceutical companies. There was an attempt made on my life. I was shot twice in the chest. I disappeared and vowed to never help in that way again. For five years I hid out in a, let's call it a cave, in the mountains near the border of California and Oregon.

"A little over a year ago, I left my cave to attend my mother's funeral. On the way back to my mountain, I met the love of my life." Looking directly into the camera to find and hold on to Nicole, I continue. "Call it chance, fate, divine intervention. I watched a strong African American woman defend her child against Devon Taylor and six of his men. Her love saved them. In that moment, I witnessed the true meaning of selflessness. In that moment, I knew that fear was no excuse for inaction, and I vowed to myself to get back in the fight to preserve humanity. Her love gives me strength." With a slight smile, I tap my heart with one finger and redirect my attention back to the audience. "My fiancée introduced me to the term 'white savior.' Maybe you all know what it means, but I didn't. In case you don't know, I'll tell you. The idea of a white savior is the notion that only whites can save non-whites from social injustices. Mr. Taylor hated me for saving my fiancée from him. But, the truth is, she has saved me more than I could ever save her. This brings me to the reason I agreed to speak here today.

"As you all have been briefed, I have provided cures free of charge for four recent virus outbreaks on American soil. I am happy to share my knowledge with anyone here who is interested. My cures have contained these attacks and prevented numbers from escalating to pandemic levels. Providing this service is my life's calling, but I have paid a steep price to make it possible. Every day I work to make a positive contribution to humanity, but every day I also put my family and myself in harm's way. My eight-year-old son participates in drills that require him to hide from gunmen, my newborn son is surrounded by armed guards, and my fiancée sleeps with a rifle next to our bed. I am not seeking financial assistance because, like my father before me, and his father before him, I do not need financial assistance. I also do not want financial pay because I have no intentions of answering to anyone in this room. My record speaks for itself. If you are as astute as I know you to be, you recognize my value in your effort to restore order to our great nation. Therefore, I come before you to ask that you pay for my services by means of protection. Declare my home, the airspace above it, and at least twenty miles around it, to be under the protection of the United States government. Do this for me and I will continue to provide my services free of charge. Take the target off my back so that I may give my wife and kids the safe life that they deserve. If you deny my request, I will relocate, and continue to defend my family by any means necessary. Yes, I will continue to help because it is the right thing to do, but I will not share any of my intellectual property. I will also put a price tag on any widely distributed drugs that I create in order to pay my security team. Furthermore, I will develop a case of amnesia regarding the prosecution of Devon Taylor.

"This is your opportunity to send a message to our citizens and the rest of the world that you intend to see peace restored, that you will not tolerate biological warfare to be launched against your citizens, and that you will defend all your citizens against oppression regardless of the color of their skin. Finally, I need an answer in twenty-four hours so that I may enjoy my wedding day without looking over my shoulder.

"I am sure you did not expect Mr. Taylor's victim to come before you and issue you an ultimatum. Likewise, I did not expect to give it. However, you know what is happening across this nation and you appear to be suffering from some sort of paralysis. I believe that you all are trying to find a solution, but in the meantime, people are dying. I am willing to help. Make it possible for me to help. That is my request. Thank you for listening and considering my proposal. May God bless each of you, and may God bless the United States of America."

To my surprise, the chamber erupts with applause. I turn behind me and shake hands with the speaker and the vice president before turning to leave the podium. Exiting the chamber doors, the sergeant at arms hands me a phone. "Hello?"

"Dr. Sinclair, it nice to hear your voice. I wish I was there to meet you in person."

"Madame President?"

"Yes. I want you to know I appreciate the wonderful service you have provided for your country. The United States government is prepared to support your work in whatever way you need. My chief of staff will be contacting your associate, Christopher Ito, to coordinate efforts. It is my sincere hope that you and your lovely wife will join me for dinner at The White House in the near future. I can't wait to meet her. I love seeing other Black women shine. Keep taking care of each other."

"Yes, ma'am, and thank you."

Chris looks at me, grinning from ear to ear. "Was that President Blake?" I nod. "Bro, you did it!"

"Chris, take me home, man!"

# Chapter 43
# The Night Before
(Nicole)

---

We shut down the compound and flew down to Thad's resort yesterday so we could have an unnecessary rehearsal that Renee insisted on, but the rehearsal dinner was a much-needed opportunity to connect with everyone. I met Jimmy and his family, and Eddie and his girlfriend. I finally got to meet Tiffany face-to-face. She didn't bring a date because she wants to keep her options open. Raptor found it hard seeing her again, but he's taking it in stride. I'm not used to partying like a youngster anymore. I find Liam and we say our goodnights. As we approach the exit of the ballroom, Renee and Chris block the door.

"Where do you think you two are going?" Chris crosses his arms as if daring Liam to try to take him.

Liam laughs. "Okay, guys, it's late. We just want to go to bed."

"Oh, you can go to bed, just not together." Renee looks at me like the mother hen she is.

"Um, Ree-ree, you know I've already given birth to his baby, right? There's not much left after that."

Liam grunts and grabs me like a caveman, humping me from behind, "I've had her in every position known to man. Pretty sure we invented a few new ones."

We all laugh. "Well, you won't be getting busy tonight. She's bunking with me and you're bunking with Chris. Besides, you have a week to play on your honeymoon."

"Seriously, sis? I hate not sleeping in his arms."

"Yes, seriously." Renee pulls me from Liam's grip. "You think I wouldn't rather be riding this stallion?" She gestures to Chris. "You need your beauty sleep. You'll both thank me in the morning. Chris, do not let Eddie keep everyone up drinking."

"Yes, ma'am." Chris grabs Renee and kisses her deeply, tongue and all.

Liam and I both protest and pull them apart.

"EW!" I yell, laughing.

"Damn, dude!" Liam laughs. "Y'all should get a room!" He playfully shakes his head. "Goodnight, Nicole. Tomorrow, you become Mrs. Simmons-Sinclair."

"Goodnight, Liam. I can't wait!"

I head off to the room with Renee. Walking arm in arm, "Nicole, I just want to say that this feels right. You and Liam, it's different. Your bond is inspirational. I'm falling in love with Chris, but I'm too old to be caught up in a fantasy."

"Why Ree-ree? You have to stop saying you're too old. You're forty-six and he's forty-two. You're never too old to find love. Besides, Chris clearly doesn't mind an older woman. I have it on good authority that he has caught serious feelings for you too."

"Wait, did Lee tell you that? Or are you just playing matchmaker?"

"He told Lee and Lee told me. Have you two not talked about what's going on between you?" She shrugs and starts to change for bed. "Ree-ree, I know you're scared, but don't let the unworthy men you dealt with in the past keep you from the awesome man in front of you. Don't be afraid to accept his love." A huge smile spreads across my face. "When I kicked fear out of my relationship with Liam is when all the magic started. That man has made love to not just my body, but my mind and soul too. I know it totally sounds cheesy, but once you let down your guard, it opens you up to a higher level of intimacy. You deserve that."

"Thanks." She looks at me like she's bursting with a question. "Nicole, can you tell me what really happened when Red was born?"

"What do you mean?"

"From the outside it looked like you and Lee were just asleep. Everyone thought it was strange, but no one had the guts to ask. I'm only asking now because it's the night before your wedding. You've lost contact with all of your girlfriends, and we didn't get to have a bridal shower. I think this story will explain the epic nature of your relationship with Liam. Will you tell me?"

I look at her and smile. "Fine, scoot over." I get in bed with her like I used to do when we were kids. "Liam likes to say that our souls speak to each other even when we're at a loss for words." Renee looks at me like I'm telling her the ultimate fairytale. "It's true." We both giggle. "The night after Lee was whipped, I asked for my gift to be increased. I prayed to be allowed to commune with my beloved. My request was granted. I literally, well I guess, we literally can meet on a spiritual plane. I was able to go to him in his dream and talk to him, touch him. I have never experienced this connection with anyone else. The next day, after the rescue, when I collapsed, he remembered what we had shared the night before. Somehow, he found me." Tears of joy fill my eyes, "Ree-ree, he found me. Liam's soul marched right onto my astral plane and kept my mind and body active in the natural world. How can I not love that man?"

Renee wipes my tears as she wipes her own. "Now hold up, who did you ask? Because I have bone to pick with them." We both laugh. "Come on, no more tears tonight. We'll be puffy in the morning if we keep this up." She kisses me on the cheek. "So, all I have to do is ask?"

"Yup." Renee turns off the light next to the bed. "Renee, will you walk me down the aisle tomorrow? I know Zion will be at the alter with us, but he doesn't need to walk me down the aisle too. I really would like you to do it since Mommy and Daddy aren't here."

There's a brief pause and sniffle. She turns over to look at me. "Damn it, Nicole. I said no more tears! Now I'm crying all over again. Of course I'll walk you down the aisle." We clutch hands between us and fall asleep.

Bright and early the next morning, I'm awakened by the familiar cry of my son. I open my eyes to find Joy standing by the bed with Red in her arms. "Good morning, Auntie Nicole. You said you wanted to feed Little Liam this morning."

"Thanks, sweetie." I reach out and take my little one. "Your hair and makeup are already done? What time is it? Why didn't anyone wake me up?"

"Auntie, you're fine. We all wanted you to rest. You are always taking care of everyone around you. Today is about you and Uncle Liam. Mom told everyone to let you sleep as late as you want. The resort is packed with wedding guests and a few special surprise guests for you. But I can't tell you, so don't ask."

"Whatever, missy. Hey, are those grandma's earrings?"

"Yes, mom said we should all wear something we inherited from grandma and pops. Justice is wearing one of pops' watches and Journey is wearing a pair of pops' diamond cufflinks. You know how they both like the bling." We both laugh. It's been too long since I've chatted with my niece. "Mom gave pops' platinum tie clip and cufflinks to Liam and asked him to make sure that Zion wears something too."

"Well, you look absolutely beautiful."

Renee walks in. "Yes, she does, looking like her mommy." She strikes a pose. We all laugh. "Okay, Joy, grab Red if he's done. I need the two of you dressed and the bride up out of that bed. Let's get this wedding started!"

After two hours of beauty prep, I'm finally ready to put on my custom made, one-of-a-kind dress. Renee helps me into the dress and then steps back to take it in. "Well, it's different. You look beautiful, but I'm still surprised you didn't go with something more traditional. You're usually so straitlaced when it comes to these things. This dress looks like something out of a dream."

I give her the most knowing smile. "It is. It's a surprise for Liam."

Remembering our talk last night, Renee gasps. "Oh, my God! You had the dress made from your dreamworld! Nicole, it is beautiful! Liam is going to lose it!" She admires it for a few moments. "You two are full of surprises today. I love it! I can't wait to see your face when you see what he's wearing. Chris sent me a picture."

# CHAPTER 44
# BUT MOST OF ALL
(Liam)

Finally, the day has arrived that I officially make Nicole mine, publicly and forever. I love that we get to exchange vows where we first met. Sergio was able to track down a few of Nicole's friends from high school, college, and work. He was even able to find a couple of Nicole and Renee's cousins. I hope it makes her feel special. I've spared no expense, and Thad loves the high-profile, political, and medical guests. It will really put this place on the map for him. As I dress, I hear a knock on the door. I had Thad give Chris a key. Maybe it's Zion. I open the door to find all of my favorite guys. My brothers, my new nephews, my sons, and Jesse are all decked out in tuxedoes. I let them in and take Red from Eddie. I kiss my big boy and my baby boy.

Eddie smiles and says, "Lee, your sons make me want to settle down and have some kids of my own. You've made a great life for yourself. Congratulations."

All the brothers look at Eddie in disbelief. Chris yells out, "Well, I plan to be next so don't pack away your tuxedoes, fellas." Justice and Journey look at him and smile. He wraps his arms around their shoulders, "That is, if it's alright with these two gentlemen."

"Yeah, yeah, yeah. Pipe down!" Thad calls out across the room to Chris. "Today is Lee's day. Besides, we came up here to help him get dressed."

"Guys, as you can see, I'm basically dressed."

Jimmy steps forward with a large box. "What you're wearing simply won't do for today."

I look at him and smile. "You didn't."

Eddie grabs Jimmy by the shoulders and grins, "But we did."

Years ago, when Thad, Chris, Sergio, and I studied abroad and met the twins, they insisted we take a trip to Scotland and trace my family's history. Though I was more intrigued by my mother's history because I loved her and hated my father, the guys insisted I had to follow my paternal bloodline. I learned that not all the men in my family had been like my father; many had been good men. My mother had been happy that I had taken that journey and it had sealed my bond with the twins. There's no doubt in my mind about what's in the box. I open it and see the kilt of green, blue, and red. "Guys, thank you." I pull out the contents of the box and now stand in my Sinclair tartan with a navy dress coat, white shirt, navy tie, and navy hoses. Jimmy and Eddie put the final touch on by attaching the fly plaid over my left shoulder. I turn to face the group; everyone in the room applauds. Justice hands me a glass. Thad and Chris flank me to the right and left. Zion stands in front of me and everyone else gathers behind him.

Journey raises his glass and toasts, "To Liam and Nicole!"

The group responds, "To Liam and Nicole!"

We sip a bit of champagne, and I am ready to go. "Get me to the altar, boys!"

As I stand at the altar with Zion at my side, awaiting my bride. I remember the very first time I saw her from the burnt building up the street. I remember the first time she looked at me with those beautiful brown eyes and the first time we kissed. The traditional wedding march song begins. I'm pulled out of my thoughts back to the present where I behold the most amazing vision I have ever had in the real world. Nicole appears with Renee at her side. Nicole is wearing the familiar gown from our dreamworld. It has been embellished with crystal jewels. She has stepped out of my dreams and into my life, like she did all those months ago. Our eyes connect and everyone else ceases to exist. Once by my side and hand in hand, I tell her how beautiful she looks.

She gives me a flirty smile. "Oh, I'm loving the kilt! You'll have to tell me the story behind it."

We recite traditional vows and then vows that we've written.

"Nicole, I promise to always put you first. I promise to always try to make you smile, but if I make you cry, I promise to wipe away your tears. I promise to always fight for you and our sons. I promise that all of our future camping trips will be glamping trips. I promise to always ask before I introduce the boys to a new extreme sport." Our guests all laugh, and I take a moment before being serious again. "But most of all, I promise to come and find you whenever darkness tries to steal your light."

"Liam, I promise to always support you while giving you the space you need to do things your way. I promise to love you when you're strong and love you stronger when you're weak. I promise to validate your feelings. I promise to let you be a fun dad to our sons. I promise to let you win family game night... some of the time." Our guests laugh again. Nicole squeezes my hands. "But most of all, I promise to always be your cure."

In unison, we say, "I love you." I almost kiss her, but the minister clears his throat. Everyone laughs at my eagerness. Zion opens his little hands to both of us and we take the rings from him. We exchange matching platinum bands and I surprise her by adding the custom engagement ring that I had designed. It has a two-carat, princess cut, vivid blue diamond, center. It's as rare as she is. She gasps at the sight of it, and I know I've done well. We gaze into each other's eyes while I listen for the magic words I've been waiting for.

"You may now kiss your bride."

I take Nicole in my arms and whisper, "Finally." I kiss her with every bit of love I have in my soul. I don't care who is watching. I hear the crowd cheering and Zion giggling. I release my wife from our kiss. We turn to the crowd and the minister announces us.

"I present to you, Doctors Liam and Nicole Sinclair!"

I turn to correct him, but Nicole stops me. "No, Liam, I told him to announce us that way. I am a Sinclair all the way!"

# CHAPTER 45

# THE HONEYMOON

(Nicole)

---

I've been Mrs. Nicole Dawn Sinclair for three magical hours. The plain ballroom from last night has been transformed into a scene fit for royalty. After lunch I danced until I had to kick off my heels. Then I danced some more. I'm tired and would love to go upstairs and take a nap since I have no idea where Liam is taking me for our honeymoon. I haven't seen my little Liam in a while, as he's been passed around by his aunts and uncles all day. Then, I spot Liam heading my direction with our baby in his arms. He smiles as he approaches me, "Is this who you're looking for, pretty lady?"

"Yes. You always know what I need."

"Yes, I do. And I think right now you and I both need the same thing." He looks at me with desire in his eyes. "I brought Red over to say goodbye to Mommy. I don't know where Zion is, but he'll come say goodbye when he sees us getting ready to leave."

My eyes get big with excitement. "Really? You don't think it's too soon to leave?"

"I want to get going while the sun is still up."

"Hmm. You're still not going to tell me where we're going?"

"No, Mrs. Sinclair. You'll just have to wait and see." Liam beckons for Renee and Chris. "Will one of you please announce our departure and ask everyone to meet us out front?"

As we make our way to the front of the resort, Zion finds us just like Liam said he would. "Mommy, Daddy, I'm going to miss you both so much, but I want you guys to have fun and not worry about Red and me. Tee-tee is going to take great care of us."

I stop even though the crowd is moving around us. I need this one moment with my son. "Zi, you have grown up so much over the last year. I am so proud of you. I see how happy you are to have a dad and a brother. All I have ever wanted is to give you a happy life."

"I am happy, Mommy." He hugs me super tight.

"Hey, you two," Liam rubs my back. I stand up. He hands me little Liam and picks up Zion. Zion squirms. "I know you're a big boy but let me hold you just for a minute. We're going to be gone for a whole week and I'm going to miss you. I love you so much. I just want to ask you one question."

"What is it, Daddy?"

"Will you please be a Sinclair too?"

"Yes!"

Sergio slides in with the official adoption papers. We both sign them, making our entire family's name Sinclair. We kiss the boys and Joy takes little Liam from me. My husband takes me by the hand and leads me out onto the dock where I fought off Devon and his guards.

"May I have everyone's attention?" Liam wraps his arm around me. "I want to thank you all for making today special for us. Today, Nicole and I stand on this dock, overjoyed to be husband and wife. For those of you who don't know, this dock is where I saw Nicole for the first time. Though it wasn't a happy time, it was the moment that changed my life and led us to this moment; the moment where I'm walking off this dock and onto our yacht the happiest man on the planet! BON VOYAGE!"

The crowd cheers as Liam scoops me up in his arms and turns to walk us to the huge yacht. I saw it when we walked out, but not for one second did I think this was the yacht he'd told me about. "Liam, she's massive!" He walks me up the ramp and onto the yacht.

"Welcome aboard the *Cassie*, pretty lady!"

"Oh my God, Liam! She's beautiful!"

"Not as beautiful as you."

I look at him as he lowers me down. "We're not going to stand out and wave goodbye to our guests?"

"No. I've given them enough of my attention today. Starting right now and for the next seven days, all of my attention will be on you." He bends down and slowly kisses me. "I have waited so long to make love to you for the first time as my wife." He kisses me again. "Thank you, for following me up the mountain." He leads me up the stairs to the master suite that has a 180-degree ocean view. I slowly walk around taking it all in as the ship departs the port.

Liam watches my every move as if recording it in his mind. I stop in front of him and rise up to kiss him. "Oh, Nicole, I don't even know where to begin." He turns me around so that I'm facing the open ocean. He kisses my neck as he unhooks all the crystal straps holding my dress up. My soft, delicate wedding gown gracefully flows down my body and onto the floor revealing my pale blue, lace corset and lace panties. "My God, you are beautiful." He caresses my skin as he runs his fingers up and down my spine. I turn in his hands so that I can face him. He kneels in front of me as I unpin his fly plaid from his jacket and push his jacket off his shoulders. I unbutton and remove his vest next. He bathes my upper body with kisses. His kisses make me weak. I moan through the sensation as I continue to unbutton his shirt and remove his cufflinks. Once his chest is bare, he stands as I kiss and lick his warm skin. His breathing is heavy, loud, and full of raw passion. He takes his time unhooking my corset. I remove his sporran and then I'm lost. I look up at him and we both smile.

"It's sexy as hell and I wouldn't mind you keeping it on, but I have no idea how to take this kilt off of you."

He cocks his head to the side and places my hands over buckles on both of his sides. He smirks. "Or do you want it to stay on? Whatever pleases you."

"Mmm, definitely some time before we disembark, but..." I undo the first side. "Right now, I want to be skin-to-skin all over you." I undo the other side and the kilt falls to the floor. He takes off his socks and shoes as I lace my fingers behind his neck and kiss him. The bed is several feet away, but it takes him no time to get us there.

Laying me on the bed he looks down to admire me as he removes his boxer briefs. He reaches down and slowly slides my lace panties off. "Perfect." He lowers himself on top of me and whispers, "Are you wet for me, Mrs. Sinclair?"

Breathlessly I answer, "Always." I spread my legs open for him and he gently settles himself between my thighs.

"Guess I'll just have to find out for myself." Before he can, I grab his long, thick cock and guide him to my opening. Slowly he pushes into me. "Yes, you are." He moves in and out of me, stroking me just right.

I move my hips up and down to receive each slow, deep stroke. "Oh, Liam, I love you so much."

"Mmm, I love you too, Nicole." He grabs my hand and laces his fingers with mine. "Making love to my wife is the best feeling in the world. You make me feel like a king." He strokes me deep and slow, over, and over.

"For the rest of my life, I am yours." With that, I have my first orgasm as Dr. Sinclair's wife. He follows closely behind me with his own.

As he comes, he whispers, "For all eternity."

He kisses me as we both recover. Liam looks into my eyes with those deep blues as our souls speak right through us at the same time on a single breath, "Forever."

…To be continued.

# A Note from the Author

Thank you for reading *The Cure for the Healer*. I hope you enjoyed the first installment of The Healer's Cure series. The second installment, *The Virus for the Cure,* will be coming your way soon, so make sure you follow me on Facebook and Instagram for information on the release date. In the meantime, go ahead and turn the page to read the first chapter of *The Virus for the Cure,* "Are you ready for this?"

## CHAPTER 1

# ARE YOU READY FOR THIS?

### (Liam)

---

Waking to the rise and fall of the waves of the Pacific Ocean onboard *Cassie*, I'm grateful that Nicole doesn't get seasick. I look down and watch my wife sleeping peacefully on my chest. Our first night as husband and wife has been amazing. She has been mine since we first met, but having her say it in front of all of our family and friends meant the world to me. Zion is officially, legally, my son, and Little Liam is healthy. I never thought that it would happen, but at this moment, my life is perfect.

I gently caress Nicole's caramel skin as the first light of a new day shines through the windows. Her soft, naked body warms mine. Though I don't want to disturb her, I can't help but kiss her on the forehead. She slowly begins to stir, smiling, and opening her eyes. Nicole holds up her left hand. Even in indirect sunlight, her blue diamond sparkles like the sea.

"Good morning, Dr. Sinclair. What are you doing?"

She smiles up at me. "Good morning, Dr. Sinclair." Placing her hand back on my chest, "I was just making sure that it wasn't a dream."

"Do you like it?"

"It's perfect. Just like this moment."

"I was just thinking the same thing. You know what would make this morning even more perfect?" With no hesitation, she takes my morning, erect cock into her hand and strokes me. I close my eyes and moan, "Mmm, you know me so well."

"Nuh-uh, husband, open those dreamy blues. I need to look into them."

I open my eyes and stare into hers. Like always, they're filled with love. Kissing me, she slowly releases me and climbs on top of me. I run my hands down her body as she positions herself to receive me. Gripping her hips, I guide her down my shaft. Nicole moans against my mouth as she accepts every inch of me. "How is it possible that every time I take you, my body experiences you in a whole new way?" I hold on to her hips as she slowly slides up and down me. The way she rolls her hips and rhythmically squeezes my cock with her sex is almost enough to send me over the edge, but I need to hold on to every second of this perfect moment.

Biting her lip and moaning my name the way she knows I love, "Ooh, Liam."

I grab her ass and hold her in place and stroke slow and deep inside of her. She's absolutely perfect. I sit up as she wraps her legs around me. I hold her tight in my arms as I lift her up and down. Even though I couldn't be any deeper in her, it isn't enough. I need to consume her, possess her. "Nicole, you're mine, all mine."

She responds breathlessly, "Yes, Liam. I'm yours."

Grunting as I continue to move her up and down on me, "And I'm yours. I love you so much." Her climax builds inside her heat as her slick tunnel tightens around my cock. She lets out the most beautiful sound of ecstasy I have ever heard. Her body trembles with euphoria. She grabs my shoulders and looks into my eyes. I catch her by the shoulders as her head drops backwards, and she arches into me. Clutching her tightly, I lay my head on her breasts as I climax with her.

Panting and trying to catch my breath, "Nicole, that was amazing. I can't believe how lucky I am to claim you as my wife, my soulmate." I scoot us across the bed and stand, lifting her with me.

"So, you're back to carrying me?" She smiles and kisses my neck. I love the way she brushes my hair back with her fingers.

"Always." I take us to the bathroom and into the shower. I slowly pull out of her, lower her down to the floor, and turn on the water. "So, what do you want to do today? Anything you want."

"I don't know. What's there to do on this magnificent vessel?"

"I'll ask the captain where we are. Maybe we can dock somewhere and have lunch. I really should have flown us to Florida and met the ship there."

"Why didn't you? Not that this isn't wonderful."

"You know me, I wanted it to mean something that we were leaving from the same place where we met."

"Is it safe for us to go ashore before we get to Canada?"

"Oh, I hadn't thought about that. I guess I'm getting used to having bodyguards." I wink at her.

"Like, oh my god, I married a rock star!"

I smack her on the ass. "Haha. You're right though. I guess we're staying onboard."

"Are the choppy waters bothering you?"

"No. I guess I'm just excited to be doing something almost normal. I'm just a bit antsy. This is the first time it has ever been just the two of us."

"I miss my babies." Nicole pouts a little.

"You know your sister and your niece are taking great care of them."

"Uh, Renee and Joy are your family now, too." Her smile turns into a smirk. "Speaking of Renee, how long do you think it will be before Chris tells her he loves her?"

"Soon. He was talking about being the next one of us to get married."

"Wow. When was this?"

"Right before the wedding. And he said it in front of all of us, including Justice and Journey. Chris has never talked about marriage. I just assumed he and Eddie would never settle down." I shut off the shower as she grabs towels for us to dry off.

"That would be amazing for both of them. Okay, feed me and show me the rest of *Cassie*." She smirks as she sashays by me. "Had me locked away for hours in your bedroom, taking advantage of me." I watch her as she walks across the room and puts on a sundress.

"Our bedroom. And as I recall, you had your dirty, wicked way with my body, too." Nicole smiles devilishly at me as I lunge towards her and wrap my arms around her. "Don't be surprised if you find yourself bent over a few times during this tour."

"Why do you think I'm wearing this dress?" She steps away from me. "And no panties." She licks her lips seductively.

"Careful, pretty lady, we're not going to make it out of this room."

Giggling, Nicole grabs me by the hand. "Come on, Lee. I'm starving."

As we open the door and head down the stairs, some of the crew greet us. "Hello, everyone. I apologize for not stopping to greet you all yesterday and introduce you to Nicole. I was just so excited to start our honeymoon." Nicole squeezes my hand, so I continue on to my point. "This is my beautiful wife, Nicole. Nicole, this is Bryce, our butler, Layla, our hostess, and Andre, our chef."

"Nice to meet all of you." Layla smiles and begins to go upstairs to clean the room. "Oh, Layla, it's a wreak up there. Let me help you."

"No, Mrs. Sinclair, or should I call you Dr. Sinclair?"

"Nicole, will be just fine." Nicole heads up the stairs behind Layla, but I grab her.

"Mrs. Sinclair, I know you may be used to doing things for yourself, but as long as you're on *Cassie*, it's my job to make sure you don't have to do anything." Layla looks at me and smiles. "Your husband pays me very well. There isn't anything up here that I haven't seen before."

"Well, thank you, Layla."

I pull Nicole back to my side and Bryce takes over. "Dr. Sinclair, breakfast is set up in the dining room. I left the doors closed because it's quite cool out."

"That's fine, Bryce, thank you."

Andre smiles big, "Lee, you found her!" He hugs me. Andre is Italian American with a mild demeanor. "I am so happy for you both," Andre hugs Nicole. "Welcome, Nicole."

"Come have breakfast with us, Dre." I just really want to talk to him.

"Now Lee, you know I already had breakfast. Besides, I'm working on something special for dinner."

"Dinner, not lunch?" Nicole asks.

"Babe, Andre is always two meals ahead." Andre and I chuckle. "Listen, I just want to catch up with you. It's been years."

"Fine." He causally slaps me on the back. "You, my friend, are on your honeymoon. Your focus should be on your lovely wife, not me."

"I'm fine. My husband is giving me lots of attention. Besides, I enjoy meeting Liam's friends." We sit down at the table. "You did all of this?" Andre nods. "It looks yummy."

"So, Andre, what have you been up to the last few years?"

"I went home to Georgia. Things have been fairly mellow there. It was smart to dock there. We picked up a few charters and a couple of aid projects."

"You've taken great care of her, Andre. Thank you so much."

"I know what she means to you, Lee. I know this yacht is one of the few places in the world you can find peace."

"Well now, I find peace wherever Nicole is." I pause to let my words root in Nicole's mind. Without looking up, she smiles tenderly.

"Whoa." Andre observes the effect my words have. He nods. "That's amazing."

I change the subject. "So, Andre, when did Bryce come on?"

"About five months ago. He's not bad for a young guy, but I don't really know him that well. Renzo up and retired. Said he was ready to go home to Italy and live the quiet life."

"Really?" This is shocking to me because Lorenzo never talked about home. In fact, he always avoided the topic.

"Shocked the hell out of me. You know he's like a father to me."

"You and me both. Nicole, Lorenzo was the butler who helped raise me and taught me how to cook." Giving my full attention to Andre, "Did he leave contact info with you?"

"Yeah, I try to check on him at least once a week. I really miss him. He would love to hear from you, Lee. He still talks about you all the time."

Nicole has been silently watching our exchange as her curiosity brews. "You two seem really close. What's the story here?"

"Dre was Renzo's last hire before I shut the house down. Fresh out of culinary school and tours in Italy and France, his food was amazing." Andre smiles and waves off the compliment. "We're close in age, so we just became buddies. When I left, I put Andre and Lorenzo on the *Cassie* and shipped them off to Georgia."

Andre drops his head. "I was worried that I would never see you again. You were one of my best friends; you were family."

"Are, Dre. I kept in touch with my other brothers, but I knew they were able to defend themselves. I wanted peace for you and Lorenzo. I'm sorry I deserted you. Please forgive me." Nicole reaches over and grabs my hand in support.

"Forgiven. At least you found amore. I wish you both all the best. I'm going to head back to the kitchen. I'll see you in a bit."

Nicole and I spend the rest of the day exploring the ship and making love in different rooms. By the time we go to bed for the evening, we're exhausted. We fall asleep in each other's arms.

*As we sit in the living room, in front of the panoramic ocean view, sipping champagne, I hear an odd sound coming from out on the deck. I get up to investigate. "Pretty lady, stay here."*

*"What's going on, Babe?" I shrug and put my finger to my lips, telling her to stay quiet. We both sit our glasses down. As I approach the door, it flies open, and suddenly, I'm looking down the barrel of a gun.*

*"Don't move, Dr. Sinclair. If I kill you, I don't get paid."*

*I can't see who he is because the coward is wearing a face mask. He waves me over to the side. Nicole jumps up to come to me, but four more masked and armed men come in and surround me. They move me farther away from her. The first man turns his gun to my wife.*

*"Don't even think about it, girlie. Walk to me." Nicole's eyes double in size. "Slowly. I can't kill him, but I would love to hurt him."*

*Then I hear Andre behind me. "How about you get off of this ship?" I look and see him pointing a gun at the intruder as he moves closer to Nicole.*

*"So, you kill me, then what? You're still outgunned."*

*"I'm pretty sure all..." Bryce hits Andre in the head, knocking him out.*

*"FUCK! That was a big mistake. I swear, I'm going to kill you." I say to Bryce.*

*Bryce smirks and draws on Nicole. "I doubt it." He walks over and taps her shoulder with the gun. "Walk!"*

*I try to get to Bryce, but the four gunmen force me to the ground. Layla walks in and screams. Bryce grabs Nicole by the back of the neck and turns the gun on Layla. "You should have let me fuck you. Now you get to die." He fires at Layla.*

*Nicole rams him and he misses. "I'll come quietly, just please don't kill anyone."*

*My assailants pin me to the floor. I yell to her, "Nicole, I love you, baby! I'll find you. I promise."*

*As Bryce drags her off of the ship crying, she yells back, "I love you Liam, with all of my heart!"*

*They beat me badly to ensure I don't follow them and then they run off the ship and speed away in speed boats.*

*Suddenly, I'm back at the compound, but I'm being hand-cuffed and taken into custody.*

Shaking and panting, Nicole and I both sit up. She looks at me. "What the hell was that? Was that what I think it was? Did you just pull me into one of your premonitions?"

I nod at Nicole. This can't happen. "Shit! This is bad. Why are they taking you?"

Fear covers Nicole's face. "Why are you getting arrested?"

"We have to get the hell off of this boat and get back to the compound." We jump out of bed and throw on clothes.

"Lee, please tell me you brought guns."

"Yes, downstairs. Come on." I reach out to hold her hand. "Are you ready for this?"

Shaking her head, "But you know I'm ready to fight for what's mine."

I grab her and kiss her. "I love you, pretty lady. Don't you ever forget it. And if you are taken from me, I'll find you. No one knows about our special connection."

"I told my sister."

"Renee will never turn on us." We move to the door. "Stay behind me. We'll get weapons, I'll take care of Bryce, and you go talk to the captain. Ready?" She nods.

When I open the door, Bryce stands in front of me with his gun in my face. I reach out to grab it and punch him in the face. I disarm him, but instead of shooting him, my anger gets the best of me. I stick the gun in my jeans at the small of my back. Nicole runs by me, trying to get to the stairs that lead to the cargo area below where the guns are. I beat Bryce to the brink of death; only then do I realize that guns are pointing towards me, and Nicole has been captured.

"Let him go, or I'll shoot her. I won't kill her because you need incentive, but I'll hurt her." I release Bryce. "Good boy." He nods to the others to grab Bryce off the floor. Andre walks up behind me and grabs the gun from my back. He draws on the gunman. I can hear fear in his breathing. He'll never get off a clean shot, and he may shoot Nicole. I reach over and force his hand down to his side.

Bryce begins to stand on his own. "We're taking your bitch, and for your defiance, I'm going to fuck her every night until you finish your job. I like it rough."

Before I can fully process my next move, I grab the gun from Andre's still shaking hand and put a bullet right between Bryce's eyes. "You'll never get the chance."

Nicole screams in pain as her captor slices into her shoulder with a blade. "Drop the gun." I see Layla and shake my head for her not to come in. The kidnappers move towards the exit with Nicole. "We're leaving now. You'll receive further instructions. Every time you step out of line, your wife will pay for it." Nicole cries and clutches her shoulder, "I don't believe in sexually violating women, but clearly some others do. Remember that."

"Nicole, I love you, baby, and I'll find you. I love you. I'll see you soon."

"I love you, Liam. I love you so much."

Andre and I follow them out and watch as they speed away with the love of my life. "I'm going to kill them all."

"What's the plan?" Andre asks.

"I need the captain to take me home or maybe have Chris airlift me out of here." I drag Bryce's body to the back of the ship and throw him overboard. We get to the bridge and all forms of communication have been destroyed. The captain is bound and unconscious. I look at Andre. "Can you get us back?"

"Of course, Lee. I got you."

As soon as the ship comes back online, a voice comes over the system. *"Dr. Sinclair, you will return to your home in the mountains, alone. Dr. Jacob Smith has been assigned to assist you on a new project commissioned by the United States government. However, when you return, I will assume the identity of Dr. Smith, who has met with a tragic accident."*

"Where is Nicole?" The voice continues without interruption.

*"I have a job for you. You will complete the job without hesitation, or I will have your wife sent back to you in pieces. If you alert anyone about what is happening, your wife will suffer."*

"Who are you? Touch her and I'll kill you!"

"Lee, I think it's a recording. What are you going to do?"

"Just get me back, please. I'm going to try to get a signal. And Andre, I'm going to need everything you have on that dumb fucker, Bryce."

He nods, "Hey Liam, I know you're eager to find Nicole, but can you help Captain Leviston? And find Layla?"

I don't want to say or do anything in front of Andre that may cost him his life. If I can just get a signal, I can use Nicole's chip to track her. I pull out my tablet and turn it on, but the signal is blocked. There's something on board preventing me from getting out. It's probably also allowing them to track me. I scour the entire ship and find three devices, one outside where they entered, one on the bridge, and one right outside my room. After an hour, I'm able to use a backdoor on our satellite to access a small, private signal. I access Nicole's chip and see that she is still moving. Her heart rate is elevated, she's afraid. I hate that she's been kidnapped because she chose to love me. Unable to stop watching the moving dot on the GPS display, I sit with tears rolling down my face, hoping she'll find a way to sleep so we can be together.

www.ingramcontent.com/pod-product-compliance
Lightning Source LLC
Chambersburg PA
CBHW020659110726
47901CB00001B/248

* 9 7 9 8 9 9 2 3 6 0 2 0 2 *